UNA TRANT

FLOTSAM GIRL

© 2007 Una Trant

All rights reserved. No part of this publication may be reproduced in any form or by any means – graphic, electronic, or mechanical, including photocopying, recording, taping or information storage and retrieval systems – without the prior written permission of the author.

This book is a work of fiction. All characters are fictitious and any resemblance to actual persons, living or dead is purely coincidental. Names, places or incidents are either the product of the author's imagination or are used fictitiously.

ISBN: 978-1-905451-50-0

A CIP catalogue for this book is available from the National Library.

Cover Photographs courtesy of Photo Images Ltd.
Cover design by Mark Daughan.

Proceeds will go to Focus Ireland in aid of the homeless.

This book was published in cooperation with
Choice Publishing & Book Services Ltd., Ireland
Tel: 041 9841551 Email: info@choicepublishing.ie
www.choicepublishing.ie

'All experience is an arch where thro'
Gleams that untravelled world, whose margin fades
Forever and forever when we move.'

Alfred Tennyson, *Ulysses*

In a wild, remote part of the west of Ireland a megalithic stone ring overlooks the sea. These time-worn boulders are sunk low in the bog like resting cattle. Although their purpose is lost in antiquity, older people still recall a story attributing magical powers to the ring. Mad Sibby Pete claimed that the stones empowered her with second sight. She foretold the great storm of 1937 and pointed the finger of doom at the island men when they put out to sea that night. But her strangest prophecy was uttered the day the coffins of John and Rosemary Fogarty passed along the road to Portree.

'The stilled music and unseen art
Lie waiting in their young one's heart.'

She shouted those words, then laughed like a seagull screaming. Those that heard wondered about the child.

Chapter One

February sun flooded the spacious kitchen in Fogartys' causing the fireside brass to shine like gold. It was nine thirty in the morning. Aine was sitting at breakfast. Delia, her aunt, sat at the head of the table, a tall regal woman in her fifties. A turf fire burned in the grate giving a warm glow. There was a smell of toast.

'You didn't spend long at Doora,' Delia remarked, busy sorting out a back-log of post.

'I came home sooner than I had planned. I was nearly killed—'

'Bills!' Delia sighed, shoving the contents back into their envelopes, 'they keep rolling in. It's so hard to make ends meet these days.'

Aine yawned and reached for the teapot. She poured out tea and pushed a loose strand of hair back from her forehead, impatiently. The white cotton blouse she had pulled on, hastily, that morning over her corduroy skirt emphasized her long slender neck, almost boyish figure. Glancing at her aunt, her lips tightened. As poor as church mice, blah, blah, blah. Would Delia never stop grumbling about how difficult it was to live? It was mind the pence ... here ... there! Not a day of the year went by when she didn't complain about something.

Nevertheless, Aine had to admit that in spite of adverse circumstances, her aunt managed, more than adequately well, to provide a comfortable living for both of them. With her strong hands, reddened by washing and scrubbing, she cut out patterns and ran up dresses on Grandma Fogarty's sewing machine charging only a handful of shillings for her skills.

On this crisp morning in February Delia sat in her sunlit kitchen, proud as the queen of England. Wearing a navy silk dress fitted with a white collar, her strong, chiselled, features and dark eyebrows lent a severity to her face which most people would be afraid to challenge.

'I was nearly killed last night,' Aine said, 'a boulder from the cliff-top passed within an inch of my head.'

Delia examined the postmark on one of the letters. 'This must be from Mollie,' she said. Her eldest sister, Mollie, had immigrated to the States after she had just turned seventeen.

'Someone tried to kill me.'

'Tried to kill you?' Delia laid aside the American letter and looked at her niece. 'Really, Aine, you'll have to make an effort to keep your imagination in check. I know that young girls fantasize a bit but—'

'I'm certain the boulder didn't move of its own accord. It was pushed!'

'It was probably loosened by all this rain we've had, that's all. Landslides are quite common on that side of Cragann. Anyway, haven't I often warned you to keep away from those cliffs? You won't find Julie or Sara rambling around out there. It's no place for a lady, wandering on the cliffs after dark on her own.'

'The ground up there is as hard as hell. There's no chance of a landslide. The boulder was pushed, I tell you!'

Delia put down her cup. 'I don't want to hear of such nonsense. Who on earth would want to kill you, a penniless waif? You flatter yourself with illusions, Miss. In future, if you have nothing better to do try giving a hand around the house. The windows haven't been cleaned for days.'

Aine tossed back her hair. 'Oh! Forget it! I shouldn't have told you. What do you care? What does anyone care? Pity I wasn't swept by the boulder. It would have ended this miserable existence.' Opening the window she gazed out at the sea, troubled after the night's storm. If only she could run away, escape to a desert island, go somewhere … anywhere. Events of the night before continued to unnerve her.

The storm was about to break as Aine set out for Doora the previous evening. She tucked her hands into her pockets and strode through the village, crunching the stones ridged on the side of the road by the floods. A westerly wind, blowing from the sea, lifted her hair and whipped it like ripened corn across her face. There was a cold nip in the air. She hugged her small figure into her coat and drew it closely around her imagining she was a ship tossing on the sea. Down on the shore waves crashed venomously against the rocks. She didn't know why she wanted to see the caves or visit Doora this evening, but even if the storm worsened she would go there ... alone.

To her right were the terraced cottages. Lean and wiry-haired, Willie Sara stood watching from the doorway. Shielding his eyes, his gaze followed his silver-blue fishing boat fighting her moorings, as green seas rolled under her keel and smashed in white sheets across the pier.

'Will she be all right?' she called, pitching her voice above the gale.

Willie shrugged, raising his hands heavenwards as if to say, what power had *he* over the run of the seas.

It was easy talking to Willie. He had hunches about things. Could tell when there would be a change in the weather.

Alas, not so with Delia! After fifteen years living with her Aine still couldn't see eye to eye with her aunt. And it didn't seem probable now that they would ever come to terms on anything. It struck her, sometimes, that Delia might have been hard done by early in her life. Perhaps if she'd met some eligible bachelor, some swashbuckling Romeo in tweed jacket and plus fours, things might have turned out differently. But there wasn't anybody like that in Delia's life.

Of course, there was that Saturday some weeks previously, when her aunt went shopping to Belmullet. It was a cold November's evening, one of those evenings when the frost around Cragann would gnaw at one's bones. Aine donned a sweater and stole upstairs to take a look around her aunt's spacious bedroom.

The Blue Room, as it was known, was situated at the front of the house overlooking Cragann's half-moon shaped bay. High ceiling with tall windows, its heavy oak furniture embossed with lily-of-the-valley cast shadows over its grey-blue walls. In a corner near the window stood a wardrobe, an oval-shaped mirror on the outside. She tiptoed across, swung open the wardrobe door. 'Ooohah!' she cried, drawing back in alarm. Squinting at her from the depths were the small beady eyes of Delia's fox furs. Beside them stood her hats, an assortment of funny little hats. She picked up one of them and tried it on. Shaped like an admiral's hat, it was broad-leafed and angular covering most of her face. 'Ship Ahoy!' she cried, saluting into the mirror. Selecting a fox fur, she arranged it on her shoulders. 'Good morning, Mrs Hegarty! And how are you this morning, my dear?' Just then, a photograph, faded and jagged, fell to the floor at her feet. It was an old-fashioned photograph showing a girl in ankle-strapped shoes, narrow-waisted skirt and bonnet, ribbon-tied, under her chin. Beside her stood a gentleman in uniform carrying a sword stick. It was late in the evening. A thin finger of light broke the November darkness. She moved to the window to get a better look. 'My! My! A dandy!' Long pointy nose and tash! She had seen men like *him* in the films. And those white gauntlets! She whistled softly under her breath, admiring him.

Delia came upon her unexpectedly. 'Give it to me!' she commanded, snatching the photograph out of her hands, two red patches appearing on her cheeks.

As she approached the coastguards' station the storm broke. A wild turbulence took possession of the sea. The ghosts of the old coastguards would have to keep a watchful eye on the Cragann fishing boats, she thought. Forlorn, the tiny flotilla rose and fell like a flock of seagulls. She picked out Colm Holohan's boat, the *Cormorant*, beyond the buoy, anchored beside the lobster tanks. Lopsided and blackened by tar, the buffeted old sea vessel resembled a *cnapan* of seaweed blown haphazardly in the wind.

Suddenly, 1n the gathering twilight Colm's figure swung into focus. Hands in pockets, head held high, his gaze was fixed on his far-off fishing boat. The wind had whipped a ruddy tint into his face, tossing his hair and flapping his tar-stained jacket.

'It's going to be rough,' she called, hoping to catch his attention.

He continued on appearing not to notice.

'Can you hear me?'

There was no reply.

'Damn!' she whispered. 'Damn! Damn! Could he not have gestured? Made some sort of sign?' She shifted her attention to the wind-blown *Cormorant* tossing precariously in the rising storm and from that to the mountains of foam surging upwards a long way off on the horizon. Something tugged at her memory. A few months previously, the *Cormorant* had gone missing from the bay while a few old tow-boats remained tied up weather-bound. Nobody had noticed it, nobody except herself.

It was well known in Cragann that Colm spent hours trying to put together the price of a deep-sea trawler. But they said he'd never have enough money. The winds and seas were against him. Savagely, she hammered a stone with the heel of her boot. If only he'd settled for a boat like Hegartys', or for a navigable old tug, something like the one she had seen anchored over at Caishlean, things mightn't be so complicated.

When she reached Doora the tide was out. Flushed with excitement she followed the irregular path zigzagging down the face of the cliff. Picking her way through the rocks she arrived at Pluais Na gCaorach, the largest of the sea caves on the far north-west side of Cragann. Inside, the drop in temperature was so palpable that it almost sucked her breath away. She chaffed her hands, flapping them vigorously against her sides and moved cautiously along by the wall into the inner chamber. In the vast cavern, gouged out of sandstone rock, daylight dimmed to near darkness. Water dripped from the vaulted roof and plopped into unseen pools. She cupped her hands to her mouth. 'Hello!' she yelled. Her voice rushed back at her from a dozen angles. She laughed but her high-pitched laughter returned to mock her. She stood still, heart pounding. In a flash she turned and fled into the light again, breath coming in gasps. She had never been afraid in the caves before and was glad there was nobody with her.

Night was falling as Aine made her way back though the rocks. Returning to the path she descended, she laboured up the steep incline. I'm going too fast, she thought with a start, slow down! But she gathered speed in spite of herself, gasping lung-fulls of cold air, almost running up the path that meandered on the face of the cliff. All of a sudden, she felt somebody watching. She looked wildly about. Below her, the sea crashed against the rocks like a raging tyrant venting his anger on some hapless victim. Foam whipped from the broken water and was driven in-shore like snow. A sea bird screamed overhead. She raised her head and stared in disbelief. A huge boulder was moving towards the edge of the cliff; it seemed to move of its own volition. As she watched, it swayed in slow motion and began its silent descent. Horrified, she flattened herself out against the face of the cliff. As the boulder hurtled down from the top, it struck a projecting rock overhead and deflected outwards raining stones down around her. There was a thunderous crash, as it landed on the sandstone slabs below splintering into pieces.

She stood rooted, scarcely able to breathe. All was silent except for the rustling of the long grass. Shuddering, she resumed her climb upwards, heart beating wildly until she reached the top.

Had she imagined it? Had a figure in Wellingtons, sack on his shoulder disappeared around the corner of the dirt track as she reached the top of the cliff? She scanned the horizon. There was no one in sight. In the dusk the revolving beam from the lighthouse cut a warning arc on the foaming waters below.

When she arrived at the dirt track it was already dark. She broke into a run. Within seconds she saw Cragann with its pendant of lights and Fogartys' house, large and sprawling, grey as iron, waiting for her at the edge of the village.

Chapter Two

Aine!' Delia lowered her glasses and peered at her niece across the room, 'Aine, do you hear me? I've been calling you for the last few seconds. Good gracious, child, what's the matter?' Short sighted as she was, Delia couldn't help noticing her niece's pallor. In the morning light Aine looked like a ghost. As she leaned casually against the windowsill, her ivory skin and flaxen hair would convince anyone she was from another world. 'What on earth are you up to, child?'

'Nothing.'

'Have you forgotten today is Monday? Nora Hartigan will be here any minute to give a hand with the week's washing.' Delia glanced at the clock. Ten minutes to the hour. Just enough time to finish her chores. She rose quickly and filled the kettle with water placing it on the fire to boil, a ritual she had enacted for years and could perform now with her eyes shut.

Aine stood motionless at the window. A few hundred yards out in the bay a currach rounded the pier. The men were rowing hard. Down on the foreshore the young Hartigans shouted, waiting for a few extra mackerel after the count for their breakfast. Kittiwakes swooped low over the sea screaming for their share of the catch.

'Aine!'

'Mmm?'

'Clear away the dishes before the girl arrives.'

'What's the great hurry? Nora's never here before half eleven.'

'For heaven's sake, you're impossible!' With an angry clatter Delia stacked up the cups and saucers and piled them on to a tray. 'Only you're my dead brother's daughter, I'd send for the gaffer and you'd be over in Scotland in the morning earning your living like the rest of your friends. Haven't I given you a home, a good education? What more do you want? God knows I can ill-afford it living on a pittance as I am. I'm not the only aunt you've got, remember.'

'Wha...t?'

'Didn't I tell you,' a hard note crept into Delia's voice, 'that your mother had a sister, a twin sister at that?'

'A twin sister!'

Delia opened the attaché case where she kept her correspondence. Having dropped in her post, she snapped it shut with a finality that brooked no argument. 'You needn't expect any help from your mother's twin. She abandoned your mother. Her whole family abandoned her after she married John Fogarty.'

What was Delia trying to say? Was she trying to tell her that her mother was a reject like one of those Indian girls she'd read about, expelled from her caste because she'd married an outsider? Words Sara Hartigan hurled at her one day came rushing to her mind. 'You're only a blown-in', Sara hissed, tossing back her carrot-red hair, 'a little nobody washed up by the tide!'

'What's a blow-in?' Aine asked Delia later.

'Don't you listen to that Hartigan one,' Delia blazed, her face going a mottled red, 'she hasn't a drop of blue blood in her veins. Not one single drop. Common as mud, that's what she is!'

'Like mother, like daughter,' Aine sighed, as she turned and clapped down the window. Suddenly, she had a passionate longing to get to know that woman in the photograph on the mantelpiece, the woman sitting close to her father. She wanted to know what she looked like, the way she smiled, the clothes she wore. She wanted to hear it from somebody who knew her, laughed with her, played with her.

Delia stood, hands clenched against her chest, knuckles showing white through her reddened skin. 'Your home is in Cragann,' she said, 'it's where you belong.' She opened the fuel scuttle and threw a sod on the fire. 'There are times, you know, when you behave like a child, a spoiled and ungrateful child. The least you can do is show a little gratitude.'

'It's you who are ungrateful!' Aine replied. 'Haven't I been a useful companion for you, doing the weekly shopping, going with you for walks? When I'm gone you'll know the difference.'

Delia's face darkened. 'I'll be judge of who should be grateful for what. Have you applied for that job in the bank yet? It's time you did something practical for a change.'

'I'm not interested in banking. I told you before ... I want to be an artist.'

'Art won't earn you a living. I can't keep you forever, you know.'

'You don't have to remind me of that! If my mother were alive to day,' Aine paused, cleared her throat, 'she'd appreciate my talents!' Picking up her coat she flounced out of the kitchen.

Delia heard the back door slam behind her. 'What will I do with her at all?' she whispered, 'she's only a child, a stubborn and thoughtless child. Maybe I shouldn't have kept her.' Outside, the rain beat softly against the windowpane like the sound of a woman's skirt swishing across the lawn. A blazing fire crackled in the grate. Her gaze fell on the gilt-edged photograph standing on the mantelpiece. Young and beautiful, halted in time, Aine's mother sat on a wicker chair, smiling. Her husband John stood beside her, tall and robust, a shock of thick dark hair falling untidily over his forehead. Two quizzical dark eyes, set wide apart, looked full-square at the camera. The photograph had been taken a few hours before they died.

'She's the spitting image of her,' Delia admitted grudgingly, 'more like her mother than her father.'

Rosemary wore a v-necked taffeta dress worn by Aine, years later, in the operetta, *Lilac Time*, staged by the students of the secondary school. On the morning of her death she picked a bunch of deepest pink lilac, arranged them in a vase and placed them on the dining room table. 'There, Delia,' she said, smiling, 'their perfume will linger on.'

The fragrance of the flowers enfolded Delia now like a cloud, drawing her back to the scene of the tragedy. Taking the photograph between both hands, she sat still staring into the fire.

There wasn't a sound, not the whisper of a breeze that sultry morning in June. Rosemary and John, home on holidays from England, took two years old Aine to the beach. Through the open window Delia heard the cry of the kittiwakes as they wheeled back and over, attracted by the scraps of mackerel left by the fishermen the previous day.

She opened the hall door and walked down to the beach. Rosemary had gone out swimming. She could see her large urgent strokes as she veered towards the circle of lobster pots. On the foreshore Pat Neddy loaded thick rods of seaweed onto his cart. All of a sudden she saw her sister-in-law begin to flounder in the water. She raced across to where John was sitting with Aine, shook him by the shoulder, pointing out to sea, 'Rosemary! Quick!'

In an instant John Fogarty was on his feet. Alerted now to the danger, he charged down the beach and plunged into the waves skimming the surface of the water like a seal. Every second had begun to count. Rosemary had ceased to struggle. Desperate, Delia ran towards the village calling out for help. The fishermen's boats had departed for the islands early that morning. Willie Sara's currach, alone, lay stranded on the slipway. Within minutes, but what seemed a lifetime to her, Willie had shouldered his currach on to the water. Dipping the oars with light confident strokes he steered it out towards the lobster tanks.

Delia stood transfixed, scarcely able to breathe. She could no longer see John or Rosemary in the water. People had gathered ... directing ... calling ...

To this day, she couldn't make sense of the drowning. And at a time like this when life was becoming difficult, she couldn't make sense of anything.

Chapter Three

Cragann, where Aine was raised, is a sprawling village situated on the tip of the Erris peninsula jutting out into the Atlantic Ocean. Overlooking this picturesque landscape, Cartra hills rise in an undulating half-circle and roll gently out towards the sea. These soft-rolling hills sweep across countless miles of sand dunes converging, in the end, with the market town of Belmullet. It was here in this harsh, but beautiful country, Aine Fogarty lived.

Aine grew up with a passionate love for the Craggan countryside. In the grimmest of winter days when the winds howled around the gable of the house and the snows fell, she donned her sou'wester and sallied forth, undaunted.

On this tranquil morning in April she sat at her desk in school, listening to the teacher inform the class that the inspector was about to pay them a visit to test them at Irish. 'He'll give you a five pound note if you pass,' Miss Cleary said, green eyes glittering, 'a great fat five-pound note that will crackle like cornflakes in your pocket ... don't let the opportunity go by ...'

When she reached home that evening, Aine was determined to go for the *fiver*. Feverishly, she tackled her lessons practising the Irish, questions and answers, until she could rhyme them off in her sleep. Delia tutored her so much that she wished she were sitting for the test herself. 'Show your cousins you're just as good as them,' she urged, 'and don't forget the five pounds. God knows I could do with it now if I had it!'

The neighbours all were of the opinion that without a shadow of doubt, Johnnie Fogarty's daughter would perform well on the day of her test. Didn't the girl have that bit of savvy in her ... that certain something? Weren't the signs of it written all over her? Ah! Young

Aine Fogarty wouldn't have to migrate to England as her father and grandfather had done before her!

'She'll come out a professor yet,' old Daniel Cassidy predicted, talking to Willie Sara over a pint of Guinness on the night before the test. 'She'll be up there in Dublin living the life of a lady.' Old Daniel remembered Aine's mother. He had seen her holidaying on the island, a young slip of a girl from London peddling at top speed down Crochan hill, hair flying in the wind. There were rumours that she was rich, but like many another had fallen on hard times.

'Her father banished her from his house,' Willie recalled, digging his teeth into the stem of his old *duidin*.

Old Daniel nodded.

'Such a heartless thing to do!' Willie drew a fresh plug of tobacco from his pouch and scaled a few pieces off with his penknife. 'Fancy, treating your own flesh like that! But the child,' he frowned, 'what will become of the child?'

Daniel said nothing. He remembered one summer's morning; a funeral procession on the hill; laughter echoing across Portree valley; an old hag's prophesy. 'Glory be to God!' he muttered, spitting on the sawdust-covered floor, 'you wouldn't know at all!'

Primroses and buttercups spangled the hedges, as Delia and her niece set out for school that morning to meet the inspector. The scent of woodbine and honeysuckle drifted on the morning air. A soft breeze blew from the sea blending all perfumes into one sweet incense.

Aine - now aged four - skipped along the road beside her aunt practising her Irish and pausing now and then to gather some flowers. Sometimes, she would recite a sentence or two letting her Aunt know how much she knew, but Delia strode ahead, face set as if carved out of granite.

As they turned at the schoolhouse gate, Miss Cleary's case-clock was striking eleven. Aine took her place in the queue outside the Inspector's door. Morning sun highlighted the dust on the pink geraniums growing in the classroom windows. A smell of ink-stained desks and stale crusts from the lunches hung in the air. She frowned, and gazed at the window facing the sea. If only the inspector would hurry and call her! Her eyes wandered to her hornpipe shoes and to the velvet dress Delia had made on her Singer machine. She tugged at the buckles and smoothed down her dress. Suddenly, she jumped up and stamped her feet on the bare floorboards raising a cloud of dust. 'Stupid! Stupid!' she exclaimed, to the astonishment of Sara Hartigan and her cousin Julie sitting beside her on the bench, 'such a stupid looking pair of shoes!' Tossing back her pigtails which Delia had tied with two yellow ribbons, she looked like a bird poised for flight. 'Why does Delia have me wear this awful dress and these shiny black shoes? Would ye look at those shoes?' She wriggled her ankles.

They gazed with envy at the offending shoes.

Aine sat down again, hot and uncomfortable in her Sunday clothes. She sneaked a look at Sara Hartigan's faded blue dress and worn boots, patched and toed by old Daniel the shoemaker. Sara's mother knew how to get money out of the inspector.

Flo and Jamsie Hartigan, with their seven children, lived in a two roomed cottage a few yards above Pat Neddy's on the road to Portree. Built on the side of the hill, the tiny white cottage would remind one, sometimes, of the proverbial shoe in which the little old woman lived with all her children. Said to be damp and unhealthy in winter, it stood directly in the way of the northwest winds as they drove their icy gusts across the moor. According to village rumours, it was the old dowager, herself, Granny Hartigan, who - metaphorically speaking - kept the roof over the family's heads in their younger days.

After her death grandma Hartigan became a legendary figure in Cragann. She immigrated to the States after she had just turned seventeen. Unable to speak English, she wore a label bearing her name and address attached to the collar of her coat on her journey out. Having spent the best part of her youth in the suburbs of Massachusetts scrubbing out kitchens and looking after children, Granny H returned, years later, with a sizeable nest egg and a posh accent.

All of the Hartigans were given the *Irish money*, but the *Grant* in itself, however substantial, wasn't enough to keep the wolf from their door. There were times when the young Hartigans went hungry, when they had to scour the shore or beg at the neighbours' doors for scraps to fill them.

Sara was the second eldest of her seven siblings. Tall and freckle-faced with a mass of carrot-red hair, she towered head and shoulders over Julie and Aine.

Wedged between Aine and Sara, Julie Brannigan sat up stiff-lipped waiting her turn to be summoned before the inspector. Julie's brown eyes blinked like a sparrow's every time the inspector's door opened.

It was late in the afternoon - Julie and Sara had gone home - when Aine was called to the inspector's office. As she entered the dimly-lit room she saw a grey-haired man in a Donegal tweed suit and speckled tie warming himself by the fire. Two large feet ensconced in suede shoes and diamond-patterned socks, were thrust out languidly in front of him. He sat up quickly as Aine entered.

'Where were you born?' he asked, checking the register.

'England,' she replied.

'Sasana?' He raised his eyebrows.

She nodded.

Glancing at her dress, he adjusted his spectacles and motioned her to sit down. 'Do your ribbons grow on your hair?' he asked in Irish.

Aine frowned. 'They don't, not in this part of the country.'

'What colour is your dress?'

'Red.'

The inspector turned towards the register and drew a line through her name. 'You may go,' he said, glaring at her over his glasses.

Aine remained seated, forehead puckered in a puzzled frown. 'What about the money?' she asked, 'Delia wants the five pounds.'

The inspector rose from his chair. 'A mhuinteoir!' he called in a barking shout, 'a mhuinteoir!'

Hurriedly, she opened her schoolbag, took out a tattered old copybook and thrust it towards him, 'you can have it,' she said, half-closing one eye. On the centre-page of the copy was drawn a giant-sized monster, an enormous tail coiled around his body, two large eyes monopolising his head.

'Imigh leat abhaile!' the inspector commanded, eyes flickering nervously, 'imigh!'

Chapter Four

As Miss Cleary cycled home in the evening after the inspector's visit, Delia stood in the front garden clipping the hedges. The day was calm, breathless. Only the snip of the shears and the clack-clacketting sound of a blackbird banging a snail against a stone broke the silence. Along the edges of the path pansies and marigolds grew in a confused mass needing to be thinned out and wed.

'Did she get the five pounds?' Delia called, as the teacher was passing.

'Not this time,' Miss Cleary replied, dismounting her bike and turning towards Delia, 'she'll have sense next year. She'll know the right answers.'

'I did know the answers!' Aine's head appeared around the evergreens. 'The inspector didn't like my ribbons. He thought they were growing on my hair.'

Miss Cleary coughed. 'Better luck next time,' she said, beginning to peddle off into the village.

'Maggie!'

'Well?' The teacher turned awkwardly on the saddle, one foot on the ground to balance herself.

'Tell me this.' Delia lowered her voice to a whisper, leaning on the handle of the hoe. 'Did Sara Hartigan get the money?'

Miss Cleary's eyes glittered behind her round-framed spectacles. She looked at Delia. 'Sara Hartigan mightn't have a whole lot of brains but she knows how to manage the inspector!'

Delia scowled. She gazed at the sea laced with foam tossing restlessly on the shore. Clutching the hoe with both hands, sunhat tilted at an angle, she thought of Aine. She had begun to doubt that she would ever achieve any kind of a grade at school. Why could she not behave like the other children in her class? Whenever she looked at her copies she found them decorated with birds and animals and every kind of reptile. Such wicked looking creatures, she thought, clucking her tongue. Centipedes and octopuses crawling around the floor of the ocean! Tch! Tch! How does she think of it at all? She glanced at the child, now drawing hopscotch beds on the pavement.

After tea, that evening, Delia sat back in her armchair and took out her knitting. It was a bright sunny evening. The sun's rays shone through the kitchen window and fell in copper-gold shafts across the floor. Determined to complete the sweater she was knitting, she counted out her stitches meticulously, one plain, one purl, two plain … her long steel knitting needles flashing like swords in the sunlight. She paused suddenly and lowered her glasses. Leaning across the windowsill opposite her, Aine was pushing their hapless cat, Pangur, bit by bit, through the half-open window.

'Aine!'

'What?'

'The priest will hear confessions in the church this evening. Maybe, its time you went.'

'I don't want to go to confession!'

'Stop that nonsense! You'll go to confession like everyone else.'

'Why should I have to confess my sins? Most of the time the priest doesn't listen to me.'

'Stop that, Aine! Stop it, I say!' What on earth had got hold of the child? Delia's eyes narrowed. She laid down her knitting and sat up straight.

Eight years ago, on the third of July, Rosemary and John were married in the chapel sacristy in Cragann. The day was etched in her memory as if it were only yesterday. Dark and austere, the sacristy, a small square room, was situated at the front of the church behind the main altar. On entering, one was assailed by the suffocating aroma of bees' wax and snuffed-out candles. An eighteenth century mahogany table with white linen cloth, lighted candles and a crucifix, stood in the centre. Two straight-backed chairs were drawn up before priedieus reminding her of a Dutch painting she had seen in the

Imperial Hotel in Galway.

Rosemary was radiant with happiness. Even her mother had to admit that. Wearng a silver-blue taffeta dress, bunch of violets pinned to her collar, she stood smiling beside John.

John wore a dark striped suit, white collar and tie, red carnation stuck in his buttonhole. She and her brother Mike, who later died of consumption in England, were witnesses. Standing beside Mollie at the back was her mother, black rosary beads slipping through her fingers. Was she interceding for her son that he might come to his senses? Or did she, in her thoughts, stand with her husband, Sean Peadar, all alone out there on Inis Begin?

As the priest performed the ceremony, a slanting sun shone through the western window bathing the room in its golden light. Birds twittered noisily in their nests. But there was no music to mark the rite of passage, no encouraging words to support the couple as they crossed from one stage in life to the next. The intonation of the priest's voice, followed by the low responses of the bride and bridegroom, were the only sounds to herald the union - *For richer or poorer, in sickness or health, till death do we part.*

Not even in death, Delia reflected bitterly, were they to be separated.

'Defection!' her mother said it was.

Nobody could persuade John Fogarty to change his mind, not even the priest who spent hours conferring with him in the presbytery. 'You understand, the … eh … implications of the *Ne Timere* decree, I mean the written condition?'

'Of course! Of course!'

'Will you be content to sign on the dotted line, to have your children brought up in the Catholic Church?'

John nodded, dismissing with a wave of his hand any complications that could possibly arise later. Protestant and Catholic were the same to John Fogarty.

But it wasn't so with everyone in Cragann. In the surrounding district there were those who remembered with bitterness the havoc wrought in the wake of the Famine in the winter of 1847. Struggling for survival, their forebears made pacts with their local landlords, forfeiting their holdings, their very religion, in return for enough food to keep themselves alive.

Years passed. The wound remained unhealed in the collective memory. It haunted their children and their children's children, as the spectre of hunger had once haunted their land.

As Delia listened to the protests of her niece a terrible fear gripped her. Was Aine behaving out of a deep-rooted instinct? Was she reverting to the beliefs of her mother? 'Glory be to God!' she muttered, crossing herself quickly, 'a high Church Protestant!' Folding her knitting she got to her feet. 'All your friends will be going to confession,' she said, grabbing her by the arm and piloting her out the door.

Minutes later, Delia and her niece could be seen hurrying along in the direction of the chapel on the hill. It was late in the evening. Most people had finished their day's work. Weary-eyed factory girls, their hair blowing in the wind, cycled past them on their way home. A donkey and cart, driven by one of the Hartigans trundled by, carrying freshly-cut turf from the bog.

When they reached the door of the little stone church they stood still outside. The sound of voices, loud and cantankerous, reached them.

'I was drunk, Father.'

'What's that?'

'I was drunk, drunk at the fair. '

'And what were you drinking, may I ask?'

'A sup o' the crathur.'

'Aaah!' the priest said, as though confirming something of great importance, *'say for your penance ...'*

Delia advanced, slowly, turning the handle of the porch door. She genuflected before the main altar and found a seat in the middle row. Kneeling at the altar rails in semi-darkness Pat Neddy listed off his sins to the priest.

A woman behind him prayed her beads.

Aine followed Delia to her seat in the middle. On her right, Julie and Sara sat up primly in their Sunday clothes. Peering through the gloom, she watched shadowy figures walk silently past, genuflect before the main altar and take their seats on the long bench. Evening sun peeped through the stained-glass window brightening the darkened sanctuary. The crimson-and-gold robes worn by the Holy Family mediated the light with a soft brilliance. After a minute or two, she leaned forward, crooked a finger in the direction of Mary and Joseph. 'Look at the holy pair!' she cried.

'Shhh!' Delia nudged her, frowning.

She shifted her attention to the picture on the right: *Jesus teaches in the Temple.* 'What are you doing up there?' she asked, nodding to the picture.

'He's letting in the light, child, what else?'

Delia left her seat and walked purposefully towards the arc of flickering candles. Choosing a candle from a long wooden box she proceeded to light it. A woman from Portree in a brown plaid shawl shuffled up beside her. She lit a candle for her son, drowned while crossing to the islands; his body was never found. As the old woman prayed, her voice, knotted with grief, rose and fell in a sibilant whisper.

Aine kept her eye on Delia. Her aunt crossed to the sanctuary, paused before the tabernacle, bowed low and sailed down the side aisle, skirts swishing as she went.

Suddenly, from the back of the church shot a more warrior-like figure. Belligerent and scabby-eyed, Tim Hegarty swaggered up the centre, pushed himself in between Julie Brannigan and herself and planted his rough muddy boots firmly on the kneeler.

Folding her arms, Aine nudged Tim with her elbow. 'I committed a mortal,' she said, loud enough for all three to hear.

'A m—mortal!' Julie mouthed from the other side of Sara, 'w— what did you do?'

'I broke the fast. A piece of Aunt Delia's home-made sausage got stuck in my tooth.'

'That's not a mortal,' Tim asserted boldly, sticking out his chest, 'you'd have to eat a fine chunk o' meat before it'd be a mortal.'

'The teacher said to be fasting from midnight.'

'Sshh! The priest will hear you.'

'I'm not going to tell him.'

'The devil will get you.' Sara Hartigan thrust her short, freckled nose into Aine's face. 'You'll be burning down below in hell.'

'Next please!'

'It's you he's looking for,' Tim Hegarty nudged Aine.

She rose and walked slowly towards the altar rails, conscious of three pairs of eyes watching from behind.

'Did you break the fast purposely,' the priest asked, looking at her sternly.

'She did, Father!' they chorused.

'It was stuck in my tooth.'

'How much ... e r ...?'

'A toothfull.'

Father Ned sighed. 'Are these all your friends out there?'

She nodded.

'Tell them go home. Their sins are forgiven.'

Chapter Five

During the war it was customary for allied ships to assemble off Craggan Bay before crossing the Atlantic to America. Travelling around the coast, those huge convoys were often attacked by German submarines. Besides wreckage, such as baulks of timber and barrels of rum, the sea often yielded up corpses, bodies of drowned seamen.

A casual visitor might be excused for staring with curiosity at the long procession of people passing along the road to Portree on a summer's evening, following the remains of an unknown sailor. He might be surprised, too, to hear the lonesome keening of those same Western sea-farers, as they mourned the loss of their own dead.

One sunny afternoon, towards the end of her fourth year, Aine raced down Portree hill, noisy and wild, playing hide-and-seek with her friend Sara Hartigan. She paused suddenly, on seeing a small knot of people gathered outside Brannigans. Willie and Daniel Cassidy were unloading a long brown box from Pat Neddy's cart on to the cobblestones. Crossing the road, she skirted the crowd and wedged herself in between Willie and old Daniel.

'Strange sort of wrack,' Willie Sara said.

'Aye, not a penny to be got from it either.'

'A British officer, I'm thinking, from the sort of clothes he's wearing.'

'What is it Willie?' She stood on tiptoe, tugging Willie Sara's sleeve. She had begun to suspect that this was no ordinary gathering. The grown-ups were silent. The brown box without any lid was being lifted again on to Pat Neddy's cart.

'A dead sailor.'

'Drowned?'

'Aye. Washed in by the sea.'

She stretched herself up to her full height. She could see the dead man's clothes, his buttons shining like gold in the evening sun. Her gaze travelled to his face, white like paper, swollen from cold and long exposure in the water. His eyes were closed. Was he praying or trying to forget about the war? Did his mother know he was here? His hands were clasped, long delicate hands. Doctor Shannon stood at the side. Dressed in a brown tweed jacket and plus fours, he read aloud from a book: *Officer of the Royal Navy. Name and address unknown. Death due to drowning. Burial* this evening *in Portree* ... His voice droned on.

Aine shivered. Her hands went suddenly cold. Portree cemetery! She fastened her jacket, stole away quietly and trudged up the hill to Holohans' farm where she sat on the style in the stone wall. Burial this evening in Portree cemetery! Two big tears welled up in her eyes and slid down her cheeks. Head lowered, strands of hair loosened from her ponytail fell across her face.

'Gotcha!' Sara Hartigan whooped, rushing in the gate. She stopped short on seeing Aine. 'Cry baby, cry! Stick your finger in your eye! Who's afraid of a washed-up sailor! Who's a—'

'Can't you leave her alone, you twit!' Colm Holohan shouted, appearing around the corner of the gable, bucket of oats in his hand, 'she doesn't put in or out on you, does she?' He walked over and gave Aine's ponytail a tug. 'Come on,' he said, 'and we'll launch the currach.'

Wiping her eyes with the tail of her dress Aine glared at Sara. 'I won't be walking to school with you tomorrow.'

'Cry baby, cry!' Sara hissed, thrusting out her tongue.

The following morning at around nine o clock, Julie and Sara landed, as usual, on Delia's doorstep to collect Aine. It was a crisp autumnal morning. Delia was busy in the scullery straining a vat of cottage cheese. Hearing noise in the kitchen she hurried back in.

'Aine!'

There was no reply.

'Aine, your friends are here.'

Silence.

Delia charged upstairs. She searched the house, all the rooms, under the beds. There was no sign of Aine anywhere. Finally, she found her hiding in the gas house under the stairs sitting on an upturned laundry basket.

'Well?' said Delia.

'Huh.'

'Are you ready for school?'

She shook her head.

'Why aren't you then? Here, let me get the thermometer and I'll check your temperature.'

'Nah!'

Delia dashed to the wall-cupboard and took out a long cardboard box with a lid on it. 'Now let me see!' Having checked Aine's temperature she shook her head. 'Doctor Shannon will be around in the afternoon. I'll ask him to call.'

'I don't want to see Doctor Shannon.'

'Tch! Tch! Come along!' Taking her coat from the hallstand, Delia bundled her into it and shepherded her out the door. 'You'll be as right as rain with a breath of fresh air in your lungs.'

Delia was of the belief that struggling against nature was a discipline that formed character. 'Fighting the winds and raging seas built a backbone of steel,' she said. This was the creed that underpinned the philosophy of the Western people. They knew from an early age that lilac won't grow in a land overgrown with weeds and thistles.

Life changed little in Craggan, not until a long time after the war. The household ration book became the axis around which the daily menu revolved. Coupons measured the amount of food, light and heat allotted to each person. Over the summer months children walked barefoot to school. During the winter they carried a sod of turf tucked under their arms to stoke the classroom fires.

Going barefoot was a passport to freedom to which Aine felt she had an indisputable right. She loved the softness of the tarred roads underneath her feet; the smoothness of the mud as it squelched around her ankles in the bog. But above and beyond all this, she felt that going barefoot was the ticket of admission into Sara Hartigan's world. She wanted to prove to Sara that she could tread the sharp stones without flinching, count her bruises as good as the rest. She rebelled against the law enacted by Delia that she'd have to wear shoes in summer.

'T'ainm an deabhail!' she protested, kicking off her sandals on a clear bright morning in May. Nature was awake; the hawthorn was in bloom; thrush and blackbird were building their nests.

'Didn't I tell you to wear your sandals?' Delia remonstrated, seeing her niece running around barefoot outside.

'Sandals?' Aine echoed, raking out the gravel with her toes, lodged at the doorstep, 'who'd wear sandals on a day like this?'

'Where are the sandals I bought you in town?'

'Sara Hartigan doesn't have to wear sandals.'

'Sara Hartigan! Sara Hartigan will never be a lady.'

'And who wants to be a lady?' Aine stormed, heading towards the door.

'Remember!' Delia called after her in a menacing tone, 'the Fogartys will always be a cut above the rest.'

'Then why does Sara laugh at my dress?'

'Which dress? Really, Aine!'

'The one with the frilly, sticking-up collar you made on the Singer machine.'

Delia wasn't listening. Her attention was drawn to the wireless set in the corner. In a second or two, Fogarty's kitchen was filled with the latest version of *Here is the News!*

Chapter Six

The year turned. Summer came again to Craggan. The sun rose in a blaze of light over the land. As Delia tackled her annual cleaning Aine sat on the windowsill, knees drawn up to her chin, idly turning the pages of Switzers' gift catalogue.

'There's a stranger in the village!' Nora Hartigan shouted, bursting noisily into the kitchen. Nora had come to give Delia a hand with the yearly cleaning.

'I didn't hear of any visitor around,' Delia remarked casually, removing dinner plates from the dresser.

'It's a woman, Ma'am. Colm Holohan met her yesterday evening.'

'Are you sure Colm wasn't making it up? He's a great one to joke. Did you see her, Aine?'

'Who?'

'The stranger. Did you see a strange woman around?'

'Never laid eyes on her,' Aine yawned, closing her book with an air of boredom.

'Colm was talking to herself. She stopped her car at the crossroads and asked the way to Portree.'

'What was she like?' Delia asked, emptying out a press and stacking the contents along the table.

'She had golden hair, sort of going grey. Spoke with an English accent.'

'Probably visiting the cemetery. Maybe there's somebody buried in Portree belonging to her.' She glanced at Aine. Her eyes narrowed.

Over the winter months a film of dust from the fire in the range had settled on Delia's willow-patterned dinner set. Clearing the table of some of its clutter - a vase with geraniums, an overflowing knitting basket - she stacked the dinner plates together for washing and filled a basin with warm suds.

'Aine, if you insist on messing with paint, why don't you take it upstairs to your room,' she asked irritably, eyeing the collection of drawings scattered untidily over the table.

'This isn't messing!' Aine replied crossly, rescuing her drawings. Bundling them under her arm, she flounced noisily out of the kitchen.

Delia picked up a watercolour she had found at the bottom of a press. She smiled, recalling memories it evoked. Dark green sea streaked with white; sea birds wheeling against a background of tattered clouds. The painting was signed, *Rosemary*. 'A real artist!' she whispered, dropping the chamois duster and holding the painting at arm's length. 'She'd have had her own exhibition if only she had lived. That was her dream.' She realized with a start that it was the sixth anniversary of her sister-in-law's death. 'Aine!' she called upstairs.

'Wha—t?'

'Put on your coat and pay a visit to the church. This is your parents' anniversary.'

'I'm busy,' Aine replied in a petulant voice, 'why don't you go yourself?'

'Really! I wish you'd be more respectful. I'll give an offering to the priest on Sunday to have a Mass said for the two of them.'

'Oh, alright, I'll go.'

A minute later, Aine trundled downstairs. She took a freshly baked scone from the batch on the tray, scooped a pat of butter from the butter dish spreading it liberally over the steaming bread and left the house.

Tall and lanky at eight, Aine was growing up fast. With her rather uncommon appearance - exotic some people might say - she often attracted the attention of strangers. As she skipped along the roads in Cragann or played barefoot on the shore, her straight tawny hair and bronzed skin prompted visitors to inquire who she was.

'I've never seen a girl run so fast,' a photographer from Dublin remarked, focusing his thirty-five millimetre camera to get a close-up shot of her. An archaeologist working on a site in Inis Begin thought the child might have noble origins, be a descendant of the high kings of Ireland. Perhaps she was related to Queen Maeve. Whatever her lineage, strangers to Cragann had come to the conclusion that Aine Fogarty was different.

As she set out that evening Aine put the hasp on the gate that opened on to the road. Holohans' cows were in the habit of pushing it in and eating Delia's marigolds. Seeing a trail of clouds moving towards the west, she turned in the direction of Portree. Prayers said in the wilderness, she thought, might be just as effective as those said in a church.

The road to Portree wound around the Coolee bog, disappearing into sand dunes that fronted the sea. She walked briskly along, skipping now and then trying to catch a glimpse of the skylarks that filled the air with their music. A heather-scented wind ruffled her hair. She clapped her hands, making as much noise as possible, to see if she could frighten the cuckoo from its hiding place. Outlined on the horizon, Sliabh Mor stood tall and majestic, silent and empty as the bog.

She passed the megalithic stone circle. The standing stones brooding on the skyline were like giant gods staring across at each other. All except one. That one seemed to be staring fixedly at her. She shivered and hurried past not daring to turn her head.

Having left the bog behind her she arrived at a dozen or more two-roomed cottages, whitewashed and thatched, standing in a row. Old Sibby Pete sat on a chair outside her half-door, spinning. A hank of wool, sheared and spun by herself, lay at her feet. 'The best you can buy for keeping out the wet,' she told her visitors.

'Are you going to visit the dead, astore?' Sibby asked.

'I am,' Aine replied.

'You won't be alone over there this evening. There's somebody gone on before you. Here, you can take this.' She reached into her pocket and drew out a small tin box. 'It's for your father.'

'My father?'

'I knew Johnnie Fogarty when he was only the height of this chair.' She gestured towards the old rocking chair on which she sat.

Aine stared. A strange expression had crept into the old woman's eyes.

'Tall and handsome he became. Black curly hair and laughing eyes. But the sea has taken them all.' She crooned softly, rocking herself back and over. 'He was only a lad when he came in from the islands. Born and bred on Inis Begin north.' She leaned forward, eyes like coals sunken in her head. 'But who'd ever think you were Johnnie Fogarty's daughter? Nobody, not even mad Sibby Pete!'

Frowning, Aine looked at the sky. She thanked the old woman. Placed what she guessed to be a tin of tobacco in her pocket and continued her journey to Portree.

As she climbed the cemetery steps she heard the roar of surf echoing across the sand dunes. Seagulls wheeled back and forth. Swooping sporadically, they flew towards the islands where the fishermen's boats were stranded. A black-backed gull flew through the rounded East window of St. Sorcha's church and soared out over the sea.

On the summit of the hillock a confusion of weather-beaten gravestones faced her in drunken disarray. She smiled at them all. They were like the children of the great standing-stones up in the bog. The long grass buzzed with insects. A butterfly alighted on her arm and then fluttered away.

She skirted the tombstones and cleared a way through the weeds, trampling them down with her feet. 'I'm related to you all,' she told the thistles. Pausing at Grandma Hartigan's newly dug grave she bent down to examine the wreath of artificial flowers encased in a glass dome. Sara had boasted that her uncle in America had ordered it specially. Lily of the valley, huh! What was so different about that? The iron frame was already rusting. She kicked at the sandy soil hoping the old tyrant would feel the impact.

A few yards to the right of Grandma Hartigan's there was a grave overgrown with dandelions. Marked by a crudely cut stone, it bore the inscription, *Henry Thornton, British Coastguard, died 1921*. There were no flowers or wreaths, not even a rounded white stone to soften its grimness. His friends and family must be dead, she thought. Half-hidden in a corner were the remnants of what appeared to be a bouquet of flowers. It was a bunch of withered forget-me-notes tied with a velvet ribbon, something like that which Delia had in her sewing box. She was glad he mattered to someone.

When she reached her parents' tomb she peeped in over the railings. She couldn't remember them. All she had to remind her was the photograph on Delia's mantelpiece. She pictured them lying in the dark, a pair of skeletons entwined. But hadn't they, after all got each other? All *she* had in the world was Delia. The wind rustled the long grass that sprouted between the graves. A twig snapped behind her. She stiffened, afraid to turn around. She was sorry she had shown disrespect for the dead.

'Aine!'

She turned quickly hoping to find a familiar face.

'Aine, I presume.' A tall stately woman stood looking at her. She was dressed in a coat of ermine fur. The western sun haloed her flaxen hair. 'Don't be afraid.' She held out her hand in a friendly gesture.

Aine's mind raced. Could this be some goddess come to spirit her away? Or was it a ghost?

'Do you know who I am?'

In a flash she knew. It was her mother, her mother standing beside her own tomb! She was older now than she looked in the photograph taken on the day she died. Aine straightened her dress and hid her hands behind her back so that the lady wouldn't see the grime that had got under her nails. 'Yes,' she whispered, too much afraid to say more.

'Good.' The lady leaned casually against the tomb. 'You're eight years old now. All those years are etched in my brain.' She paused a moment, lost in thought. 'How are you getting on at school?'

Aine raised her eyes in despair. 'Dreadful!'

She laughed, deep throated and musical. 'Well, you're honest about it at least. But don't be discouraged, my dear. All you can do is your best. Are you interested in art?'

'Yes,' Aine replied, 'I love it!' She frowned. 'But Delia knows absolutely nothing about art. Oh! She's so hopeless.'

'Delia has her own way of doing things,' the lady remarked.

'But she doesn't understand!'

'My dear, you're so terribly like her.'

'Like Delia?'

'No! No! I was just thinking aloud.'

'I wish you were always here. We could talk about so many things. Painting, books. Can I visit you again, here at the tomb?'

'The tomb?' She touched the crude stone wall, thoughtfully. Her eyes misted. 'There's part of me here, already. This will be the link between us. I was in Portree last year, you know, and the year before but you never came.' She sighed. 'It's not easy for me to get here, you understand?'

Aine nodded, but she wasn't quite sure what she meant.

'Well, I'll do my best. So we'll meet a year from to day. Agreed?'

'Agreed.'

'We can meet at the tomb,' she said, pointing to where Aine's parents were buried, 'and you can tell me all about yourself. How about that?'

'Great!' Aine said, her face glowing.

A wind laden with rain spattered heavy black drops across the graveyard. The lady shivered and drew her coat closely about her. 'I'll have to go if it rains.'

'Look!' Aine said, pointing to the clouds careering across the sky. 'It's down for the night. You had better be off.' She reached into her pocket and drew out the box Sibby had given her. 'Here, this is for you.'

'For me? ' She stretched out her hand to take it.

Aine's hand brushed against hers. She had expected it to be as cold as death and was surprised by the warmth of her touch.

As she hurried across the sand dunes to Cragann, Aine's mind was in turmoil. Her mother! She had seen her at last. She recalled her gestures, intonation of her voice, shape of her face. She had said so much in so little time. *Catherine* she said was her name, *Catherine!* But it didn't really matter. She knew the lady was her mother. *Nothing can take the past away,* she said. She frowned. What did she mean by that? And then she skipped and laughed. The tomb would be their *chord of communication.* What a strange way to talk! She bent her head against the heavy drizzle sweeping in over the Atlantic. Her hair was wet, matted on her forehead. She resolved not to tell Delia that she had met her mother in the cemetery.

Chapter Seven

'I'd like to point out, Miss Fogarty,' the headmistress said, speaking to Delia at a parent-teacher meeting, some years later, in St Aengus' Secondary School, 'that it isn't for lack of brains that your niece is falling behind. Aine is an intelligent girl. She could easily be one of our best.'

'Why isn't she then, why isn't she one of your best?' Delia asked, crossly, annoyed by having to listen to the same rigmarole of complaints, year after year, about her niece.

'The trouble with Aine,' the headmistress explained, flipping through a pile of copybooks stacked on her desk, 'is that she tends to be lazy. Look at these essays!' She paged, quickly, through one of the copybooks. 'Some of the words here are spelled backwards.'

'What do you mean, backwards?'

'They read back to front.'

'Why in ...?'

The headmistress shook her head. 'God alone knows. Sometimes I think she does it out of spite. She doesn't want people to know what she's thinking. But really it's the same with everything. If she doesn't like a subject, she'll simply ignore it and spend her time doodling or drawing pictures of the teachers.'

'I see.' Delia opened her handbag, took out a bottle of lavender water and dabbed a few drops on her forehead. 'What kind of pictures?'

'Drawings, sketches, that kind of thing.'

'You mean to tell me ...?'

'Well, I ... eh ... Lowering her eyes, the headmistress blushed. 'There hasn't been an incident recently, but in the last few months, I can assure you, we did see some eh ... unflattering studies.'

Delia said nothing. Things were even worse than she had anticipated. But come to think of it, wasn't it this the kind of thing that worried her, made her afraid that, one day, Aine Fogarty would turn out to be like that aunt of hers over in London. Those cantankerous moods of hers; the way she'd concoct a story. One day it would be the lumps in her porridge. 'Can't eat it, Delia,' she'd say, pushing away her plate and offering it to the cat. Another time it would be her hair. After Mass, one Sunday, she attempted to slice off her ponytail complaining the boys were pulling it. And there was the morning she flung the *Dear Daughter* book out the window, the book she'd taken so much trouble to get her in Dublin.

'Another thing I'd like to discuss,' the headmistress said, putting away her records and eyeing Delia warily, 'is the subject of Aine's art. Your niece is a talented girl. The quality of her painting far surpasses that of the rest of her class. But as you, yourself, know, art isn't an academic subject. It won't get her anywhere.'

'Ahh!' Delia sat bolt upright, nodding her head vigorously. 'That's just what I was thinking all along. Only dunces become artists. If I had my way ...'

'Now! Now! I wouldn't go as far as all that!' The headmistress held up a reproving hand. 'Art does have its use when it comes to church fetes and that kind of thing ... But before you go,' she waved Delia back into her seat, 'there is one other matter, something that was brought to my attention recently.' She rose, walked to the window and looked down at the playground. 'Your niece,' she said, 'has acquired a voracious appetite for books. She reads non-stop, everything she can lay hands on, in between classes, while she's waiting for the bell, at every possible moment.'

'Reads? But the child never read. What kind of books, may I ask?'

'Well, fiction for a start. Mostly literary stuff, her form teacher tells me. Novels, poetry, all that kind of thing.'

'Novels!' Delia had heard enough. She snatched up her handbag and headed towards the door. Aine was going to the dogs. Her worst fears were being realized. 'I'll speak to her,' she said, turning and wagging her finger, 'I'll tell her a thing or two. We'll soon see who's boss in Fogartys.'

'Be careful now, the headmistress warned, 'go easy chastising her.'

It soon became evident, however, that no amount of threats or scolding would change Aine. When Delia confronted her the following morning reprimanding her for her laziness, she merely tossed back her head and ran out the door. What the headmistress said or didn't say didn't bother her.

On the twenty first of May, her seventeenth birthday, Aine was awakened early, a strange sound echoing in her ears. It was like the sound of somebody keening. She sat up straight and listened. Then she realized she had been dreaming, dreaming of ghosts. She jumped out, crossed to the window and flung it wide open. A gust of wind whirled through the room swelling the blue cretonne curtains out like sails. It was raining heavily. Huge drops slid down the windowpane and ran in rivulets along the path. On the opposite side of the road oleria and furze bushes dripped. Everything in nature looked sodden. She slammed down the window and hurried downstairs.

In the kitchen a scent of wild flowers greeted her. Somebody had placed a vase filled with violets and primroses on the windowsill. Bending, she smelled them, a pure sweet smell bearing all the memories of childhood. A pile of folded sheets, freshly laundered, were left on the table. Nora had come and gone. There was a note from Delia standing against the milk jug: *don't forget the groceries.*

She lingered over breakfast debating with herself how she'd spend the day. Would she continue painting or...? Impulsively, she put down her cup and ran upstairs to the attic.

The attic, at that hour of the morning, was as dusty and dry as Pa Holohan's greenhouse. Eddies of hot air, mixed with particles of dust, swirled around her as she entered. She opened the window to let in a breeze. In a corner, near the door, stood a long wooden box. Squatting on the floor, she began to rummage through its contents. There were books on gardening and cookery; an assortment of magazines and Readers Digests. An illustrated book of art which she hadn't noticed before caught her attention. Quickly, she leafed through its pages. The drawings were true-to-life sketches executed in the open air. Brushwork broad, sometimes unfinished but very real. There was much sunlight, greenery, water and many parasols in evidence. Happy pictures! Intrigued, she gazed at a jungle of flowers - poppies and cornflowers - growing in a garden in France. A pond filled with water lilies spanned by a trellised footbridge reminded her of a bridge she had seen in a Japanese painting. She marvelled at its beauty. She felt she was looking into a newly discovered world which nobody hitherto had imagined. She read out the artist's name: *Monet, Claude Monet*. Written on the flyleaf were the words: *To my dearest pupil, Rosemary*. Who gave the book to her mother? Pensively, she closed it and sat back listening to the silence of the house.

The rain cleared. She took out her bike and cycled to Brannigans' for the weekly groceries.

'Well, my dear, what can I do for you?' Mary Brannigan beamed, appearing from the back room, purple pencil lodged behind her ear.

Squinting, Aine read the shopping list: *a pound of rashers, Donnelly's sausages, tea, butter and a* pot *of little chip*.

She couldn't understand why Delia liked the *little chip*. Marmalade with the chunky bits of rind would be more of a chew. There were no cakes or biscuits on the list. Her aunt baked a loaf of soda bread each night that would be cool and settled by morning. Sometimes, she'd add a batch of sultana scones or a caraway cake for the evening tea.

The sun was sinking in the Atlantic as Aine emerged from Brannigans. A pink glow tinged the clouds banking up over Cartra. She slung the shopping basket over the handlebars, left the bicycle against the wall and walked briskly along by the sea. When she reached the boathouse she paused. The sound of hammering, followed by the screeches of a handsaw, could be heard inside. She ran across the grass and around to the front.

The old boathouse in Craggan was a limestone structure built in the early nineteenth century. Grass around it was overgrown with weeds; windows were boarded. She lifted the latch and pushed open the wood-stained door. Inside, it was dimly lit and smelled of tar and axel grease. Strewn across the floor, in the light cast by an overhanging lantern, was a pile of tangled-up ropes and a few cans of paint half-used. It was raining again, pattering on the roof with a hollow sound and tapping on the boarded-up windows. Suddenly, a tall muscular figure, dressed in dungarees and a *bainin* sweater, emerged from the shadows. Colm was mending his planking intending to smarten up the *Cormorant*. A gallon can of paint stood beside him on the floor.

'Maybe you'll give us a hand,' he said, stooping and picking up a paintbrush.

Aine's eyes shone. She caught the shaggy-headed brush as it hurtled in mid-air. 'Going to row in the races?' she asked, slapping the paint on to the warped wood, heedless of it dripping on her shoe.

'Maybe. All depends.'

'You'll row for Cragann?'

'Maybe.' He sat back on his heels surveying his handiwork whistling *The Rakes of Mallow*.

Her lips thightened. Over the past month, whenever she tried to talk to him about music or art, he deliberately ignored her, shuttering her out as if she didn't exist. Angrily, she drew the brush over the rough wooden surface. Close by, the drone of bees could be heard. A swarm had settled on the fuchsia bush growing over a neighbouring wall. She stole a glance at his profile, dark, inscrutable, grim line of mouth, long slanting eyes. Blinking hobo! she thought. Who does he think he is? Bending, she dipped the brush in the paint can and flung it against the timberwork, spattering him from head to toe with wet paint. 'You'll have time to clean up the mess,' she shouted over her shoulder, bolting out the door like a colt untethered.

Straightening, Colm stared after her. What would she say if I told her, he mused, if I ...? He threw back his head and began to laugh. Then his face changed. Frowning, he lifted the mooring ropes, dragged them out and threw them into the swirling waters.

Later as he put the finishing touches to the *Cormorant* Colm saw an old discoloured rag caught between the planking. White with pink flowers, it was stained with oil from the bilges. The initials A.F. were embroidered on one corner. Aine's handkerchief. She had dropped it the day they were out fishing together. About a month ago now, he reflected ruefully, stuffing the soiled handkerchief into his pocket.

Silhouetted against the horizon, two diminutive figures walked slowly down towards the beach. As they approached, the soft thud of their puttees could be heard squelching the grass.

'Another fine evening,' one of the fishermen remarked, recognizing Colm.

'Aye.'

'The weather should hold for another few hours.'

'T'will last till morning at any rate, but after that I'd be making for port.'

The fishermen collected their belongings. Having donned their oilskins they shouldered their currach and walked slowly down the slipway. In the fading light Colm's profile could be seen sharply outlined.

'Old Stevie's son looks troubled,' one of them remarked.

'He's become like an old man over night,' the other agreed.

Close to where they stood the newly painted *Cormorant* lay glossy and garish, her rock-battered hull exposed recklessly to the sky.

Chapter Eight

On reaching the caves, Aine stood white-faced gazing at the scene below her. Still calm, the waters of the bay looked dark and swollen like a ripened blister ready to burst. Maybe, I shouldn't have attacked him, she thought, but Colm had no right, no right to behave like that ... as if I were only a rag doll! She tugged at the ribbons on her ponytail, tied them firmly and squared her shoulders. About to enter Pluais Na gCaorach, the largest of the sea caves, she stopped suddenly and wheeled around.

'Bad cess to you, Miss, you'll be drowned yet!' Pat Neddy rasped, glowering down at her from the top of a giant rock.

'Mind, you're not drowned, yourself,' Aine retorted, glaring at the irascible old sea veteran, towering above her like the Archangel Michael guarding the entrance to Paradise. A pair of corduroy trousers, tied with twine at the knee, spiked out over his Wellingtons. As his raincoat swung open she noticed the shape of a bottle bulging through the lining of his pocket.

'The tide will soon be on the turn,' Pat Neddy warned, 'its not safe to be in the cave when the tide comes in.' With a sweep of his blackthorn stick he struck the rock as if expecting water to gush forth from its centre.

A seasoned beachcomber, Patrick Edward O Donohue - to give him his full title - was never too far off whenever there was wrack. Whatever wreckage floated in came from cargo ships sunk in the Battle of the Atlantic. Bales of rubber, hulks of timber and crates of coffee were often included in the loot.

As well as beach combing, Pat Neddy also kept a distilling business, which his neighbours acknowledged with a wink an' a nod. He distilled and fermented the poitin, himself, selling it illicitly to trusted customers.

From where she stood, balanced on a rock below him, Aine eyed the old beachcomber. She couldn't help thinking what a *gombeen* he was, frittering away his life distilling poitin. But on second thoughts, wasn't that what people said about her? That she spent her time daydreaming, turning out useless paintings. And if that wasn't enough, didn't Ma Hartigan say recently that Delia Fogarty's girl acted so strangely, that she wouldn't be surprised if she were one of those changelings, someone in tow with the fairies. She and Pat Neddy might have a few things in common, she thought, grinning. Seeing his gimlet eyes staring at her, she pulled herself up quickly. 'I've been surrounded by the sea before,' she said stiffly, 'you needn't worry about me. Anyway, I know how to swim.'

Pat Neddy pursed his lips. He swayed back and over a few times as if trying to ascertain what her intentions might be. 'Take a look over there,' he said, dropping his sack and pointing with his stick to the crumbling walls of an old cemetery, 'they come out of their graves. Walk and walk all night.'

Aine followed the direction of the blackthorn. Cresting the nearby hill stood a line of crosses. Beyond them a megalithic circle of dolmens rose starkly against a changing sky. There was nobody in sight. During the weekends, city people, tired of their contrived lifestyle, travelled down from the city, tents, primus stoves and blankets on their backs. She had always distrusted the city people. They belittled the landscape, leaving behind them sweet papers and empty cigarette packets. With a start, she realized what Pat Neddy had said. 'You believe in ghosts?' she asked.

With an air of authority, Pat Neddy raised his blackthorn, 'there are plenty of ghosts around these parts.'

'Does Sibby Pete ever see any?'

'Huh?'

'Does Sibby Pete ever see any ghosts?'

'Sibby Pete! Sibby Pete! What would that woman be doing wandering around here? It's too many ghosts *she* has in her head.' He stepped back and spat venomously into a hidden ravine. Picking up his sack, he turned to go in the opposite direction.

'Wait!' Aine said, hurriedly, gesturing with her hand, 'what kind of secrets does Sibby Pete keep hidden over there?'

'Eh?'

'What does she think she knows about my parents?' Annoyed by the old man's evasiveness, she felt like catching him by the shoulders and shaking him.

He turned and looked at her. 'Some years ago now,' he said, drawing circles on the surface of the rock with his stick. He stopped suddenly. A guarded expression crept into his eyes. 'Be off,' he shouted, 'this is no place for your sort!' Throwing his sack over his shoulder he shuffled off over the rocks muttering to himself.

'Drunken old scoundrel!' she hissed, shaking her fist after him.

Having watched Pat Neddy disappear up the cliff, Aine turned her attention to the caves. It was a long, long time since she had visited Pluais Na gCaorach, not since the evening she had been almost killed by the boulder. Sculpted by the sea from a meandering fault line, the dome-roofed cave was the oldest of its kind on the far west corner of Cragann. On entering, she paused, blinking the glare of the outside world from her eyes. It took her sometime before she could adjust to the saturated gloom within. The chamber inside sloped downwards creating a drainage pit for the water-laden air. The smell of the recently departed sea made her feel she was trespassing in its lair. Water dripped from the moisture-filled roof echoing like clanging cymbals.

She leaned her head against the cave wall, smooth as glass from the chemical action of the sea. At last she was free. Free of Delia's constant worrying, telling her to stand up straight and scrub her teeth. Scrub! Scrub! Scrub! Free of the eucalyptus rubbings, the tins of goose grease and layers of brown paper that went crack, crackle, next her skin every time she moved making Sara's eyes roll. Above all, she was free of Sara; Sara's cat-green eyes watching, pointing out her mistakes, hinting in so many ways that she didn't have the right kind of smartness for her sort of world.

A few paces more and she was in the cave's inner sanctuary. She placed the palms of her hands against the damp wall and felt the moisture seep in through her skin. She thought of Colm. These last few weeks she couldn't understand him at all. Her anger, which had erupted so suddenly, had just as quickly subsided. She felt confused, bewildered. She remembered the nice bits; the time they landed the thirteen pound pollack out beyond Carrageen causing commotion in the village; the day they went skating on the frozen pond at the Puchan. There were no shadows then, no darkness. Frowning, she recalled something else. It was the evening, so many months afterwards, when sitting in the alcove of a window she saw him walk down the slipway and lower a punt into the water. Clad in yellow oilskins and Wellingtons, he rowed out from the shore and hurriedly boarded the *Cormorant*. A few false starts, agonizing splutters and the *Cormorant* was off, ploughing its way around the pier and disappearing into the depths of the night. That's where all the trouble began. She ran the tips of her fingers along the ice cold wall. Glancing at her watch she saw it was after six. She donned her cap, drew her jacket around her and set out for home.

As she emerged from the cave the evening star had already appeared in the sky. Pat Neddy was stooped amongst the rocks filling his sack with *dilisk*.

'D'you want to get yourself drowned or what, like the rest of them?' he rasped, looking up.

Tossing back her hair, Aine pretended not to hear. She headed straight towards the cliff conscious of his blood-shot eyes staring after her.

She walked quickly back through the village humming softly. Brannigans was beginning to fill up. Men in white homespun jerseys dismounted their bikes and filed in. As she approached the coastguard station the sound of voices reached her. Julie and Sara Hartigan stood at the Sergeant's gate discussing a ceilidh to be held on Sunday night. Over the summer there was a ceildh held on the first Sunday of every month. Neither of them missed a night during the holidays. She withdrew into the shadow of the boathouse before they could see her.

'Jack Deneghan's band doesn't play old time waltzes,' Sara said.

'You can always make a request,' Julie pointed out, 'that's if ...'

'There's to be a ladies' choice,' Sara drawled, finishing her sentence.

'I know who you're going to choose,' Julie remarked, laughing. 'Watch that he hasn't got his eye on Aine. Didn't you see him the night of the ceilidh at Christmas?'

'Aine doesn't bother about boys and Colm, certainly, wouldn't be bothered with her,' Sara replied peevishly, in a high-pitched voice.

Aine pressed her shoulders against the gable wall, hands clenched against the cold stone.

'I heard her aunt talking to my mother last week,' Sara continued. 'She said she's as wild as a March hare, always mooning around on her own. Drawing pictures when she should be ...' A seabird's scream drowned the remainder of her sentence. 'And d'y'know, she has this pipe dream about wanting to be an artist. Fancy that! An artist! Far better that she'd get herself a job.'

'But everyone knows she's artistic.'

'Art! For heaven's sake, where is her art? I haven't seen any of her pictures. And look at her clothes! She doesn't know the first thing about fashion, wearing that green corduroy jacket to Mass Sunday after Sunday. No wonder the priest gets confused in his sermons.'

There was a peal of laughter as they walked past Aine hidden in the shadows.

She took the short cut home across the strand. The tide was coming in. Waves lapped around the base of the boathouse, advanced, retreated in confused battalions. The breeze was scarcely audible. Seagulls screamed as they swooped on the carcase of a sheep floating in a mass of seaweed out towards the south. She drew the collar of her jacket up around her throat. The night air was cold but her face burned. When she reached the house she pushed open the hall door, tossed her coat over the banisters and ran upstairs.

'Aine doesn't bother about boys! She doesn't know the first thing about fashion,' she mimicked in a high-pitched voice, taking two steps of the stairs at a time.

The room where she painted was at the back of the house facing the western hills. It was the room where she had played as a child, weaving dreams through the long winter evenings, dreams that sometimes threatened to tip over into nightmares. Loss … grief …were ghosts that haunted the night.

She opened the window letting in the cold night air. Mounting the sketch pad firmly on her easel she began to draw. Furiously her pencil flew over the paper. Curved lines and circles wove madly in and out. After a few quick strokes of her paint brush the impression of a woman became visible, a woman bearing a child in her arms. She selected her paints, cadmium yellow, burnt umber, ultra marine, alizarin crimson. Squeezing out worms of thick slimy paint from the tubes of watercolours, she mixed them with her palate knife. She picked up the hake brush Colm had given her, dipped it into the water and swept it quickly over the rough surface. A few broad brush strokes and the woman's dark features became visible, her gaze fixed on something far off. Taking out the rigger brush, a fine sable-haired brush that had belonged to her mother, she tapered the leaves and branches. Task completed, she laid down her brush. Her eyes drooped.

She was awakened by the grandfather clock in the hall striking midnight. The house was silent; Delia would be asleep. Through the open window came the sound of music. Willie Sara was practising his accordion in his cottage. Away out at sea there was a low rumble; the wind had risen. Somewhere beyond, Colm's yellow fishing boat wrestled with the waves. A full moon shining over Cartra filled the room with its stolen light. She leaned back in her chair. Through half-closed lids she viewed the painting. The woman's ravaged face shone with a transparent brilliance under the silver light of the moon, evocative of, yet different from the face she had seen in the cemetery.

Chapter Nine

For days Aine avoided meeting Colm. His indifference towards her that Saturday still rankled. 'He has no manners,' she complained to Willie Sara, as she helped him beach his currach, 'even Pangur could do better than that.'

'You must be patient, he's got a lot on his mind,' Willie replied, giving her a knowing wink.

'Like what?' She couldn't imagine Colm being bothered about anything.

'Well, things men worry about.'

'Hmm.'

'Look at it this way. Whenever he's in the humour you be around. See!'

'You reckon he'll forget about the paint spattering?'

'Not a doubt in the world. You wait and see.'

She didn't have very long to wait. Midsummer's Eve was almost upon them.

The festival of Midsummer had its origin in pagan times. It was the shortest night of the year, a night when fairies and goblins were believed to be abroad. Around the country they were preparing for bonfires and Cragann was no exception.

Early in the morning, soon after sunrise, Aine set out in search of turf. It was a fine summer's morning. A thick white haze had settled on the land. A mile or so north of Cragann Bay, on the road to Belmullet, she came to a straggling cutaway bog blanketed in purple heather. There hadn't been any rain for days; the soil was dry and crusted. Stalks of bog cotton swayed in the breeze along its borders like thousands of fairy lanterns.

With the aid of a *slean* left behind by somebody the previous evening, she dug out slabs of *spalach* and threw them into her basket. *Spalach* was the thing for banking a fire. Some distance away men were footing the turf. She could see their strong, rhythmic, movements as they passed and stacked the sods, but she couldn't figure out who they were. It came to her that if they were travelling her way she'd get a lift home on their cart. On second thoughts, it might be better if she didn't bother. Who was to say, Colm might be among them. And she couldn't bear to meet Colm just then.

Soon afterwards, she was out on the road laden with a basketful of turf. There wasn't a sound, except for the twittering of robins in the hedgerows and the murmur of the distant sea as it washed in on the shore. As the sun mounted the sky its rays burned her back and shoulders. She walked slowly along, basket of turf creaking against her hip, thin arms stretched to breaking point. Suddenly she heard the sound of tyres crunching the gravel. Somebody was peddling furiously behind. She half-turned as the cyclist drew up alongside her.

'Give me that! I saw you back there in the bog.' Colm jumped off his bike and threw it in the ditch. Hoisting the basket on to his shoulders he walked beside her, big as Fionn Mac Cumhaill.

Aine kept her eyes on the road. A feeling of unease swept over her. What if he held the paint incident against her and refused to forgive? Maybe he'd finish with her altogether? Her hands clenched and unclenched behind her back. She sneaked a look at his profile. Head high, hair tousled, his eyes were fixed on something in the distance. A powerful strength emanated from him. After a minute or two she plucked up courage. 'I could manage it myself, she said, through dried lips, 'I could—'

'Nah.'

'The road's going down hill—'

'It isn't right for a woman to be humping. Besides, look at your hands.'

'My hands?'

He stopped suddenly and shifted the creel to the other shoulder. 'Why didn't you call me?' he asked, glaring down at her, 'why didn't you tell me you were over there?'

Overcome with confusion, she stared at the marks on her fingers, great red indents like the imprints of a red-hot poker. 'I didn't know it was you. I was busy cutting.'

He jerked the basket up high and walked on as if he hadn't heard her.

When they reached Cragann he lowered the creel and threw it on the grass beside the rest of the pile. 'You've enough fuel there,' he said, pointing to the cairn of driftwood stacked up high, 'it should hold for the night.' He turned on his heel and bounded down the slipway to take a look at the boats.

Aine stared after him, forehead knitted in a puzzled frown.

That night almost everyone in Cragann gathered on the green. Tim Hegarty came with his young brothers, Johnnie and Phil. Sara and six small Hartigans could be heard shouting to each other from the other side of Cartra. Nora, their sister, had cycled into town to give a hand with the cooking in Donnellys' hotel. Old Daniel Cassidy stood at the top of the road roaring encouragement to the helpers.

Flushed with excitement, Aine and Julie dragged baulks of timber up from the shore and threw them into the flames. Sparks whizzed and crackled; smoke belched around their ankles blackening their summer dresses. 'Keep piling on!' Aine cried hoarsely, 'it might reach the skies. They'll see it up there in heaven.'

When evening fell they all drew in around the fire. Leaping and spluttering, flames made patterns on their upturned faces. Daniel Cassidy told stories, great awe-inspiring tales of ghosts and puckas. He spoke till he was hoarse from the fumes of tobacco and woodbine cigarettes. Sitting cross-legged on a stool, shoulders hunched, a hat like a tea cosy pulled over his head, he quickly got the measure of his audience. 'The banshee can be heard keening outside certain houses at midnight,' he said darkly, 'people with Os or Macs in their names.' He threw Mags O Connor, sitting opposite him, a sinister look.

Poor Mags took a fit of screaming. She clutched Tim Hegarty by the arm almost knocking them both into the middle of the flames.

'A red-haired woman was seen spinning outside Holohans' gate the other night,' Willie remarked.

'That would be Sara,' Tim winked, 'spinning and spinning. She'll have a ton of ould socks knitted agin' Christmas'.

'Whoosha!' Sara cried, grabbing a sally rod. She ran after Tim, whacking him soundly on the shins.

But everyone knew Sara was pleased

Steam hissed from the greenwood. A silver moon colluded with nature casting its spell on the revellers.

Daniel smoked another woodbine. Having finished his last fag he ground the stub into the earth with the heel of his boot. 'Did I ever tell you,' he asked, 'about the time I was cabin boy on the *Veronica Jane?*'

'No!'

'I was, then! Did a few trips around the Straits O'Gibraltar some years ago. Was shipwrecked twice!'

'Well, well.'

'Pirates raged everywhere in those days. They roamed the seas plundering every sloop and schooner within range of their telescopes. I caught one single-handed myself.'

'You didn't, man?'

'I did faith! A devil of an old salt he was too, from somewhere in the Outer Hebrides. I trussed him up and locked him below in the hold. But what do you think? Wasn't there nearly mutiny on the ship that night.'

'Go on! How so?'

'Your man broke loose and cleaned out the cellar. Every noggin of rum disappeared.'

They roared laughing.

'Did you see any mermaids?' Tim asked.

'Aye. I remember one fine lass with a tail a couple of feet long. She sat outside my cabin one morning. Very nearly had me in tow.'

'You're not joking us?' Julie looked at him, round-eyed.

'Cross my heart.'

'A real mermaid?'

'As real as yourself!' Hair flowing down her back the colour of ... eh, well, something like Sara's there.'

Sara sat up preening herself. She shook back her hair flashing a grateful smile at old Daniel.

Colm sauntered down towards them from the top of the road. Hair combed, he had changed into a clean white shirt. Glancing at the fire he prodded it with a stick, pushing back the darkness crowding in on them. Flames leaped, licking the branches of gorse causing it to spit like a snake.

Aine rose and moved up higher where the air was cool and sweet. Sitting on a hillock, she watched the bonfires light up across the bay, smelled the meadowsweet as it wafted over the fields. In the half-light, before darkness blotted out the land, shadows lengthened. Down in the valley strange faces appeared. Pucas peeped from their hiding places and danced in and out between toadstools.

'It's cooler up here,' Colm remarked, emerging from the shadows.

'Oh!' she exclaimed, with a quick intake of breath.

He sat down beside her on a clump of heather. 'It's not shivering you are?' he asked.

'No ... It's ... it's just this time of night ... makes me feel a bit queasy ... Maybe it's my imagination...'

He hitched up his dungarees, stretching his legs to a more comfortable position. 'I know how it is,' he said, 'I used to be afraid like that once.'

She laughed. 'Afraid! I couldn't imagine you being afraid of anything.'

Silently, he looked at her. 'Everybody's afraid of something, sometime or other. When I was a lad,' his voice took on a low note so that she had to bend to hear him, 'I had a bit of a handicap.'

'A handicap?'

'Well, its years ago now. For a long, long time I couldn't make sense of the reading. I didn't make any headway at all, not till I was fifteen. I hid it from them, but I was always afraid, afraid they'd find out. I used to put up a show for the old man, I remember. When he'd come in from the fields in the evening I'd pretend to be reading the newspaper. But it was only myself I was fooling. Now as I look back I realize he knew, knew all the time. I never told this to anyone before.' Frowning, his eyes smouldered in the firelight. Sun-tanned face flushed.

Aine sat, hands resting in her lap. Below them the noise grew louder. People were laughing, shouting. Some roasted potatoes or fried slivers of black pudding on red-hot coals. There was a great clamour, everyone calling for something. She looked at Colm. 'But you've such a vivid imagination! Oh, God! You've missed out on so many things, books, poetry—'

He shrugged. 'I managed to get by.'

'Why didn't you tell them? Anybody ... Somebody would have—'

He shook his head. 'I don't know. I suppose it was my pride. I couldn't bear to think of what they might say. Hated to imagine how they'd pity me, see me as a weakling. Maybe it was the way I was brought up.'

She drew her knees up to her chin. Frowning, she gazed at the orange-red flames flickering in the valley. Everything looked so extravagantly beautiful. But underneath it all, were things really like that? Wasn't there always a shadow somewhere? 'Funny how people behave, isn't it?' she said. 'They miss out on each other all the time. Pass each other by as if they didn't seem to notice. 'I painted a picture, once. It was a water-colour, I remember, a study of Achill at sunset.' Nervously, she pushed a loose strand of hair back from her face. 'My art teacher, the unassailable Mr Grinley, tore it up and threw it in the bin. What would you do with a philistine like that! Delia thinks I'm a fool, wasting my time on art.'

Colm moved into the shade. He cracked a match on a stone and lit a cigarette. Exhaling slowly, he watched the smoke curl upwards. 'Who'd listen to Delia? What does she know about art, for God's sake? Go for what you want, yourself!' He caught a stick, rounded by the sea, and pegged it into the middle of the fire where the flames licked it greedily. 'I plan to buy a new boat, myself, a fifty foot fishing boat. As soon as I've enough money put together, I'm off. Some day, maybe,' he leaned towards her, smiling, 'I'll be master of the Cragann fishing fleet.'

At that moment Sara ran towards them, eyes luminous, dressed to kill. 'Music's what we want,' she cried, 'where's Willie Sara?'

Aine sat up with a jerk and stared at the vision in front of her. Arms akimbo, feet planted apart, Sara wore a sequined dress of gauze, something like the straining-cloth Delia used for her cottage cheese. 'Like it?' she preened, thrusting out her chest in a catwalk turn, 'do you like my dress?'

'Do I like what? For heaven's Sara, what is there to like? Julie and I have been here all evening. You only show up when the work is done. Go and look for Willie Sara, yourself!'

'Nasty little spitfire!' Sara blazed, her face going a mottled red. Turning on her heel, she swaggered off up the road.

From the corner of her eye Aine saw Colm's tall figure disappear across the green. She hauled herself up from the grass, flattened the creases in her drindl skirt, blackened by fire, and scanned the scene below her. The crowd had thickened. People were running here and there. Daniel had taken advantage of the night and was cooking his supper on the coals. The Hartigan boys frolicked at the water's edge splashing each other. There was no sign of Willie. Come to think of it, she hadn't seen Willie Sara all evening. Sometimes he went off on his own and spent the day fishing or maybe he'd cycle into town for a few hours. It couldn't be ... No! No! He'd said last night he hadn't touched a drop for weeks, yet ...

Panic stricken, she was off like a shot. She charged across the green and on to the foreshore, tufts of grass piercing the soles of her sandals, heels crushing the cockleshells. 'Willie!' she called, her voice drowned by the crashing of the waves on the far shore.

There was no reply.

'Willie! They're waiting up there for the music!' The sharpness of her own voice startled her. A seagull flying low wheeled in the opposite direction. Finally, she found him lying against the slipway asleep, feet crossed in front of him. 'You're needed,' she said, nudging him with the tip of her sandal, 'the dancers are waiting.'

Willie opened one eye, heaved himself up into a sitting position, took an ounce of tobacco from his pouch and began paring some of it off with his penknife. 'Easy now, easy! It'll do them no harm to wait, no harm at all!' He uncovered the marble-topped melodeon, pulled out the stops, ran his fingers over the row of buttons. One last draw from his pipe and he followed Aine across the green

Ever since Aine could remember Willie Sara had played the melodeon. It was said in Cragann that music was the legacy he received from his father. Both Michael Og and Sean Michael, his grandfather, had been playing before him. They performed at every wedding and funeral that took place between Belmullet and Westport. Wllie believed in music, in the power it had to overcome darkness. 'It's the language of the gods,' he said, 'needing to be played wherever people gather.' On this Midsummer's Eve he sat like Jupiter in his *sugan* chair playing the Carolan reel. Softly at first, then louder, the music faded in and out inviting whatever wasn't there to be present.

'Come on!' said Colm, leaping to his feet. He crooked an arm offering it to Aine.

They took their places on the boards. Around and around they went, eyes glinting with laughter. Not that Colm was any good at the dancing, but the girls in Cragann never seemed to notice.

Tim beckoned to Sara.

Sara rose to her feet, twirled and turned, passed over and under.

'Your petticoat's showing!' somebody called.

'It came from my aunt in the States!' She steered Tim through the dance, counting hop one, hop two, as expertly as if she were driving a donkey and cart.

Half-set over, the dancers threw themselves on the grass, breathless. The music stopped; the fire went out and people drifted away. Ma Hegarty called to her son Johnnie, the youngest of the Hegartys, to gather his things and come home. Having searched the green she found him, in the end, hiding behind Willie Sara's chair clinging to the last few minutes of magic. Jimmie Hartigan, Sara's four year old brother, had fallen asleep at the fire. His grandfather, old Shamie Cattigan, came out to look for him. He hoisted him up on his shoulders and carried him home.

After the crowd had gone a great stillness settled on the green. There wasn't a sound, not even the rustle of waves on the far shore, nor the cry of a seagull. Cragann was suddenly empty.

Aine cast a quick look around her. Debris was scattered everywhere, lodged between stones, strewn along the rocks ... lemonade bottles, sweet papers ... Further away Colm sat with his back against a rock, smoking. There was something detached, almost solitary, about the droop of his shoulders.

Julie and Tim were quietly dozing.

'I'm parched with the thirst,' Sara croaked, rattling her throat, 'anyone with anything to drink?'

'It's after midnight. Brannigans are closed,' Aine yawned.

Colm turned. He darted a quick look around at the three of them. Scrambling to his feet he ran to the boathouse and returned with a bottle in his hand. 'Water from Brannigans' well, eh, Sara?' he grinned, unwrapping a bottle of poiteen. He unscrewed the cork, sniffed the contents and took one long swig, swirling it around in his mouth.

'Is it lemonade you have there?' Julie asked, sitting up, blinking.

'Lemonade with a difference. It'll blow the top off your head!' He winked at Aine

Aine struggled to her feet. 'Give it to me!' she cried, 'give us the bottle. You're not the only one here who's thirsty.' Tussling, she wrenched the lemonade bottle from Colm's hand and raised it to her lips. 'Ouch!' Tears stung her eyes. Spluttering, she thrust it towards Sara.

Colm crept up and caught her by the waist.

'Let go!' she yelled, struggling to free herself, 'let go, you oaf!'

A shadow crossed the grass.

'Hand over that bottle!' Sergeant Maloney commanded in a cool and authorative voice, 'it's a bit late for young people like you to be out. You need your night's sleep.' He stared at Colm under bushy eyebrows. Removing his cap the Sergeant mopped his brow. This particular job wasn't his choice of work. Hadn't he a daughter, himself, once? She'd be the same age as these if she had lived. But all the same, the law was the law. Later on they'd thank him for observing it.

A wave of anger swept over Aine. She watched as the Sergeant lumbered across the grass, the bottle of poiteen tucked under his arm. Hell! she thought, how did he know? Neither wife nor child, living alone up there in the Barracks!'

'He'll probably drink it himself, the old rascal!' Colm spat, angrily.

Julie's face had turned pale. Sergeant Maloney was the man who raided her father's pub, locked people up if they got too out of hand. Julie gave the Sergeant a wide birth.

But Sara Hartigan knew better. She staggered to her feet, brushed the grass from her clothes and shook back her hair. In her nightly prowls Sara had often taken a turn around the Barracks. Like many another she knew the Sergeant could down a few glasses.

As Aine got up to go, she saw the jagged outline of Pat Neddy standing on a charred patch of grass beside the dying bonfire. Her lips tightened. Like the devil himself, she thought, standing in the middle of the embers!

Chapter Ten

The following Monday Cragann pupils were all back at school. It was just another school day where St Aengus' secondary school was concerned. Always on time, the pupils from Cragann were sitting at their desks long before the town scholars arrived.

Standing at the classroom window, Aine perused her weekly timetable. The door opened; the school secretary put in her head. 'Miss Reynolds wishes to see Aine Fogarty!'

'Me!' Aine gasped, 'Why does she want to see me?'

The secretary made no reply.

Once or twice every year, Aine encountered the headmistress and then only for a fleeting minute at the opening and closing of the school term. Sometimes, in the evenings, when she'd slip out early, she would see her watching from her window. What she was staring at, she had no idea.

Frowning, she left her books on her desk and walked sedately down the green-carpeted corridor. Miss Reynolds' office was on the right hand side at the far end. Her name was inscribed in gold letters on her door. 'Come in,' she called, in answer to Aine's knock.

Tall and spare, wearing dark rimmed glasses, the headmistress sat at a long mahogany table reading an official looking document. She glanced up, quickly, as Aine entered. 'I have a report here on my desk,' she said. 'Can you explain your conduct last Saturday night in Cragann?'

'Last Saturday night?'

'Yes.'

Aine felt the blood drain from her face. 'I don't know what you mean, Miss Reynolds. It was Midsummer's Eve. We were having a bit of fun at the bonfire.'

'According to this report your behaviour was, to say the least, disgraceful. You were drinking poiteen.'

Somewhere in the room a clock struck twelve. Julie and Sara would be preparing to leave their classroom. 'I didn't know it was poiteen,' Aine said, through dried lips.

'Who was instrumental in bringing it to the bonfire?'

No reply.

'Who was responsible for the poiteen?'

Still no reply.

'You realize how dangerous those spirits are. You know they're the source of blackguardism, of every evil deed committed around here, how they affect some people to the point of madness.'

Aine stood motionless. 'If only Miss Reynolds would go away, disappear, be spirited to Timbuktu, go anywhere out of her sight.'

The head teacher removed her glasses, folded them carefully on her desk and looked at her. 'If your father could see you now!' Trembling with anger, her voice was no bigger than a whisper.

Through the open window shouts of laughter floated up from the schoolyard. The pupils were out at play. Aine thought of Portree, of the surf rumbling at the Srutha where the mountain river tumbled into the sea. In her imagination she saw it, seething mountains of foam tossing restlessly on to the shore. Beyond the lobster pots seagulls swooped low over the currachs as they veered towards the islands. Calling ...

'He was somebody I could trust, honest, truthful, never touched drink,' the headmistress continued, as if talking to herself. She stood up, walked over to her desk and took out the slim black rulebook of St. Aengus'. 'Sit down!' she commanded, motioning Aine to a chair. She adjusted her glasses, cleared her throat and was about to speak.

Aine pushed the chair out of her way with a clatter and glared at the woman in front of her. 'Hump your old secondary school!' she cried.

'And when you go home,' the headmistress said coldly, 'stay for a month. Your aunt will deal with you!'

Chapter Eleven

As she stood looking out to sea, Aine recalled the previous few days. She still bristled when she thought of her row with Miss Reynolds. The headmistress' malevolent green eyes and bloodless lips haunted her. What right had she to speak of my father like that, she raged, flinging a stone into the foaming water, my dead father! Why wasn't it Delia's or the priest's or somebody else's name she invoked? Poiteen indeed! Pity she wouldn't try a drop, herself. It might brighten her up!

But apart from the odd vitriolic outburst, Aine's days out of school passed harmoniously enough. In the mornings she would sit at an upstairs window and watch the sea swell into great mountains of water, the boats sway up and down like seagulls. If the day were wet she'd don a sou'wester and walk across the hill to Portree, where she'd have a better view of the islands.

The first of July crept in unnoticed. All over Cragann the air became heavy with the scent of summer. Roses and marigolds grew in profusion in Delia's garden.

As Aine was leaving the house one evening, Delia called her.

'I've invited the new bank manager and his wife to dinner.'

'So?'

'You might give me a hand with the cooking. He's a man of powerful influence.'

'What kind of influence?'

'Well for one thing, he's known to get people jobs. Mags Doherty, for instance, after a word or two in his ear was given a position in Donnellys' hotel the next day.'

'Bah!'

Delia pretended not to hear. She opened the cupboard, took out the weighing scales and placed the ingredients for rhubarb pie on the table. Though an experienced cook, Delia never left anything to chance. She weighed and measured every ingredient.

Aine eyed her coldly. Was this another of Delia's schemes to get her to work in a stuffy old bank? What did *she* know of bankers and their swanky wives? Frowning, she yanked open the drawer of the dresser and rummaged for her cookery apron. Having measured the flour she scooped it on to the scales and shovelled it into a bowl. Better look after the bank manager, she thought, throwing in a few extra fistfuls. And of course the old dowager, herself. Chances are, she'll have a ferocious appetite. They always do. How did Delia manage to acquire such an assortment of cronies? Here she was, a prisoner all evening, having to listen to a load of codswallop. Afterwards, of course, there would be the usual compliments, unctuous farewells.

'Aine!'

'What?' She jumped at the sound of her aunt's voice.

'Have you washed your hands?'

'No'

'For God's sake! Are you ever going to be trained as a housekeeper?' Delia stared at the mounds of flour spilled on the table and floating on top of the milk.

'I never said I could cook.'

'Well, high time you learned. It's the first thing a woman must know before she gets married?'

'Who said I'm going to marry? If ever I do I'll have my own housekeeper, somebody who'll do all the cooking and washing as well.'

'Hmm! And what will you do all day, may I ask?'

'Paint!'

'Paint?'

'I'll work in my studio. Paint wonderful pictures, landscapes, places I know ... and yes, far away places,' she added dreamily.

'Do you really believe that art alone is going to boil the pot?'

'Money isn't everything. There are other things in life besides money.' Meditatively, she rubbed the margarine into the flour with the tips of her fingers, letting the mixture fall in a fine powder over the sides of the bowl.

'Fool!' Delia snorted, 'you'll soon learn sense!'

Punctuality was an important virtue in Delia's books. At five to seven that evening Aine put the final touches to her aunt's dinner table. Four wine glasses, linen serviettes and side plates. All in order. Mr Finnegan would sit at the head of the table. She removed the cat from her place on the hearth rug and shooed her out to the kitchen. Through the open hatch, between the kitchen and the dining room, she saw Delia's angular figure bending over the range. A fragrant odour of cooking drifted in towards her, crisp brown pastry, apple dumplings ... mmm!' Even the percolated coffee was beginning to smell good.

'Potatoes are boiled,' Delia called out, 'the carrots will take another few minutes; prawns are almost cooked.' She peered anxiously in through the hatch. 'Everything all right in there?'

'Yeah, unless, of course, he wants to be fed from a silver spoon.'

There was a knock on the hall door.

'Close that hatch!' Delia commanded tersely, hurrying to answer it.

Aine made no reply. She had disappeared to the scullery to remove the flour from under her nails. The kitchen hatch was left wide open.

'It's so kind of you, Delia,' Mr and Mrs Finnegan gushed, as Aine returned to the dining room a minute later.

'Delighted you were able to visit us,' Delia replied, taking her visitors' coats and hanging them out in the hall. 'It will take some time for you to get used to the people in Cragann.'

'Well, if they're anything like you we've nothing to worry about,' Mr Finnegan replied gallantly, removing his hat.

A portly man with a large pot belly, Bill Finnegan looked every minute of his sixty odd years. Having been transferred from a bank in Dublin's inner city, he looked forward now to a more tranquil life in Cragann. His wife, Tess, seemed a good many years younger than her husband.

'This is Aine,' Delia said, introducing her niece. 'She's been with me ever since she was a child. But she's more than a child now, let me tell you!'

The Finnegans laughed. 'Hello!' they both said, simultaneously.

There was an awkward silence.

'Well, no point in standing,' Delia said quickly, 'let's go inside.'

A cheerful fire burned in the dining room grate creating shadowy patterns on the pale-green emulsion walls. The cherry red curtains, which Delia had made on her Singer machine, hung in folds over the bay window giving the room a warm glow.

'I'm sure you'd like a nice glass of whiskey,' Delia said, addressing her guests, 'something to warm you up. Tess, what will you drink? Sherry?'

'Whiskey for me, please. I feel a bit chilled.'

'And what about you, Bill?'

'A whiskey will do fine, thank you.'

'I'll have a sherry, myself. Aine, will you get two whiskies and a sherry?'

'Have one yourself, girl,' Mr Finnegan called, seeing Aine's figure disappear around the door.

Delia rose and followed Aine to the kitchen. She opened the window to release the steam. Checked the oven for the correct heat. The rhubarb pie was browning nicely; cheese sauce smooth as cream on the back of the spoon. Frowning, she stared at the sink. It was full to the brim with unwashed saucepans, bowls, cutlery, everything Aine could lay hands on. The kitchen had been bright and shining a few minutes earlier.

Though a trifle shabby, Delia's kitchen was her pride and joy. High and spacious, its long rectangular window looked out over the Western hills capturing the gold of the evening sun. In the past, all the young Fogartys sat at that same scrubbed table. And though the walls were faded, curtains threadbare and the tiles the same old terra cotta red, Fogartys' kitchen still had that indefinable air of grandeur.

'You won't be having whiskey?' Delia asked anxiously, ignoring the pile-up in the sink.

'Why not?'

68

'There just isn't enough to go around. We've only got half a bottle.'

'Well that can be rectified. We can top it with water.'

'For heaven's sake, Aine! Water the Bank Manager's whiskey!'

'Of course! It wouldn't do to send the gentleman home footless, would it?'

'But he'll know!'

'That old codger wouldn't know whiskey from tomato juice.'

'Slainte!' Delia said, a minute later, raising her glass as she sat sedately in her leather-backed chair facing her guests. Things were going according to plan; Aine appeared to be in one of her good moods; Mr Finnegan had replied to her toast though with a somewhat watery smile.

Sipping his whiskey, slowly, Bill Finnegan's glance wavered in the direction of his wife.

Tess drank hers in silence.

'Well, I'd better begin serving,' Delia said, rising and moving towards the kitchen.

'Can I help?' Mrs Finnegan called after her. Tess had begun to regale them with stories of her childhood. Brought up in the south suburban area of Dublin she had been accustomed to many of the modern conveniences.

'Thank you,' Delia said, smiling her appreciation, 'we can manage.'

Aine followed her aunt to the kitchen. 'Can I help?' she mimicked, closing the kitchen door. 'I bet she couldn't make a decent cup of tea without calling in the fire brigade.' She stopped suddenly. Delia stood in the centre of the floor, speechless.

'What's wrong?'

'The cat!'

'Well, what about her?'

Her aunt's face turned a mottled red. 'The prawns! She's eaten the lot.'

Aine stared incredulously at the empty plate. The pound of prawns bought in the fishmonger's the evening before had vanished holis polis, devoured almost before their very eyes. All except pieces of slimy skin, which old Pangur had considered unfit for consumption. 'Well, she's certainly got one up on the Finnegans,' she observed, wrinkling her nose. 'Now what?' She opened the cupboards and scanned the shelves. 'I have it!' she cried, snapping her fingers, 'we can try something else. A tin of sardines! Sardines make a delicious main course.'

'Sardines!'

'Yeah. Cooked in batter they can be really quite tasty. And the Finnegans won't notice the difference. Colm said they do this in France all the time. And what's good enough for the French is good enough for the Bank Manager.'

Delia said nothing. Stony-faced she watched as Aine fumbled with the tin opener. Having emptied the tin of sardines on to a plate, she cracked a few eggs against the side of the bowl. Humming cheerfully, she added some flour and milk and whisked all three to a creamy batter. 'Ready!' she cried. Lifting the sardines-in-batter off the pan she arranged them neatly on plates, picked up the loaded tray and sailed into the dining room, followed by Delia.

Sitting opposite Mr Finnegan at the table, Aine eyed him curiously. A heavily built man with massive shoulders, his brushed-back hair and high forehead suggested a man of intellectual leaning. 'Like a stuffed rabbit,' she thought, appraising his immaculate white collar and waistcoat. 'I couldn't imagine *him* mucking it in Cragann. What with the roads flooded, gales blowing at ninety miles an hour—'

'Pass the butter please!' Delia threw her a withering look. 'Oh, what a wonderful shade of blue!' she exclaimed, turning and complimenting Tess on her royal blue two-piece suit.

'Bill's favourite colour, isn't it, darling?' Tess' pink-and-white complexion was more pronounced than usual. She gazed with admiration at Delia's Dresden dinner set and smoothed back her ash blonde hair, displaying a set of sparkling rings on her middle fingers. 'Cragann's such a charming little village,' she sighed, 'such wonderful people! The scenery's so incredibly unspoiled. A shame, something can't be done to put it on the map. A new hotel, perhaps?'

Aine fidgeted with her table napkin. Stupid old bid! she thought sourly. Could she not imagine something more interesting than a commercial watering hole?

'Don't you think an hotel would be a good idea to attract tourists I mean?' Tess asked prettily, turning to Delia.

Delia nodded. 'Something we could have done with a long time ago, I assure you.'

'But, there's the question of electricity,' Bill pointed out. 'It would take an amount of power to supply an hotel. And since the houses aren't wired it would be rather awkward, wouldn't it?'

'I don't know why there's all this fuss about an hotel!' Aine burst out. In her mind's eye she pictured it, a sprawl of concrete disgorging a bevy of sunbathers on to Cragann strand. They'd set up their sun shades and leave behind them a trail of litter, beer bottles and cigarette packages. Water in Cragann would soon lose its sparkle. Basking seals wouldn't be seen anymore ...

'But don't you believe in development, my dear?'

'Development?'

'This place needs to be modernised. There are plenty of enterprising people around to develop the village, open a sports complex, a few restaurants ...'

'And a night-club, perhaps?'

Tess fingered her pearl necklace. She threw Aine a sidelong glance. 'Well not exactly,' she purred, 'something more practical, a profitable investment to attract strangers.'

'People have lived happily around here for hundreds of years. We don't need hotels or tourists to make life more exciting. It's a question of attitudes. Animals and birds have their rights too.'

'I agree entirely with you, Tess,' Delia interrupted. 'Tourists and holidaymakers are just what we need to bring new life to the village. There would be more houses and money. Emigration has drained our village of its population. There isn't enough work. Those who stay have either to pick winkles or carrageen moss or work in the factory. The only other option they have is to emigrate to England or Scotland.'

Mr Finnegan was silent. He was busy trying to mop up coffee

spilled on Delia's tablecloth without attracting the attention of his wife. Having wiped his hands on his table napkin he lit a cigar and sat back. 'And what about you, Aine? What do you plan to do when you leave school?'

Delia coughed.

'I'm going to be an artist, a professional artist.'

'She knows there's no future in art,' Delia rushed in, refilling the coffee cups, 'it might be better if she applied for the Bank.'

The Bank Manager's eyes were fixed on a butterfly caught between the panes of glass in the window.

'It's difficult to get into the Bank,' Tess remarked sweetly, plunging her teeth into a granny smith's apple.

'She has a good head for figures, knows all about book keeping, is excellent with—'

'Now, now, don't misunderstand me, my dear,' Tess cooed, placing her heavily jewelled fingers on Delia's sleeve. 'I'm sure Aine's quite a smart young lady.' Her eyes flickered. 'But the standard of education required in a bank is, well, shall we say, rather high. There are excellent opportunities out there, shop assistants, waitresses ... The list is endless.'

Delia's face darkened. She chewed a crisp oatmeal biscuit with concentrated fierceness. Thrusting out her chin, she stared into space determined to ward off any further comments.

Bill reached for the ashtray, flicking a mound of ash from his cigar. He glanced at Aine under half-closed lids. 'The Bank is a good steady job, my dear, something worth aiming at. There's plenty of free time, good holidays and the salary's not bad. More importantly, there are plenty of opportunities for promotion. A girl like you would do well—'

'But I don't want to work in a bank!' Aine protested. 'All my life I've wanted to be an artist!'

Raising his eyebrows, Bill picked an imaginary piece of food from his teeth. He glanced at his watch. No use in arguing with this young woman. Like many another, she'd have to learn by experience. 'If you'll excuse me,' he said, nodding to Delia, 'I'm meeting a colleague of mine in Westport. The golfing bug, you know,' he added, laughing.

Tess cast a covert glance at her husband. 'This is my night out for Bridge, darling. Delia, my dear, we've had such a wonderful evening. You'll have to visit us sometime ... when things settle down, perhaps. So many jobs to be done, carpets, curtains, you know how it is.' She drew the collar of her jacket up around her throat.

Delia disappeared to the hall to fetch the coats.

Aine scraped back her chair and stood up. She piled the dishes on to a tray and carried them out to the scullery. Evening light was already fading. Coals from the fire cast a steady glow in the room.

'Good Lord!' Bill nudged his wife. 'Just look at this!'

Stacked along the sideboard, close to the window, lay a pile of recently finished paintings. He walked over and leafed through them. There was a variety of scenes, some painted in the open, sketches of animals and birds. An oil painting of a Western seascape; yachts counter-changed against a background of distant hills; a water-colour of Achill with Sliabh Mor in the background. And another of the Atlantic coastline painted in swirling yellows, oranges and browns reminding him of boyhood holidays spent in the Donegal Gaeltacht. A pencil-sketch of a windy day with fluffy cumulus clouds scudding across the sky; a fast-moving river scene; misty morning on the coast of Mayo and a view of Craggan Bay seen from Belmullet heights. At the bottom of the pile was a painting of Portree, sea edged with white, beach, rocks ... 'An astounding amount of work for such a young artist,' he breathed, his eyes becoming hazy. His thoughts drifted back to the days of his youth, to the dreams he had had of becoming a painter, those idealistic days when the whole world lay at his feet. Nothing was impossible then, no mountain too high to climb. But, alas! His father ... With a sigh he placed the paintings back on the sideboard, rearranging them one by one as he found them. No point in useless regrets, he thought. The past was over; what was done was done. He walked back to rejoin his wife.

Delia returned, scarves and overcoats thrown over her arm. Beaming, she handed them to her guests.

'Keep an eye on that hatch!' the Bank Manager winked, as he followed his wife to the door.

Chapter Twelve

It was time, Delia thought, for Aine to sort out her grievances and forget the past. She still brooded over the row she had had with Miss Reynolds. The penalty imposed on her by the headmistress still galled her. Whenever anyone mentioned her name Aine stiffened with temper, and it was nothing compared to the hostility she entertained towards the unsuspecting Sergeant. A mission, Delia decided, was what Aine needed. A mission would settle her.

Soon afterwards, it was announced from the altar that a mission would take place in Craggan. 'The missioners will travel from Galway the previous evening ,' the parish priest said, 'to give them enough time to settle in.'

Old Daniel Cassidy hobbled from the top of the hill with news of the missioners' arrival. From his vantage point up high, Daniel saw a green Volkswagen with a Galway registration drive past the village pump and pull up at the presbytery gates. Two robust clergymen, cloaks over their shoulders and sectioned birettas on their heads, got out. The priest's housekeeper met them and carried in their cases.

'It's those Friars again!' Daniel informed the neighbours, gathered in Delia's that night for a game of twenty-five.

'Glory be to God!' Willie Sara exclaimed, 'we're in for a time of it. They'll frighten the wits out of us all!'

'Some people could do with a fright,' Delia remarked, glancing at her niece.

'If it's me you're looking at,' Aine warned, 'I'm not going. Why should I go to a stupid old mission?'

'Holy Jerusalem, if it isn't the joker she has!' Willie remarked as Delia pounced on Daniel's knave of hearts.

Aine shrugged her shoulders.

The following evening as the church bells were ringing, Delia set out for the mission. She wore her black suede coat and boater hat which she had purchased specially in Galway.

As she reached the chapel gates the mission stalls were already in place. She paused a moment to take a look at the statues. She'd have to buy a new Infant of Prague; Nora Hartigan had knocked the head off the old one the day they were doing the spring-cleaning. There was an assortment of scapulars. Pictures of Our Lady, eyes rolling to heaven, hung at the back.

Inside, the church was in semi-darkness. She genuflected before the altar and found a seat in the middle aisle. Nearer the communion rails she recognized Flo Hartigan's hat. Maggie Holohan sat in the seat behind Flo saying her rosary. Delia opened her prayer book and began her novena: *Thou, O Lord, shalt open my lips ...* Whispering from behind distracted her. Her new boater hat obstructed the view. She changed places and settled down again to await the missioner.

A second later, Aine slipped in behind Delia. In a candy-striped dress and red beret, she sat next to Julie and Sara, close to the side door.

The tiny church filled up quickly. People came from every direction, down from the mountains, over the hills, even as far away as Bangor Erris. They crowded the side aisles and filled the sanctuary. The air in the church bcame heavy with the smell of mothballs and newly mown hay. Smoke billowed from the thurible and rose towards the rafters. The congregation coughed.

As the missioner mounted the pulpit the coughing ceased. A vigorous man in his thirties, he was tall and fresh faced. His sleek dark hair, brushed smoothly back, reflected the flickering light of the candles. He wore a black cossack and leather cincture into which a crucifix was thrust like a crusader's sword. A string of rosary beads brushed his thigh.

What doth it profit a man if he gain the whole world and suffer the loss of his own soul?

With a sweep of his hand the missioner began his sermon. There wasn't a sound. Willie Sara, standing beside Daniel on the side aisle, shuffled his feet. His fingers closed around the stem of his *dudin* buried deep in his inside pocket.

'My dear people, I've come here this evening—'

'Hah!' Daniel grunted, 'pity you don't stay where you were!'

'Women and men sitting before me to-night, you'll all have to die some day. It doesn't matter how or when or where but if you die in mortal sin'- his voice rose and descended to a whisper -'you'll be buried in hell for all ... eternity.'

Delia nodded. She was pleased with the way things were going. A black and yellow butterfly flew in through the open window and fluttered around the sanctuary. It landed on the statue of the virgin and then came to rest on top of Flo Hartigan's hat.

The men at the back cleared their throats. Bronzed and weather-beaten, they were men of the sea, accustomed to raging storms.

Aine stifled a yawn. Through the open window a chorus of birds could be heard fighting for their place on the trees. She craned her neck. Ten minutes to eight on Delia's watch. Half an hour more before the missioner would finish.

'Young men and girls!' the missioner thundered, pointing a finger in the direction of Sara Hartigan.

Sara tossed back her hair. In the gathering darkness her hazel-green eyes were a phosphorescent glow.

'If there's anyone down there among you guilty of the sin of concupiscence, of gallivanting at midnight, loitering on the boreens ... larking at the crossroads, he's dancing on the cobblestones of hell!'

Aine sat bolt upright. There was a sharp in-take of breath behind her.

Delia looked back at her niece. She caught sight of Sara's flaming red hair gleaming in the candle light. Impudent hussy! High time her mother did something about *her,* roaming the countryside flaunting herself, not to mention playing up to the inspector! And now she's throwing her cap at young Holohan! Delia folded her arms and fixed her attention on the missioner.

The missioner lowered his head. 'As for you poitin makers,' he bellowed, 'you good-for-nothing hoors! Get rid of those stills! Get rid of those stills I tell you!' He leaned forward, throwing his weight against the edge of the pulpit.

The Sergeant looked across at Pat Neddy. Pat Neddy wiped his nose on his sleeve.

'And let this be my final warning. Anybody before me this evening who stores up barrels of poiteen or spends nights in drunken stupors, it would be better I say, better if he were never born!'

'That's about the lot of us,' Willie Sara whispered gloomily.

Somewhere a woman sighed. A breeze under the door lifted the cords on the window causing them to flap like a funeral knell.

Delia clasped her rosary beads tighter. Opening her handbag she treated her neighbours to a cloud of lavender.

Aine looked slowly around. From the corner of her eye she could see the women's faces, tilt of their chins. What were they thinking of? Were they ...? Suddenly, memories of the Midsummer bonfire came rushing back, memories of figures dancing ... Sweat broke out on her forehead. Her heart began to thump. She leaped to her feet clutching the holy water font bought at the stalls, lunged past an old woman in shawls and charged down the aisle.

Through a cloud of incense Colm's tall figure disengaged itself from the shadows. Wearing the green and gold Local Defence uniform, he stared up at the rafters as if he were seeing them for the first time. As Aine reached the last row of seats he glanced across. In the twinkling of an eye he had elbowed a path through the men, brushed the black shawled women out of his way, grabbed her by the arm and piloted her out the door. 'Bloody old hypocrite! He should have seen me the day of the February fair!'

'Did you see old Reynolds sitting in the middle aisle, ogling?'

'Pity we didn't offer her a drop ... eh?'

Without a word Aine began to laugh. She laughed till the tears rolled down her cheeks. Hoops of laughter rang across the fields and resounded in the church. People leaving by the side door looked at each other. Others hurried home, eager to return to their ordinary tasks.

As they approached the crossroads they paused. The evening air had grown damp. Drops of dew had settled on the hedges and on the tall grass.

'I'll have to head back,' Colm said, 'Hegarty will be waiting at the schoolhouse gate.'

Aine wiped the smudges from her face. She watched as Colm's tall figure disappeared across the hill. Removing her beret she stuffed it into her pocket. A cool breeze lifted her hair and fanned her cheeks. She began to walk fast then faster. Finally, she broke into a run. When she reached the spot where the village came into view she paused. *Dancing on the cobblestones of hell diddle-ee-i!* she sang, pirouetting in the middle of the road, her only audience being the birds perched on the telegraph wire. Suddenly her face changed. She thought of Miss Reynolds. She pictured her at school calling the roll. *Aine Fogarty?* Nobody would answer. Nobody ever did. Miss Reynolds despised her, had despised her a long time. Was it because she was the daughter of a Saxon or because *her* man had been stolen, the handsomest, most sought-after man in the whole parish?

In less than a minute she had reached the house. She rushed upstairs, took out her pencils, laid a fresh sheet of drawing paper on the table stretching it full-length and began to draw. An image of a woman took shape, an angry virago swirling in the arms of a beleaguered policeman. Choosing strong vibrant colours, crimson, ultra marine and chromium yellow, she mixed them with the handle of her brush.

The painting was an ordinary watercolour. It would pass unheeded at any exhibition but for its garish colours. Aagh! The Battenberg pink of the woman's hat and blood-red orange of her dress would smack one straight in the eye. She flung the brush on to the table and ran downstairs. Opening the front of the range she dried the painting before a few resurrected coals and left the house.

As Colm strolled home that evening, he paused before entering the village. The evening air had grown cold. A sharp breeze blew from the sea rustling the leaves of the evergreens. He was joined, a minute later, by Tim Hegarty and Pat Hartigan; they began to discuss the happenings of the day at the training camp. Tim unfastened his rifle, took up position in the middle of the road and began to demonstrate his newly acquired skills. 'Attention!' He clicked his heels. 'Aim!'

Seeing a passing cormorant he lifted his rifle. 'You might as well be dead after that sermon to-night!'

Exclamations from behind distracted him.

'Holy Jerusalem! What's this?' Pat Hartigan was peering up at the telegraph pole. Pinned half-way up was a life-size drawing of a woman, a woman in the arms of a bemused policeman. 'Sergeant Maloney, I'll be damned, in a tango with old Maggie Reynolds!'

They all dissolved into guffaws of laughter.

'What a lark! Wait till old Maloney sees himself in action. Say, look how she stares as if she were about to jump off the pole!' Hartigan pulled the collar of his coat up over his head in mock horror.

Colm scrutinised the poster. There was something familiar about that style, the boldness of line, exuberance of colour. 'A stunning piece of work!' he exclaimed. 'Well whatever about you guys, I'm positively starving.' Signalling to his companions that he was leaving, he turned on his heel and headed towards the village.

When he arrived at the crossroads where the road forks for Portree, he paused and retraced his steps. Passing by Fogartys he gave a quick look in. Aine was sitting at the table, writing. He could see her head, her outlined profile. Her burnished hair was braided in an Alice-in-Wonderland plait, magnificent luminous hair sufficient in itself to light up any room. Flames from the fire were reflected in the Sacred Heart picture hanging on the opposite wall. He averted his gaze and looked out to sea.

On the outskirts of the village he stood before the telegraph pole and looked up at the poster. Only one person in Cragann could draw like that. It was the work of an artist, a born artist. But who in God's name could help her? Glancing around, he met the impassive stares of Hartigans' cows being driven home by a tottering sheep dog. He looked at the poster again and began to laugh. Old Maggie Reynolds mightn't see it up there! Standing on tiptoe, he dragged it down and stuffed it into his pocket. Glancing at his watch he found it was after eight. He retraced his steps and took the road to Portree.

Miss Reynolds occupied a two-roomed cottage about three quarters of a mile from the village in from the road. Fronted by lawn and box hedge, a tired old hollyhock growing at the corner relieved it of its otherwise bare appearance. Colm gazed up at the windows. Painted in dark yellow ochre they were tightly shut, lace curtains and half-blinds drawn. Every bit as drab as *her*, he thought. He took the poster from his pocket, strode over to the pillar and fastened it to the side. About to turn on his heel he paused. But she mightn't see it up there! He removed the poster again and tried the gate. It was padlocked. Without a moment's hesitation he scaled the wall and strode up to the window. Through a parting in the curtains he could see into the living room. Everything was in order, house, garden, the same as if nobody lived there. He went to the door, flattened himself down on the doorstep and shoved the poster under the lintel. All was silent. The only sound to be heard was the gentle swishing of the evergreens. It was already dark. Lights in the village twinkled in the valley below. Humming softly, he climbed the wall and set out for home.

Chapter Thirteen

It wasn't so much that she was missing school that annoyed Aine. Deep down, she felt she wasn't missing anything. She explained this to Willie Sara.

Willie was inclined to agree. 'But all the same,' he told her, 'it mightn't be a bad thing at all if you went back to the schooling. Things will settle, you wait and see. It's only a ripple in the ocean.'

The nub of Aine's problem was Delia. Delia never let an opportunity pass without reminding her of the terrible disgrace she had brought to the Fogartys. 'Never before in my whole life,' she said, 'did I have to endure anything like this. Where did you get your wildness?'

'Where do you think?' Aine asked, biting into a piece of fresh apple cake, 'not from the wind surely!' She and her aunt were sitting at the kitchen table having their evening meal.

'Well,' said Delia, as she buttered a slice of bread, 'there's one thing sure, you didn't take after me or after your father. John Fogarty, God rest him, was a law-abiding man.'

Aine put down her cup. Her lips tightened. Would Delia never give up? Never relax for at least one minute without getting into a sweat about the poiteen? Through the open window came the sound of laughter. High and boisterous, the Hartigan boys were on their way home from school. At any other time she'd have been part of them, swapping bits of gossip, slagging. Frowning she shook back her hair, took her jacket from the hall and left the house.

She walked briskly along by the sea. Turning to her right, she headed towards Portree where she wouldn't have to meet the scholars. She continued on until she came to a spot beyond the hill where there was a better view of the islands. Straight ahead, were

81

those smoky grey stacks carved against the skyline. The sandy white beaches of Inis Begin beckoned her. She pictured those azure blue skies, the barnacle geese flying low at evening. Tired from walking, she sat at the side of the road and contemplated the prospects of getting there.

Some minutes later she rose, shook the pebbles from her shoes and straightened her skirt. It was then she noticed the old woman. From a distance she saw her, traipsing along the rutted road, basket hanging from her arm. As she drew nearer she could see her clearly, multicoloured shawl wrapped loosely around her, check kerchief knotted at the back of her neck.

'You must be Delia Fogarty's girl,' Sibby Pete said, drawing up close to her.

'I am,' Aine said, surprised that Sibby hadn't recognized her.

Sibby's beady eyes scanned her up and down. 'D'you want your palm read?'

Aine dug deep into her pockets. 'There!' she said, thrusting a sixpenny piece towards her. 'Seeing you were smart enough to prophesy the drownings, maybe you'd read what's in the stars for me.'

Sibby Pete glanced at the coin. She turned it over a few times. Shifting the basket up higher on her arm she examined Aine's outstretched palm. 'You're an orphan,' she rasped.

'You don't say!' Aine tossed back her head, derisively.

'Wait! It's the sign of the Zodiac. Sign of the crescent moon. Those high and mighty notions you have, Miss, will get you nowhere, nowhere at all. In the end, it's your heart that will tell you what you want. But you're going to have to pay. He! He! He! You're going to have to pay.'

Aine caught the sixpence and threw it in the dust. 'Be off you old rogue!' she cried, stamping her foot.

Sibby Pete picked up the coin and stuffed it into the folds of her dress. She drew her shawl closely around her and shuffled off down the road as if she hadn't heard her.

Darkness was falling. A new moon shone through the clouds. Before setting out for home Aine took another coin from her pocket, flipped it a few times in the silver light, laid it on the flat of her hand and blessed herself. In Cragann a new moon brought a special warning. It was never to be seen through glass.

The following day she set out for the islands, accompanied by Julie, in Willie Sara's currach. It was early on Saturday morning. As they sailed from Cragann the sun was rising over Achill creating a thick haze. As Willie rowed, the currach slid over the bottle-green sea creaking and knocking at the rowlocks. Further out, the call of the curlew could be heard far off across the water. Aine leaned over and gazed into the depths. 'Aren't we very close to it, Willie?' she asked, in an awed tone.

'Aye. Only a half of an inch between us and it. Another little bit and we'd be landed down under.'

'There's a great swell out there beyond Carrageen.'

'A wonderful pull altogether.'

'Can you swim, Willie?' She trailed her hand through the churning sea.

'Naw.'

'Never learned to swim?'

'Sure I've been in a currach all my life. Where would I get time for swimming?'

Somewhere near Carrageen Mast, within sight of the islands, she rose to her feet, eyes shining. 'Faster, Willie! Pull harder!' Swinging her hips she rocked the currach.

'D'you want us to drown, or what?'

'Who'd be talking of drowning on a day like this?'

'Be careful now, don't put your foot through the canvas.' Willie scanned the horizon, blue eyes crinkling at the corners. The day was sultry. He removed his jersey, turning his seaman's cap backwards on his head to protect his neck from the sun. His open-necked shirt revealed a brown sinewy body glistening with beads of sweat.

Julie sat quietly beside Aine, eyes flickering, nervously. When the currach mounted a wave she clutched the sides knowing there was nothing underneath to balance them. Through the tarred canvas, separating them from the Atlantic Ocean, the sliding waters could be heard. 'Aine, stop!' she cried, gripping her seat as the currach began to rock from side to side.

'You're safe with Willie!'

'Stop it, I say.'

'There's nothing to fear.'

'Willie!' Julie screamed.

'Can't you leave her,' Willie Sara said, turning a reprimanding eye on Aine, 'don't you see she's frightened?'

Contrite, Aine glanced at the ashen face of her cousin. 'Oh, alright!' she assented.

As they approached Inis Begin Willie Sara brought the currach in fast. The stone pier had been washed away; the beach was their only access to the island. He jumped out as the bow of the currach touched the shore and pulled it in the remainder of the way.

Aine stepped lightly on to the sand followed by Julie. As she lifted her face to the sun she felt like Oisin as he landed on Tir Na Nog. The conflict of the previous days had rolled away, lost in the clouds scudding above her.

Having deposited their luggage in a safe place, she helped Willie beach the currach. Crunching the cockleshells, they pulled it up on the grass where it would be safe from the marauding Atlantic. For all its size the currach was surprisingly light. Skilfully crafted by an intermesh of plywood, its delicate frame had a covering of tarred canvas. The acrid aroma of tar reminded her of those long lazy days in summer, mornings when she'd lie in bed and listen to the fishermen's voices echoing across the water.

They collected their baggage, a picnic basket, two sleeping bags borrowed from Holohans' and Willie's fishing tackle. Like most of the fishermen in Cragann Willie fished off the islands in summer and grazed his sheep on their sandy hills in winter.

On entering the village on Inis Begin they were immediately struck by its silence. Only twenty odd years since it was inhabited by people. Already it had lost all signs of humanity. Nobody passed by the broken doors; the roofs of the houses had collapsed. In the distance they heared the gabble of the barnacle geese as they clapped their wings over the water.

'We'll have to search for a well,' Julie said, dropping her knapsack.

'Over there!' Aine pointed to a nearby field where they saw a running stream glinting. 'All we need is a container.'

The cottage where they deposited their luggage had been deserted for years. A thicket of nettles and ragwort spread out from its walls; sand sifted across the hearth. Inside, the rooms were crammed with wreckage; rolls of cotton, baulks of timber. Crayfish pots were piled on the floor. Stacked in a corner there were a few wooden stools, a bale of rubber, a billycan and a candle stuck in a jar.

Using the kindling gathered from the shore, Aine prepared a fire in the hearth. With a match she had got from Willie she set it ablaze. 'Speak!' she commanded, waving her hands over the pile of kindling.

'Incantations and spells!' Julie cried.

'Speak! Tell me.'

'That's a sin!' Julie accused, quoting from the catechism.

'Shh!' Aine put her finger to her lips. She pointed to an orange green flame fluttering in the grate.

Julie snatched up the billycan and walked off haughtily. When she returned, a minute later, Aine was still on her knees communing with the flames. Placing the can of water on the fire she laid two tin cups and a parcel of sandwiches on one of the stools.

'Is it proof you are looking for?' she asked, as they sat at an improvised table having their meal.

'Proof? What d'you mean?'

'Well, you know.'

'Careful, we're not alone!' A robin had alighted on Aine's plate and was pecking the crumbs dropped from her sandwiches. They looked on in silence as it stood boldly, head sideways, watching them. A second later, it flew upwards beating its wings off the rafters of the old house. Aine made an effort to catch it but the agitated bird stayed in the far corner refusing to stir.

'Take this.' Julie offered her the handle of a broom.

Gently, she guided the robin to the open door. A minute or two later, they heard the whirring of wings as it flew out, up into the sky.

Having finished their lunch of sandwiches and tea they washed their cups.

'Going walking?' Julie asked, as Aine began to study an old map she had taken from her pocket.

'As far as the ruin of the old monastery. I'll take a look at the settlement.'

'The day's warm,' Julie yawned, 'I think I'll hang around for a bit.'

As she walked south from the village Aine came upon a landscape of stone. Leaping, sometimes stumbling over a wild terrain, she spotted a chasm in the cliffs. It reminded her of Hennesys' pond in Portree, a jagged causeway sculpted from the rocks. The gorge was roughly shaped, well rounded inside by the relentless pounding of the sea. Staring at her from the depths was a grey seal. She disappeared instantly only to return a few minutes later with four of her young, pert noses visible as they swam. 'You're alright, you lucky little sea dogs, you know who you are!' She dropped a few pebbles into the water. Somewhere from the depths of the chasm she thought she heard a reply.

Having left the seals behind she scanned the landscape. There was practically nothing on Inis Begin that wasn't a memorial, adapted to something new. Pagan pillars and monuments had been carved with a cross. Columba's old church was built on the site of a druid's temple. Even the god Baal was converted into a respectable looking image of the devil.

Chapter Fourteen

'You almost missed out on the mackerel,' Willie Sara said, as Aine rejoined them after a leisurely walk around the Island. Stooped over the fire, cooking, Willie was enveloped in a thick column of smoke, a sack apron tied around his waist.

'I'm starved,' Aine sniffed, eyeing the steaming food.

'Well, nobody's going to stop you from eating.' He passed her a plate of heaped up floury potatoes and a crisp brown mackerel.

'You've a fine crop of spuds this year, Willie,' she said, sampling a potato from its jacket.

'Better than the last crop of poreens, I'll grant you.'

'What happened to make such a difference?'

'The land needed a rest. Overworked it was. The priest came in a currach on Brigid's Day and blessed it.'

'Are you sorry you left it?' She looked around at the scattering of monuments and remains of beehive huts.

'Left it!' Willie drained his last drop of tea. 'We never left the island.'

'Didn't you all go ashore?'

'Aye! That was after the drowning, the night of the Great Storm. It was an evening like this when it happened. There wasn't a ripple on the ocean. It was flat calm. Twelve of them, the strongest of our men set out from the island, out for a night's fishing. Ah! You never can tell, never can trust the sea.' He paused, took a pull from his pipe. 'Around midnight the storm broke. And its likes nobody ever saw before and will never see again. By morning there wasn't a trace of them. The currachs were driven against the rocks, smashed to smithereens. All lost.'

Julie sighed and shifted to a more comfortable position. A lighted sod became dislodged and fell into the ashes. Willie retrieved it with the lid of the billycan. Below them, on the tiny beach waves broke on the sand.

'Was it shortly after that you came ashore?'

'Aye! Bad luck had fallen. Every man, woman and child of us packed and went. But we never really left, we've always come back.' He unearthed a small keg of poiteen from its hiding place in the ground. 'It's the best that there is around here,' he remarked, tasting it reverently.

'Not half as good as Pat Neddy's.'

'What?' Willie paused, eyeing her suspiciously as he poured some of his smoky-blue vintage into her cup.

'Did you not hear?'

'Eh?'

'The Sergeant caught us the night of the bonfire drinking poiteen. That's why I was kicked out of school.'

'Merciful God! And what did he do with the poiteen?'

'Kept it himself.'

'You bet he did, the old rascal.' Willie wiped his mouth with the corner of his apron. 'And I'd say he drank every drop of it too.'

Sparks from the fire landed at their feet. There was light enough still to see the outline of houses around them. Here and there an animal moved looking for fresh pasture. Willie struck a match on a rock and re-lit his pipe. 'You know,' he said, 'he used to sit here on this hillock on a summer's evening making up songs.'

'Who?'

'Your father.'

Julie and Aine exchanged glances.

'What age was he then?'

'Not a whole lot older than yourself.'

'That'd be about twenty-five years ago, roughly. 'Was he born on the island?'

'Aye. Born and bred in that cottage over there. The very house you're sleeping in tonight.' He pointed to the two-roomed cottage where they had left their belongings. 'Your grandfather built it, every stick and stone of it. And mind you, the family never saw a hungry day. If the catch was poor the neighbours would help out.'

'They must have missed it after they came ashore?'

There was no reply. A breeze lifted the smoke and flung it in the opposite direction. Only a stone's throw away a white-bibbed rabbit sat on a mound, ears pricked, then scuttled away.

'Och,' Willie said, after a few minutes, sitting up shaking himself, 'there was an awful row the night he told them he was going to be married. Your grandfather flew into a terrible rage. He accused Johnnie of marrying a Saxon, one of those heretics.'

'Phew! And what did my father do?'

'Nothing. He just walked away without a backward glance. John Fogarty was like that. He wouldn't get involved in their fights. Always had that bit of pride in him.'

'Ahh!' Her eyes were luminous.

Willie took a fresh square of tobacco from his pouch, sliced it in pieces rolling them between his fingers. Light from the fire flickered on their faces drawing the three of them into a silent conspiracy.

'Was my mother often on the islands?' Aine asked after a while.

'They used to come and stay in the cottage over there.'

'You remember her?'

'Ah! She was a beautiful lady. Tall and stately. Whenever they'd go out walking she'd be the talk of the parish.'

'And she a Protestant?'

'Only some people cared what Church she belonged to?'

'They say her family were rich?'

'Rich or poor, she'd give you the last crust of bread she had in the house. A grand lady, that's what she was. Dressed like a princess. Long silk robes down to her toes. And golden hair coiled around her head. Whenever she laughed it was like the music of angels.'

Aine sighed and closed her eyes.

Willie eyed her quizzically. He reached over and took another sup of poiteen from the keg. It was clear he had forgotten his audience.

The evening had turned chilly. A cold breeze blew from the Atlantic. Aine shivered. She pictured herself back again in Portree cemetery talking to a woman identical with her whom Willie had described.

After the meal they gathered up the scraps for the seagulls. Willie Sara replaced the poiteen in the ground. The moon was full casting a silver path on the water.

'No sign of the barnacle geese tonight,' Aine remarked.

'They're upset by the growing moon. Whenever the moon is full they fly to the other islands.'

'Julie!' Aine called, shaking her cousin. 'Wake up!'

'Its time we hit the hay.' Willie extinguished the last of the fire and dampened the cinders.

'Night, Willie!' Aine called, as she and Julie got up to go.

The path through the sand dunes was uneven and stony. Stumbling in the moonlight, they arrived at the cottage where they planned to spend the night. Aine stood a moment at the door outside. This was the house where her father had been born and bred. A great sadness gripped her. She looked up at the sky. It was studded with millions of twinkling stars. Suddenly her heart lifted. She knew then there was something out there ... something beyond, around her ... It filled her being, suffusing her. She raised the latch on the cottage door and stepped lightly over the threshold, followed by Julie.

It was a two-roomed cottage built at the turn of the century. The kitchen reeked of damp from the crumbling walls. There was an aroma of soot and rotting rafters. Two small windows faced the sea. She pictured it on a starry night in January; storm gusts booming in a roof welded from tin and concrete; firelight flickering on the spars slung beneath the rafters. Having lighted the fire she drew up chairs and they sat warming their hands. Pieces of willow-patterned dinner plates standing on the dresser caught her attention. She walked over and traced her finger around the edge of a plate.

Seeing the bedroom door open she tiptoed in. There were two iron beds corroded by rust standing in the far corner. She stood, motionless, on the moon-lit floor.

When she returned to the kitchen, a minute later, Julie was already asleep, enveloped in her sleeping bag.

During the night the wind rose. Aine was awakened to its whistling under the cottage door. She revived the fire in the hearth and sat gazing into the flames. Bits of conversation she had had with

Willie echoed in her mind ... *her father banished ... exiled like a common criminal ... by a bitter old man afraid of outsiders.* Tears stung her eyes. She extended her hands towards the flames for warmth. As the wind rattled in the chimney she moved up closer ... *the islanders will always come back ... will always come back ...* After a few minutes the warmth of the room and the rhythm of Julie's breathing lulled her to sleep.

By morning, the wind had dropped. Willie Sara pulled out the currach. Aine and Julie brought down their baggage. The sea was as clear as glass, rippling under a soft breeze.

'Look!' Aine shouted, pointing towards the sky.

Clapping their wings, the barnacle geese were flying in a straight line over the island.

As they were leaving, she heard the first low quack of the geese as they returned ... and somewhere beyond, far, far off, the sound of a bell tolling ... She felt a great calm as the three-man currach skimmed over the water.

Chapter Fifteen

Reinstated in school, Aine forgot about the mission. Neither was she upset when the poster of the headmistress and the Sergeant vanished mysteriously from the telegraph pole.

'It was blown out to sea in the night's gale,' she assured Willie Sara, chatting to him at the door of his cottage one evening after her return.

Willie took out his tobacco pouch and emptied the contents on to an oilcloth-covered table. Lighting his pipe, he eyed her quizzically through the smoke. 'As a matter of interest,' he asked, after a few pulls, 'what night of week did your picture vanish?'

'First evening the missioners were here.'

'Och,' Willie said, shaking his head, 'the portrait of Miss Maggie didn't end in the sea.'

'Where else could it go then, Willie?'

'An admirer, maybe.'

'What!'

Willie caught her eye. She burst out laughing.

Aine was scarcely landed back at school when she noticed that a change had taken place in the classroom. There was an hostility in the air ... a certain something ... It screamed at her ... glowered at her from the very walls. Whenever one of her classmates looked at her she froze.

It was on the following Monday - when she had believed herself safely installed - that she learned the full truth. Having missed the Craggan school bus she got a lift into town with Pa Brannigan but was late arriving into class. Breathless, she sank into a seat beside Julie noticing at the same time that a pecking order had been put into play in the classroom. The pupils from the town sat in the front row; the

92

rest were at the back.

Weeks later she admitted to Julie, that on that particular morning in November, she was totally unprepared for what happened next. As she entered the dimly-lit room she was met by a stony silence, followed by loud coughs. Bugsy Cattigan, son of Mike Cattigan of the Hardware shop sprang from his seat, staggered across the floor and began to imitate the actions of someone intoxicated. 'Poor little drunkie!' he sneered, 'she couldn't swallow a mouthful of poiteen without getting herself clobbered by the law!'

'Seargie Maloney's little pet!' a voice in the back row jibed.

They all roared laughing.

Dumbfounded, she stared. Then in a flash she was on her feet. She struck out blindly, one right, one left ... small fists cleaving the air like someone possessed.

Somewhere from behind, a strong hand descended upon her. Tim Hegarty's rough bony arm encircled her, pinning her to the wall.

Let go!' she yelled, struggling to free herself, 'let go, you mutt!'

'They'll kill you!' Tim hissed, holding her and dragging her away, 'they'll leave you for dead.'

It was then it dawned on Aine that this bunch of scumbags hadn't forgotten, hadn't forgiven her the commotion she caused on the eve of the Midsummer. In their books, to flout the law was one thing, but to get caught by the Sergeant was a different matter. A curfew had been put into operation in St Aengus' on the night immediately after the Halloween bonfire. All nightly excursions were ended. The pupils from the town were under surveillance.

Towards noon, on the same day, Aine closed her books, fastened her schoolbag and blew vigorously on the tips of her fingers trying to restore life to them. The room where she had sat all morning was cold and cheerless, a place where the sun never shone. Suddenly, as if by magic, a ray of light fell across the floor like a spotlight. She rushed over flinging out her arms. 'Aahha!' And then the spotlight went out.

For many of the pupils in St Aengus' a light shining across the floor at midday could be explained easily in scientific terms ... the sun's rays refracted in the greenhouse ... were reflected back ... But for Aine it was a numinous affair, a message from beyond. Starry-eyed - escapade of the morning forgotten - she returned to her seat and sat chin in hand. 'If only Mr Grinley could understand ... realize ... Time was when the pupils at St Aengus' would have clapped for joy at the sight of such a thing. Dejectedly, she folded her arms and rested her head on the desk. She got a queasy feeling the teacher was watching her. She sat up straight and began to draw.

As if reading her thoughts, Mr Grinley removed his glasses and snapped shut his brief case. 'Class is over,' he said, 'I'll inspect your work.'

'One minute,' Aine requested.

'Class is over!' he rasped. He moved to the sink and began to rinse out his thermos letting the water run in sucking gulps down through the pipes.

Aine reached for her paint brush and dipped it in a jar of water ... translucent tones, broad-brush strokes ... more or less what she had envisaged.

The teacher turned and gave the bell an authoritative ring.

'Oh God!' she breathed, 'he's such an impossible bore ... rushing to be in time for his golf.'

Born and bred on Inis Begin north, George F Grinley had studied art in the Royal College of Art in Edinburgh. Returning home some years later he took up a position in St Aengus' Secondary School. But the reception he got on his homecoming was anything but civil. The fishermen ignored him. He was one of themselves, yet not quite. Not even his brusque manner or pin-sharp eyes would convince them he was one of them. Having once flown the nest, they decided, Grinley would forever be an outsider.

Old Daniel attributed the art teacher's eccentricities to his training. The professor in Scotland who discovered him, he said, found that young George had a talent for measurement and advised him to train in technical drawing. George took the professor's advice but some years later turned to the painting. All this Daniel heard at the post office.

The women admired him. The attention he paid them whenever they visited the school made their hearts beat faster. At end-of-term meetings they would flock to his door, eager to hear reports of their sons and daughters.

'He's such a conscientious gentleman!' Maggie Holohan sighed, seeing the art teacher emerge from the church one Sunday morning, prayer book in hand.

Delia nodded. 'Ah! You know where you stand with old George. A pity that English teacher, the big fellow from Dublin, wouldn't take a leaf out of his book. I hear he spends a lot of his time in *Lost Property* retrieving his belongings.'

'Foreigners were never any good,' Maggie agreed, throwing Delia a sidelong glance. Maggie believed that Delia's niece, Aine, was growing too big for her boots. And what's more, she thought, she exerted far too much influence over her son, Colm.

As he began his weekly inspection on this dreary Monday afternoon, Mr Grinley donned his teacher's gown, adjusted his spectacles and stepped heavily down off the rostrum. The added exertion caused his brushed-back hair to fall in wisps over his low forehead. Taking the pointer between both hands, he stood stiffly facing his class. 'What's this?' he barked, pointing to Aine's sketch book.

'My painting, Sir.'

'Your painting?'

She nodded.

'Hah!' Picking up the sketch pad he began to leaf through its contents. Still wet, the drawing paper on which she had worked all morning had buckled in places like a sheet of corrugated iron. On it was a painting of shimmering light. In the background were trees, foliage, birds set against a sky of lapis blue. Mr Grinley gritted his teeth. He ran his short stubby fingers through his hair. 'Did you follow my demonstration, Miss Fogarty?'

'Which demonstration, Sir?'

'What I drew on the blackboard.'

'I watched while you gave the lesson.'

'Why then didn't you paint it? Why this ... this hideous ... piece of rubbish?'

'Because that's what I saw.'

'Never mind what you saw! Did you follow my instructions?'

Aine flushed. She fidgeted with the ribbons on her ponytail and began to rub off paint embedded in her fingernails with a flimsy white handkerchief. Out of the corner of her eye she saw Sara, Sara with her short stubby nose ogling the teacher. Sucking up to the old barnacle, hah! She steeled herself quickly for the next onslaught.

Mr Grinley's eyes flashed. 'Who ever saw the sun appear like that at noon?'

'It happened—'

'Forget what happened. Look!' He tapped her painting with the tip of his pointer. 'Draw what I demonstrated on the blackboard. I'll examine it on Wednesday.' He reached for her painting, tore it in two and threw it into the wastepaper basket.

Aine said nothing. She flounced out of school in rage.

That night she was unable to sleep. Her thoughts drifted back to the sombre classroom; to the will o'the wisp light dancing across the floorboards; particles of dust scintillating. Was it real or had she imagined it? Deep down she felt it was real. What would Mr Bluebeard know about such things, blinkered as Pa Holohans' farm horse? At last she fell into a troubled sleep and had an unusual dream. She told it to Julie the following morning on their way to school.

'I met an old woman on the road to Doora. She told me to look for a box in the caves. There I would find a linnet. When I found the box I put in my hand and drew out the quivering body of a bird. It was my pet linnet. I had forgotten all about him and was afraid he'd be dead when I removed him. Cradling him in my hand I lifted him out ...' She paused and looked at her cousin.

'Go on,' Julie prompted.

'I began to cry, my tears falling on his body scarcely more than bones. Immediately he transformed into a baby boy and d'you know what he said?

'What?'

'I only want to sing my song, the translation of every tune I ever knew.'

'Oh, for heaven's sake, Aine, you're far too superstitious. The teacher said it's against the teaching of the Church to believe in dreams.'

'There are dreams in the Bible. The Bible is the teaching of God.'

As they approached the school Aine lapsed into silence. Her blue eyes became pensive. She was convinced more than ever that her dream had significance. In some strange way it was telling her something. 'As a matter of fact,' she said, turning to Julie at the school gate, 'I did have a linnet once, a brown linnet.'

'Don't tell me, you're still brooding over that old bird? Where did you find him, anyway?'

'Lying in the snow. D'you remember that heavy snowfall we had some years ago?'

Julie laughed. 'Could I forget? It was the time I fractured my ankle. There was such a commotion at home! What did you do with him?'

'Oh, I wrapped him in my scarf and fed him until he flew away.'

The following Wednesday the art class in St Aengus' began as usual. A heavy fog descended on the hills. Unable to see out Aine allowed her gaze wander around the room; the bare floorboards spattered with mud; pallid walls cluttered with pupils' paintings. On the opposite wall hung a portrait of a woman, another of a country gentleman with his dog, standing at a gate. All dull imitations of Mr Grinley's work. Down at the back was an empty fireplace adding to the surrounding gloom. To avoid having to look at it she fixed her eyes on Michelangelo's bust adorning the mantelpiece.

Standing before his class, Mr Grinley rubbed his forehead. Some of the pupils looked tired, disinterested, particularly those at the front. The fresher more attentive faces belonged to those at the back. He began his demonstration. A house fronted by lawn, flanked by flowerbeds. Demonstration completed, he laid down his chalk and began to explain, advising on each important detail. In full flight, he paraded back and over before the blackboard like a melodramatic Shakespearean actor.

Aine fidgeted with her copybook. She tore off the corners of a page, rolled them up and stuffed them into the inkwell. She stood up.

'Sir!'

'Well?'

'Describe the mood in the picture?'

Somebody tittered.

Mr Grinley threw her a baleful glance. He didn't like the tone of her question. He had a set formula from which he refused to depart to satisfy the whim of any young chit. 'Where's the picture I told you to paint?'

'Which picture?'

'The one I demonstrated on Monday.'

'I was unable to copy your work, Sir.'

Tim Hegarty coughed. There was a scraping of throats in the back row.

The art teacher reddened. He paced up and down, wisps of hair flying out over his ears. He whirled around, gown swinging open like a bullfighter's. 'Why study art if you won't keep the rules?'

'Art isn't about rules.' Aine remembered her dream and looked him straight in the eye.

'Then how do you propose passing your test? Don't you realize the amount of work that's involved?'

'I won't be doing any test.'

'What?'

'Art is an adventure not a test.'

'According to whose authority, Miss Fogarty?'

'The greatest painters, Sir.' She felt an inner force driving her and refused to capitulate before his cold stare. 'Monet was a pioneering artist. He introduced new methods of doing things. Like Christopher Columbus he charted a path ... In the *Giverny Gardens,* for example'

'Where did you learn about Monet and the ... the ... This ... is preposterous!'

Her gaze swept the room, eyes blazing with intensity.

The pupils leaned forward, chins cupped in hands. Some began rummaging in their pockets wagering bets as to which of the protagonists would be the winner.

98

Speechless, Mr Grinley stared at her. 'He'd have to get rid of the wench! Like her father before her she was never done stirring up trouble. He took a turn about the room, paused and took out his file.

Without a word Aine snatched up her schoolbag. She rose to her feet, opened the door quietly and let herself out.

The day had suddenly brightened. Instead of going by the road she took a short cut home across the fields. Scrambling on to the rocks she followed a pathway leading to the sea.

The grandeur of the ocean leaped at her as she reached the sea, separating her from the Lilliputian world of Mr Grinley. Waves crashed beyond the pier out near Carrageen. A flock of geese appeared and disappeared catching the sunlight as they zoomed and glided.

At the water's edge she kicked off her sandals and bathed her feet in the shallows. Picking her way through the shingle she came to barnacle-covered rocks, great shining slabs of schist, old as Methuselah. She stood still.

When she rounded the corner Cragann pier broke into view. The bay was empty; the fishermen had left for the islands that morning. Two remaining currachs rested upside down on the foreshore. Crayfish creels were weighted along the pier. She slung her sandals over her shoulders and tied her cardigan around her waist.

Up above her on the heights the fields looked dark under a coat of purple heather. In the space between the valley and Cartra the men worked. Loading their carts with hay they carried it down to the haggard. One figure disengaged itself from the rest and ran down towards her.

'You're home early,' Colm said, arriving on the shingle beside her.

'Yeah.'

'Anything wrong?'

'Not much. Had a bit of a row with Mr Grinley.'

Colm's face darkened. A furrow of disapproval lined his forehead.

Guessing his thoughts, Aine laughed. 'I left of my own accord. Mr Grinley's as stubborn as a mule. He refuses to see anyone's view but his own.'

'Well, I suppose there's no end to view points. But who's to know who's right in the end?'

Aine said nothing.

'Care for a swim?'

'Yeah.'

'Be with you in a minute after I've delivered this load.'

She ran up to the house. The day was calm; there wasn't a sound along the road, not even a breeze to rustle the evergreens. The scent of roses wafted towards her as she approached the gate. Delia was in the lawn clipping the hedges. The snip, snip of the shears drowned her approaching footsteps. She slipped in around the back, collected her bathing togs and raced on to the beach. In the shelter of a stranded currach she changed quickly. Without a moment's delay she plunged into the coral blue sea disturbing its tranquil surface.

Colm arrived on the slipway, towel slung over his shoulders. He watched as Aine swam outwards, cleaving the water with quick bold strokes. Each time her head surfaced he could see her face, tilt of her chin. In less than a minute he dived in after her.

She reached the lobster tanks a second after him. Breathless, she hoisted herself up on the floating tank. They sat in silence dangling their feet in the ice-cold water. Straining against its moorings the tank rose and dipped. They could hear the clacketting of lobsters inside like human bodies in coats of mail. About a hundred yards in, the village drowsed in the afternoon sun. The fishermen, working with their nets, looked like cardboard figures in the distance.

Sitting in the middle of the bay - events of the morning forgotten - Aine felt as richly bejewelled as the Queen of Sheba. Salt water drops shimmered on her arms and ran in rivulets along the tank. Her skin glistened like gold in the sun. She gazed into the depths of the sea and watched the fish swim. Beside her, Colm kicked sheets of water into the air.

'What happened to Grinley?' he asked, after a while.

'You mean what happened to me?'

'Well, which ever.'

'He tore up my painting. Told me to paint it again the way he wanted it done.'

'And you did?'

'Like hell I did! Artists don't behave like that. They create new things. Don't repeat them over and over as if they were walking a treadmill.'

'You told him so!'

'Yeah.'

Colm laughed. He dug his heels into the sides of the tank. The clacketting of lobsters had ceased; they had fallen asleep. Would she ever make her way in the world, he wondered. What training did she have? Artists like her were ten a penny. Real artists underwent rigorous discipline. They spent years studying. He recalled some of her drawings, impressions of boats, windmills, people, some framed, others still without frames, all evidence of her talent but a talent that would need to be harnessed. He smiled, remembering the poster of the Sergeant. Pity the old codger hadn't the chance to see it! 'You're a bit of a genius,' he said, turning to her, 'you'd make your living from art. Knock spots off old Grinley. But you'd need someone with influence, someone with money to back you.'

She threw him a sidelong glance. His face was as sharp as hewn granite. Drops of salt water glistened on his arms as he gripped the edges of the tank. So different from the pasty-faced townies she had encountered that morning. She leaned forward and placed her sun-tanned hand over his. They lay back on the tanks and gazed up at the sky. White clouds scudded lazily above them. Close by, a seagull hovered and flew off again. Water swished around the base of the tank rocking them into a drowsy stillness.

Suddenly Aine roused herself. 'I'll race you in!' she cried. She pulled her bathing cap over her ears and dived into the sea-green depths scattering the sprats swimming in the shelter of the tank. Carried by the buoyancy of the water, she struck out for shore.

A second later Colm followed. Together they swam side by side. As they approached the shoreline he slackened his speed allowing her to pass him. 'You won,' he grinned, traipsing after her through the shallow water. They walked up the beach picking their way over the shingle, hard and white under their feet.

Aine draped a towel around herself and removed her cap, shook the salt from her hair and wiped her face. 'You're slowing down!' she laughed.

Colm wasn't listening. A brooding expression had settled on his bronzed face. Studying a yacht that had appeared on the horizon, he drew his shirt down over his head and bounded up the slipway, towel thrown over his shoulders.

Chapter Sixteen

Things settled as Willie predicted. In a few more months Aine would complete her years at school. She applied for work in the Bank and was placed on a waiting list, but knew deep down that she would never be a banker.

There was little rain the whole month of August. A sharp breeze scattered the petals on Delia's marigolds. Sitting on the step of the hall door one sultry afternoon she watched the clouds roll by over Cartra. So imperceptibly did they glide across the sun that she was momentarily stunned. She closed her eyes, shutting out thoughts of the departing summer. The cat nudged her into action. She sat on her lap and stared morosely up at her.

'Scut Pangur!' she cried, jumping to her feet. She ran to the house, collected her paints and set out for Doora

It was downhill all the way to the pier. On either side, blackberry bushes, denuded by starlings, heralded the winter. Ox-eyed daisies, heads bowed, were brown and withered at the stalk. Over on the slipway Willie Sara, aided by Tim Hegarty, shouldered his currach. She could see Tim's gangly legs underneath as the currach advanced up the slipway like a monstrous four-legged beetle.

'Glass is falling,' Willie greeted her, lowering the currach, 'boats are coming into the bay.'

'It won't be much … only a summer storm.'

Willie shook his head. 'Summer is over, m'girl. There's a murmur out there beyond.'

Aine laughed. She wrung her hands in mock horror. Continuing on, she hurried in the direction of the lighthouse.

Willie Sara frowned. He watched as she turned at Brannigans' corner, spindly legs barely touching the ground, ponytail flying.

'She'll get caught, yet,' he muttered, shaking his head.

Tim Hegarty laughed. 'I wouldn't put a bet on it. It would take more than a storm to catch that one!'

The road stretched in a straight line all the way to the pier. Here and there potholes yawned in the tarred surface. The council men hadn't been around for sometime to fill them with tar and loose stones. Aine left the road and followed the dirt track until she came to *An Poll Donn*, a large pond enclosed among the cliffs. She sat at the edge dangling her feet in the ice-cold water. A boat crossed the horizon, Hegarty's fishing boat running to the islands for shelter. The barnacle geese would have their peace shattered. She tried to recapture an image that had evaded her mind all morning. However hard she tried, it eluded her. The wind freshened. Beyond Cragann, the sea, which a few minutes before had been tranquil, was dark and threatening. Seagulls flew in a haphazard direction wheeling in broken lines. Rain fell in heavy drops. She no longer had a desire to paint. She gathered her painting gear quickly, picked her way along the rocks and hurried to the cave for shelter.

At first the total blackness, not just the darkness of the cave, shocked her. She took a torch from her pocket and shone it along the walls letting its minuscule light do a will o' the wisp dance. The damp air clung to her. She tried to imagine hibernating in a place like that where the temperature never changed ... every moment of the day would be the same. Suddenly, an angular-shaped object leaning against the wall caught her attention. On inspection, she found it to be a large copper pot half-hidden by seaweed, a coiled pipe of lead running through it. She tapped it gently with her shoe. The sound echoed in the darkness like a brass gong. But over and above all this was a sound more ominous. It was the roar of the sea driven by its own inner force. Could it be possible? Had the wind risen, pushing the tide to the mouth of the cave? She rushed out and ran through the tunnel. Her worst fears were realized. The threshold of the tunnel was wet. Driven by a strong wind the tide had come in.

Aine was prepared for a long night, four or five hours' delay at least.

People had been caught in the caves before. Visitors, sheltering from the rain were often marooned when the tide crept up unexpectedly. Daniel Cassidy had it that he saw a skeleton, a shaky-bones swinging from the roof of Pluais Na gCaorach, teeth bared in a grin. Och! Old Daniel was making that up! A storm didn't last more than twenty-four hours.

She marvelled at the ferocity of the wind. It pelted the waves, hurtling the spume on to the floor of the tunnel. Not only was she trapped by the sea, but she was caught in a raging storm. Increasingly, the wind drove the tide on to the rocks, advancing, withdrawing in gulps.

She returned to the inner chamber, propped her fisherman's satchel against the wall stretching her legs to a more comfortable position. Water dripped from the roof echoing like tinkling glass. At first the sound enthralled her but after a while its repetitiveness became irksome. She could hear the droning voice of old Grinley, *paint it again, Miss Fogarty* ... clickety, clickety, clack!' The dripping began to resound through the cave like the relentless tapping of typewriter keys. She glanced at her watch. A minute to seven. Delia would be having her tea, munching a slice of buttered toast and a boiled egg.

Rising, she went to the mouth of the cave. A searing flash, a crash of thunder, made her head reel. In a second, the image she had been trying to capture became clear. Hurrying back she set up her easel. In the light of the torch she sorted out her paints, ultra marine, raw sienna, alizarin red. She picked up the chinchilla haired brush that belonged to her mother and stroked its head. Then she returned it to its box and took out the Japanese hake that Colm had given her.

There was another streak of lightning. In the blue atmospheric light Aine saw an object hidden in the corner. Beaming her torch, she found it to be a storm lantern camouflaged by seaweed. Beside it was a box of Safety matches containing four unlit matches untouched by dampness. She lifted up the lantern, tested the wick and struck a match. The match flickered and went out. She struck a second, a third. The flame of the last match survived in her hand.

In the glow of the lantern she began to paint. Like a prehistoric artist her shadow mirrored her brush strokes on the cave wall. Every stroke of the brush had its purpose. She painted fast, fearing that if she faltered or looked over her shoulder like Lot's wife, the image would vanish. She hummed a tune, something she had heard in childhood, whispering encouraging words to her shadow. *Keep going! Keep going!* she laughed at her flickering image. In the dim orange light she painted, not pausing once to check the time. Paint marks streaked the sleeves of her jacket. Outside, the waves crashed; thunder rolled overhead. Plying the paint quickly her tones became richer. Loose patches of colour were set beside patches of white. Finished, she laid down her brush. Her eyes drooped.

After what seemed an age Aine awoke. She sat up blinking in the ghostly light. Her hands were stiff. She rubbed them a few times trying to restore life to them. Then she noticed the stillness. She ran to the mouth of the cave and looked out. The storm had ceased. The tide, though turbulent still, was receding. Water tumbled over rocks glistening under a weak but persistent sun. Wrack, thrown up by the tide was scattered along the shore. Corks floated on the water; plastic bottles and pieces of timber from ships' fenders were strewn everywhere. Along the shore, between the rocks and the lighthouse, seaweed had piled up. She ran back to the cave, collected her painting gear and packed it into her satchel.

As she reached the cliff top a rainbow appeared. Its diffuse band of colour shone triumphantly through a curtain of drizzling mist.

Chapter Seventeen

Cragann got two weeks of the wettest weather in the century. The rain fell in buckets. It pounded off the sheds, struck the barns and filled up the dikes. Daniel Cassidy said it was a curse from God, such terrible things were happening. Young people drinking, smoking ...

Aine pretended not to hear. Old Daniel was losing the run of himself. What did *he* know about God or heavenly things? Far better he stayed at home and said his prayers.

She hadn't painted for weeks, not since the evening she was trapped in the cave. After she returned home that night she hid the painting in the attic where Delia wouldn't see it and refused to look at it again for several weeks. As the evenings grew darker she became pensive, drawn into herself. Around her everything was changing. A smell of rotting leaves floated in from outside. The swallows were migrating from the land sick of the damp. Hundreds of starlings flew through the rain in disappointed flocks. Following their leaders, they huddled together on top of the oleria, cold and wet.

One evening, as the rain continued to fall, Delia hurried in from the garden. Her back was troubling her again. More tired than usual, she peeled off her gloves, washed her hands in the sink and sank heavily into the armchair. Suddenly she sat up straight. 'You forgot to take out the bread!' she sniffed, springing up and darting across to the range. Thick black smoke billowed around her head as she opened the door of the old Stanley. Having scraped off the burnt crust, she planked the ruined caraway cake down on a tray. I should have known better, she thought, the child's head is like a sieve!

Sprawled across the sofa, hair in curlers, Aine looked as if she were spirited to another world. Wearing a short denim skirt and polo-necked jumper, her small feet dangled over the edge of the sofa. A pair of sandals lay on the floor beside her.

'Time you got ready for the dance,' Delia remarked, shortly, glancing at the clock.

'Mmm.'

'What are you wearing?'

'Does it really matter?'

'Of course, it matters!' Delia's sharp eyes missed nothing. She knew instantly that something was wrong; the way Aine fingered her hair; the droop of her mouth. 'Your friends will be wearing their best. I heard Nora Hartigan say yesterday that she was lending Sara her drop earrings. You bet, Sara won't let the grass grow under her feet, especially when Colm Holohan's around.'

'What's Colm got to do with it?' Aine swung her feet off the sofa and sat up straight, two red patches appearing on her cheeks. Her pale ivory skin, normally flawless, showed angry spots.

Glory be to God! Delia thought, the child hasn't an ounce of sense! 'Did anyone ever tell you,' she asked, turning to her, 'that you're remarkably like your mother. Same straight nose and finely chiselled mouth. Rosemary was a beautiful woman. No one around here could equal her in looks.'

Aine was silent. Why did Delia have to keep on talking about appearances, always drawing comparisons? Everyone was given something. Like Santa at Christmas, if you didn't get one thing, then you got another.

The night had turned cool. Delia opened the front of the range letting heat into the room. She took out her knitting and settled into her chair. The rain had lightened. Drops fell softly on the pavement outside. 'As well as being beautiful,' she said, rising to close the window, 'your mother had a gifted pair of hands. There was nothing she couldn't do between this and high heaven, tapestry, needlework, painting. She was a genius at painting. She'd sit on the rocks down below for hours, easel in front of her.'

'Where are those paintings now?'

'Her sister claimed the lot of them after her death, just as she took the rest of her belongings. We managed to salvage a few personal things in the end.' Returning to the hearth she sat down and continued her knitting, long steel knitting needles flashing in the firelight. Peering at the pattern she spread it out on her knee and began to read the directions aloud.

Strange, how her aunt should harbour such bitterness. Was it because of the few odd necklaces and baubles that her mother had owned or was it because of something else? 'My mother had great talent?' Aine remarked.

'Aye. Buckets of it. But you're not a bad hand at the drawing yourself. You must have taken after her.'

Aine reached for her sandals and slipped them under her feet. She was about to go when Delia called her back.

'Aine!'

'What?'

'There are times when I wonder what will become of you, what strange path you're going to take. The world's a tough place, a hard taskmaster. People out there—'

Aine frowned. This kind of *palaver* always irritated her. It was worse than Delia's customary scolding. Didn't she know by this that she was nineteen, older than—

'Well, I hope you'll be lucky. Some day you'll meet somebody suitable, somebody your equal who'll make you happy.' Her head began to nod. Spectacles, already on the loose side, slid from her nose on to her lap. In a minute she had dozed off.

Smiling, Aine noticed the lines around Delia's mouth, relaxed in sleep. She'd look years younger if it weren't for the telltale grey around her temples. A suitable husband? Huh! A man with a bulging bank account, no doubt! Out in the bay an engine throbbed. It started, stopped then started again. Colm would find it choppy tonight. A lighted turf fell on the hearth with a soft thud. Delia sat up blinking. 'What was that?'

'A lighted sod. You forgot to put back the fireguard.'

'I get tired much sooner than I used to. I suppose the years are beginning to tell.' She picked up the tongs and settled the fire. A wistful smile crossed her face. 'But I reckon I can't complain. I had my day and plenty of opportunities.'

Aine's eyes lit up. She leaned forward. 'Who was that man in the photograph?'

'Which photograph?'

'The one you've locked up in your trunk.'

'You've been rummaging again. That trunk—'

'Was he a friend?'

'Yes. He's dead many years now. Buried in the cemetery over there.' Face flushed, Delia began tightening the hairpins that had loosened in her sleep. As she rearranged each one, a slight tremor showed in her hand.

'Were you … did you go out together?'

'We were going to be married. He was one of the coastguards, a captain at the station. He picked up tuberculosis in his twenties. Nothing could be done for him.' She folded her glasses and was about to go but changed her mind. 'His parents knew I was a Catholic but it made no difference. We had it all fixed up. Then over night he became ill, struck down with a fever.'

The clock in the hall chimed seven. Another hour before the dance would begin. The flames in the old Stanley leaped and crackled engulfing them both in a warm glow. Aine rose, took the photograph of her parents from the mantelpiece and held it in front of her. 'I know what I'll wear to-night,' she said, a determined look in her eyes. Crossing the floor in quick strides, she left the room.

Half an hour later, as Delia was raking the fire Aine stole up behind her. 'Well, what do you think of it?'

Delia straightened. Aine stood in the centre of the floor, hands gripping the back of a chair. Her hair swept up by a comb was piled on top of her head. She wore a long silk skirt edged with white, matching a Carraigmacross blouse. Fronting the blouse was a row of satin-covered buttons. 'Where did you get it?' Delia asked, her hands going to her face.

'In a box on top of the wardrobe. It seems to have been there for sometime.' She backed away nervously.

Delia laid a hand gently on her arm. 'Wait, I've something to give you, something I've kept over the years.' She disappeared upstairs and returned seconds later, a small square box in her hand. 'I'd like you to have it,' she said, opening the box and handing her a brooch, 'it was your mother's.'

Aine paled. The brooch was long and oval shaped, beautifully crafted, wrought in gold and pewter. There were two ivy leaves carved at the base. Inscribed in the centre, in slanted letters, was the word *Mizpah*.

'Mizpah?'

'It means covenant. Look! The message is engraved around the edge.'

Moving to the window Aine read the inscription. *May the Lord watch between you and me when we are absent, one from the other.* Looking up she met Delia's gaze. 'When did she give you this?'

'It was on her dress the day she was found. I was keeping it till you got older. But somehow, I think the time is right. You're a young woman now, the same age as *she* was when she married. When your mother and her twin turned eighteen they were presented with a brooch each by their parents. It was meant to be a symbol of their closeness. I'm sure the twin has still got hers. I haven't seen her for years; somebody said she got married.'

'Was the twin very like my mother?'

'At first glance you couldn't tell them apart. But after a while, when you got used to them, you'd notice the difference.' Something caught in Delia's throat. 'Rosemary was of a sunny disposition, bright like the sun. Everywhere she went she radiated happiness. Generous to a fault, she kept nothing for herself, not even her clothes. You know the ermine coat upstairs in my wardrobe?'

Aine nodded.

'That was hers. She gave it to me for my trip to London. And the Russian hat that Mary Brannigan wears. She got it from Rosemary.' Smiling, Delia gazed into the fire. 'Amazing how she loved a bit of fun. Whenever she came here for Christmas she'd throw a party, dress John up, togging him out in red furry boots and coat. The Brannigans would come over. We'd sit around chatting, exchange gifts and sip a glass of punch.'

'Would she have been happy in Craggan?'

'Without a doubt. But that sister of hers! That woman was different.'

'How do you mean?'

'Catherine was a worldly bit of goods. Close as you could meet. She went after pleasure, parties and fine clothes. She never could understand why your mother married John.' Delia's lips curled. 'She had no nature in her. Cold as ice. After Rosemary left home she didn't want to hear of her again.'

Aine fingered the brooch, turning it over in her hand. Did her mother have a premonition of her death the morning she wore it? She walked to the window and looked out. It was still bright. She could distinguish the shape of the pier, the figures of fishermen entering and leaving Brannigans.' She spun around quickly. A veil had descended over Delia's face. Lips tightened, she had retreated once more into her own private world. 'Pin it to my dress,' she requested, handing her the broach.

Delia undid the clasp and pinned the brooch to Aine's collar. 'There!' she said, standing back, 'take a look at yourself.'

Peering in the mirror, Aine scarcely recognized what she saw. A pair of sombre blue eyes stared soulfully back at her. Her burnished hair, swept up by a comb, made her look years older. Was this how her mother had looked the day she was drowned? The stricken expression on Delia's face confirmed her suspicion. 'I'll have to go,' she said, hurriedly, 'I'm calling for Julie.' Turning, she threw her arms around Delia. 'Night, Aunt Delia,' she said.

Delia heard the staccato sound of her footsteps in the hall below as she let herself out. She recalled, as if it were only yesterday, the day the mizpah was found on Rosemary's dress. A tear trickled on to her hand. Looking up she met the smiling gaze of the couple in the photograph. 'She's changing,' she nodded to them, 'Aine is growing up.'

Chapter Eighteen

It was her secrecy, lately, that annoyed Delia. For a fortnight or more Aine had been arriving in late for meals. She'd snatch something to eat, charge off again and spend the rest of the day in her studio. Delia couldn't understand what was happening.

Determined to investigate, she climbed the narrow stairs leading to Aine's studio early one Saturday morning. In a corded green dressing gown and camel-haired slippers, she tiptoed quietly across the corridor careful not to awaken her. Saturday was Aine's day for a lie-in.

As she opened the brown panelled door she drew back quickly. A blinding sun flooded the small square room, spilling in over the primrose walls and worn mahogany furniture. Half-hidden at the back, among a confusion of potted plants, Aine sat on a stepladder, palate in one hand, paintbrush in the other, daubing a painting propped against the wall. Her flaxen hair fell around her shoulders like sheaves of ripe corn.

'So this is where you are!' Delia's glance swept the room. An old kitchen dresser, wood untouched by paint, occupied most of the space. In a corner near the window stood a table stacked with watercolours, unframed but neatly mounted. A jam jar containing wild flowers, woodbine and meadowsweet stood on a shelf. 'You're not forgetting your parents' anniversary?' she asked.

'Mmm?'

'Your parents' anniversary, you're not forgetting it?'

'Oh, I'll be going to Portree in the afternoon, after I've finished this job.'

'Looks like it's going to rain. Better take your coat; it wouldn't do to get a drenching.'

It was then Delia saw Colm. Bending over the table on the opposite side of the room he was busy polishing a picture frame. A stream of light pouring through the skylight window highlighted his head and shoulders. Sleeves rolled-up, his shirt neck open, he hummed softly. A lighted cigarette lay on a saucer in front of him.

'Well, if my eyes aren't deceiving me! A man about the house, at last!'

'Yep! That's me.' Colm removed the smouldering cigarette butt, squashing it on the floor with the heel of his boot. Running his finger over the edge of the picture-frame, he continued polishing.

Glory be to God! Delia thought, rolling her eyes to heaven, he'd burn down the house in a minute without batting an eyelid. If Maggie Holohan could see him now! Every time they met, Maggie hinted at Aine's influence over Colm as if she, Delia, could do anything about it. 'You're around a lot lately,' she said, addressing him, 'are you going to move in, or what?'

Colm laughed. 'Is that supposed to be an offer?' He winked at Aine. Reaching for a polishing rag he dipped it in turpentine and began rubbing the paint-stains off his hands.

'I've been hearing rumours.'

'Rumours?'

'You're investing, aren't you, investing in a boat?'

'Och, not for a while. When the time is right, maybe. I've my eye on a fishing boat in the north of the county. But it'll take time before it's all sorted out.'

'Mmm. Everything takes time.' Delia glanced quickly across at her niece. Perched on a stepladder, mouth firmly set, Aine looked little more than a child. Yet she was nineteen, a grown-up woman about to take her place in the world. Delia felt a tightening in her chest. Was she really prepared? Would she be mature enough to meet the problems that awaited her? After all what did she know of life, of men, their masterful ways, one-tracked minds? What if she got into trouble, became pregnant like young Mags Donnelly? What then? She cast a sidelong glance at Colm pushing a loose strand of hair back from her forehead, uneasily. A breeze from the open window fluttered the curtains scattering sheets of drawing paper across the floor.

Aine beckoned to her. 'What do you think of it?' she asked, stepping down off the ladder.

'Of what?'

'The painting?'

Delia stepped back awkwardly. Hands on hips, she pursed her mouth. 'Looks like a blackbird to me, but then I'm no expert. Things can be anything nowadays according to the meaning you give them. When did you paint it?'

'One evening lately over in Doora. The tide came in. Somebody left an old lantern behind so I took out my paints. And ... well, that's it!'

'You shouldn't be going to Doora alone. I told you before to keep out of it. But you'll listen to nobody. Just like your father before you, you'll please yourself.' She moved over to the table and scrutinised the newly-made picture frame. 'Not bad,' she remarked, turning to Colm, 'where did you get the wood?'

'In the shed outside. It needs a fair bit of polishing though. It's a very light beech. Rather colourless, in fact, but it catches the tone ok.'

'Mmm. All very interesting. Who's the painting for anyway?'

Neither of them spoke.

Delia frowned. 'Well, amn't I going to be let in on the secret? Who is it for?'

'It's not for anyone in particular,' Aine replied quickly, noticing Delia's colour beginning to mount. 'I hope to show it to a friend,' she added,' somebody who knows something about art.'

'Have you nothing better to do? For goodness sake, Aine, go and get yourself a job!' Delia yanked the door open, closing it noisily behind her.

'You ought to have told her,' Colm chided, a few minutes later, as they heard the sound of Delia's footsteps on the corridor and echoing in the hallway below, 'you ought to have explained ...' Holding the sweeping brush between both hands, he leaned back against the studio wall.

'Explained what?'

'About Catherine ... the painting ... the whole damned thing!'

'For heaven's sake, Colm!'

'She's all you've got,' he shrugged, 'the only relative you have who really cares.'

Aine frowned. She stood the newly framed picture in a shaded corner where it wouldn't catch the sun. Peculiar the ideas people had, she thought, haughtily. Of course, she had relatives. What about that well-to-do aunt of hers over in London? Wasn't she as closely related to her as Delia? She watched as Colm swept up the wood shavings. Bits of wood twisted this way and that like a family of glow-worms. Shifting the finished picture out of his way, he propped the sweeping-brush against the wall. Her eyes followed the movements of his hands, workman's hands, supple and strong. 'Catherine is a private person,' she assured him, 'she wouldn't like her visits to be made known. I don't really know why, but I'm sure she has her reasons.'

'She'll be pleased with this. It's quite an impressive piece of work. Different from the rest.'

'How different?'

'The child is alive, present. When you look at him, it's the same as when the teacher used to call out our names in class. D'you remember? When you used to answer *Anseo*?'

She laughed. 'Strange how you should notice that. Not everyone does. There are so many different ways of seeing things.'

'I know. But how can you tell how the child is feeling, I mean get under his skin like that?'

'Well, it's like this. If you paint a tree, flower, anything, you'll see the sap rising, flower opening. That's how it is.'

Frowning, he hacked off a piece of plywood with a rusty handsaw. Paring it carefully with his penknife he stood it against the wall. He looked at her quizzically. 'Tell me,' he said, 'how can you tell a man's feelings, I mean his real feelings?'

She flushed. Fumbling with the measuring tape, she folded it neatly and returned it to the sewing box. Glancing up she met his gaze.

In a flash he pushed the chair out of his way, leaned across the table and kissed her. 'I'll have to go,' he said hurriedly, 'shout if you need me.'

'Wait!' she cried, 'wait!'

A second later, the sound of his footsteps could be heard clattering on the stairs and across the hall.

Soon afterwards, Aine was out on the road walking in the direction of the cemetery. It was a fine summer's day. Though the morning had threatened rain, the sky was clear. Fleecy clouds moved across the sky like snowdrifts. *Mares tails*, Delia called them. She frowned, thinking of her aunt. She'd never be satisfied until she saw her working in a stuffy old bank. After some minutes walking she forgot about Delia.

On reaching the cemetery she paused and stood beneath the old stone wall. Below her the sea stretched for miles, sloping out from the land. The cemetery, built on a hill, was etched like a citadel against the skyline. Tall white crosses, faithful custodians, brooded over their dead. Clutching the parcel tightly to her side, she rose, crossed the style and strode up the hill.

The grass around the graves was long and unkempt. She cleared a path, avoiding unknown graves. Some of them were marked by stones arranged in the form of a cross. Others had no mark at all. She paused at the grave where her grandparents were buried; *John and Bridget Fogarty, late of Inis Begin*. It was overgrown with dandelions. Letters in the name were missing, erased by the searing wind. These are my people. I'm related to the dandelions, she thought. The grave was sunken in the middle, a sign that the coffin was decayed and the dead had departed for heaven.

Suddenly, the figure of a woman became visible. Tall and slender she was leaning back against the tomb. Even from a distance one could see she was beautiful. As she gazed out at the islands the sun highlighted the contours of her face.

Aine tiptoed across, fearful of frightening her.

But Catherine had seen her. She half-turned, relief and watchfulness in her dark eyes. 'Ah! I thought you had forgotten me.'

Aine dropped the parcel on the grass, confused and happy at once. 'Good gracious!' she cried, 'I'm not as scatter-brained as all that!'

Together they sat on the wall facing the sea. Aine was reminded once again of someone she had seen before. Perhaps it was the Grecian goddess in the picture hanging in the school library or, maybe, Niamh Cinn Oir as she sat behind Oisin on his winged horse? Her classical features and burnished hair struck her as being strangely familiar. 'I've a painting to show you,' she said, picking up the parcel.

'A painting!' There was a hint of amusement in Catherine's voice.

Clumsily, she untied the string and removed the layers of brown paper dropping them, one by one, and held it up for inspection. Then she began to feel afraid. What would she think of it? But urged on by her dream she rose and moved the painting into a better light where it could be seen to advantage.

Catherine threw it a cursory glance. She was about to turn away when something else struck her. Her eyes narrowed. She unhooked the spectacles from around her neck and placed them firmly on the bridge of her nose. 'Did you really do this?' There was frank incredulity in her voice.

'I've already told you I painted it one night when I was marooned in a cave.'

'Strange, I haven't seen anything like it. There's an originality here that might prove valuable.' She spoke softly, as if trying to convince herself of something. Placing the painting against the wall she stood back examining it. 'Is it completely your own?'

'Of course it is!'

'What I mean is, does your aunt or your friends have a stake in the ownership?'

Aine laughed. 'Certainly not. Most of them don't even know I painted it, except for Colm of course.'

'Colm?'

'A friend of mine, a fisherman in Cragann.'

'Oh, I see. Well, fishermen don't matter much, do they? We'll have to have it exhibited. There are several exhibiting forums in London. An exhibition is the only way you'll be able to present your work to the potential buyer. You understand?'

She nodded.

'Every year there's an official exhibition in the Tudor Gallery. Works there have a chance of being sold. Collectors are more inclined to buy what's displayed in the Tudor. I attend many of those exhibitions, myself, works by Henry, Keating, Yeats. I love the exuberance and colour of you Irish artists.'

'But how could I possibly—?'

'Everything is possible, my dear. I happen to be a member of the Gallery Jury. There's a big demand for subjects like this. Because you're a friend of mine, you'll be sure of the approval of the panel.'

Aine looked at her, puzzled.

'But remember the immediate aim of exhibiting a painting is to find a buyer.'

'Oh!'

'There's a gentleman, a close friend, who's a well-known art dealer in London. I think he'll be able to help you. After all it's the agent who persuades clients to risk their money.' She re-wrapped the painting and flicked an imaginary speck of dust from her dress. 'But you'll have to come to London. There are some magnificent shopping malls, Harrods, for instance. You'd love the neon lights, cinemas, theatres and of course the galleries. The galleries, in particular, are simply superb.'

'But I haven't any money.'

'I'll send you the fare.'

Aine thought a moment. Was this the chance she was waiting for, the opportunity she had dreamed of for years? She felt a sharp thrill of excitement. Everything around her began to glow. The sun looked brighter, the sky bluer ... 'You seem to be busy in London,' she said, trying to control the tremor in her voice.

'There's plenty to do. Lots of openings, premiers ... dreadful things! I attend charity functions; visit homes for the handicapped, children's hospitals. Yes, you might say I'm kept occupied. The estate is extensive, an enormous responsibility really with heavy overheads. Between servants and gardens, my husband and I have very little time for ourselves.'

'Your home must be beautiful?'

She frowned. 'It's my ancestral home. A country house like *Netherby* requires a lot of attention. But it still remains in reasonably good shape, at least for the present.' Her eyes flickered. 'But you must see it, my dear.'

As Aine turned for home, minutes later, the sun was beginning to sink behind Cartra. A cold breeze lifted her hair blowing it in wisps across her face. Her skirts billowed around her knees. Drops of rain, driven by the wind, pelted against her, streaming down her legs and entering her shoes. She paused at her grandparents' grave, pulled a few dandelion roots and tossed them over the wall. Drawing her jacket closely around her she ran the remainder of the way.

Chapter Nineteen

It was a stifling hot day, a day when anything could happen. The sun bathed the countryside in its harsh light. Sauntering along the road to Belmullet, Aine paused at the narrow bridge separating the old market town from Cragann. She still marvelled at the turn of events the previous evening. Her painting would be exhibited, not in any two-pence-halfpenny gallery, but in one of the most sophisticated art galleries in London. She leaned over the parapet, contemplating the grandeur of it all.

Across from her, Cragann headland towered over a shimmering blue sea. The fishing boats, *Cailin Bawn* and the *Cormorant* swayed gently on the morning tide. Further towards the hills sheep wandered in the meadows. A donkey had broken loose and strayed into Holohans' field trampling the growing barley. She turned quickly as Julie approached. 'The men have fallen asleep,' she said, 'there's not a soul working in the fields over there.'

'Phew! How could you blame them?' Julie pealed off her sweater and tied it firmly around her waist. 'Amn't I nearly half-dead, myself!' In the intense morning heat Julie's round face had become blotched and patchy.

'Maybe they're all gone in to the fair. I heard Pat Hartigan say yesterday they were taking the day off. Come on, Julie! We'll see what's going on'.

Turning their backs on Cragann they crossed the bridge and walked into Belmullet.

As they approached the Square old Lizzie Harper thrust her head over the half-door. 'Come in, my beautifuls!' she chirped, 'come in, come in!' her faded blue eyes lighting up at the sight of them.

Julie hesitated but Aine pushed past her, opened the half-door and walked jauntily in, followed by her cousin.

Lizzie's premises were part of an old stone building situated on the right hand side of the Square as one enters the town of Belmullet. Green painted woodwork framed a small latticed window over which her name was written in block letters, *Lizzie's Fashions*. Hanging in the window was a cage containing a yellow canary. A dark blue curtain hung behind it making a backdrop for the canary.

'Where has she gone?' Aine asked, peering into the depths of the shop where a minute before the old lady had stood.

Julie shook her head. 'Try a little cough,' she suggested, 'maybe she'll pop out.'

Aine cleared her throat. An explosive sound burst from her lips. A door opened. There was a sound of feet descending steps followed by silence. Close behind the curtain, cardboard boxes were being shifted and placed one upon the other. They heard a rustling of paper. The curtain twitched, shivered, swung open. Lizzie stood in the archway staring out at them. She wore a multicoloured shawl draped over her thin shoulders. A cloud of feathery-white hair, swept up by a comb, crowned her head. From the light of the small square window Aine could see a row of cardboard boxes stacked along the shelves. She had seen them before and knew their contents. In former years when she had visited Lizzie she helped her sort out her wares. There was a conspiracy between them in those days, an unwritten agreement.

As Aine advanced into the shop she was assailed by a familiar odour. Pungent and sweet, it floated towards her tickling her nostrils and making her sneeze. On the shelf, near the window, stood a row of glass jars full to the brim with red and white aniseed balls. She manoeuvred her way to the counter. 'Sixpence worth of aniseeds, please.'

'How much have you there?' Lizzie peered at her out of the darkness.

Aine counted out her coppers, two three penny bits and a halfpenny.

Lizzie removed the lid from the sweet jar, twisted some newspaper and filled a cone-shaped paper bag with a fistful of sweets.

'There, my pretty,' she said, handing them to her. Taking the coins she dropped them, one by one, into a rusty old till. She unfolded a stepladder and began to climb to the top returning with an armful of boxes. 'Make yourselves comfortable, m'dears.'

Aine laughed. 'What's it to day, Lizzie?'

There was no reply. Settling herself on the top rung of the stepladder with the air of a high priestess Lizzie pointed to a box marked *Fragile*. 'This, my dears,' she tapped the box with the tips of her fingers, 'is my masterpiece! What we have here is a dress designed by one of London's Big Ten, the great *Melanie Sherard,* herself.' She drew herself up to her full height and pursed her lips. 'This magnificent gown is made from the sheerest silk, bodice trimmed with Brugienne lace and matched with a sequined bolero.'

'Wow!'

Throwing them a sidelong glance, she arranged her skirt in a canopy-like fashion over her bony knees and resumed her sacred ritual. She continued on, weaving layer upon layer of colourful extravaganza. Suddenly, she stopped. 'So what do you think? Stunning eh?'

'Oo ... ooh!'

'It's the bridal dress of a lady, a beautiful rich heiress, once a customer of mine.'

'From London?'

'Yeah Yeah.'

'Posh?'

'Very grand entirely.' As the old woman spoke, her long yellow teeth clapped against her lips like a pair of Spanish castanets. 'The lady of whom I speak was exceptionally beautiful, fair as the evening star with long golden ringlets and eyes like diamonds that would rob the sun of its brightness. But alas! Along came a prince, a handsome young stalwart.'

'Aahh!'

'Just look at this!' She began to root in one of the boxes. 'Would you believe it, a handmade shawl matching the white Brugienne lace?' Lifting up the box she placed it firmly on the flat of her knee. 'On the day—'

'The prince!' Aine interrupted, quickly, 'you were telling us about the prince.'

'Wait! Wait! On the day of the wedding the whole village turned out dying to catch a glimpse of the bride. But what do you think happened?' Her eyes glittered, darting from one to the other.

'She became ill.'

'Oh dear! No! No!'

'She got sorry.'

'Never!'

Julie leaned forward and nudged Aine. 'She's stone mad. She forgets we're not children anymore.'

Aine flushed. 'She's not one bit madder than the rest of us!' she snapped. Was Julie forgetting? Was she beginning to act silly like Sara, nothing in her head only fashion and boys? 'Go on, Lizzie,' she urged, turning to the old woman, 'tell us what happened.'

Studying them out of the corner of her eye, Lizzie gave a consequential little cough. 'On the morning of the wedding,' she said, 'the townsfolk assembled. They waited and waited ... The couple never showed up.'

'Skedaddled?'

'Yeah. There wasn't sign or sight of them between here and Westport. They'd taken the boat and skitted off to London.'

'That was the end of them?'

'Naw. A girl child was born but they didn't live to see her grow up'.

'Died?'

'Drowned. They were drowned out there in the middle of the bay one morning in June and buried in the cemetery beyond.'

There was a long pause. The canary in the window began chirping madly.

The old woman rose and descended the stepladder. She stood over Aine and gazed into her small pale face. 'The strangest thing of all,' she said softly, 'is that, that same lady, the lady of whom I speak bore an extraordinary resemblance to you, my dear!'

Aine gathered her purchases and rose to her feet. It was as if an ice cold hand had touched her. 'Good bye, Lizzie,' she whispered.

Beckoning to Julie, she threaded her way awkwardly through the dingy little shop and stepped on to the pavement.

Out on the street they plunged into blinding sunshine. Everywhere there were raucous sounds; cattle lowing, pigs squealing. The sun beat relentlessly down on them. A truculent farmer with a blackthorn stick brushed past them, leaving behind a smell of dung and an unwashed body. Aine fanned her face with her handkerchief, staving off the wasps that swarmed around her.

Having arrived in the square they were surrounded by a bevy of traders. Some had stalls selling second-hand clothes and gaudy patterned delph. Others displayed their wares from tarpaulin-covered trucks. Further over, fishermen's wives sold winkles, carrageen moss and dried mackerel hoping to buy a churn or a dresser with the proceeds before evening.

They strolled down Abbey Street. Stopped at a stall and haggled with a woman selling sunhats. Julie bought a red-ribboned Panama and settled it jauntily on the side of her head. Busy swotting flies, she failed to notice the winks and nods of the townies. They paused before a stall selling cotton dresses. 'Here's something for you, Aine,' Julie said, pointing to a dress with polka dots and a peter pan collar. Removing it from the hanger she measured it against her. 'Perfect!' she breathed, 'that goray skirt does something for you. Well, what do you think?'

'Of what?'

'Of the dress, silly! Aren't you going to buy it?'

Aine's eyes glinted. She took the polka dot down off the rail, held it against her chest and began waltzing in and out over the cobblestones ... *I could have danced all night ...*

'Shut up!' Julie cried, horrified.

... I could have danced ...

'Put back that dress, young scallywag!' the stall woman screamed, appearing from under a tarpaulin, 'put it back, d' you hear me! Gu ... ard!'

Aine jammed the dress back on to the rails.

They took to their heels, fled across the Square and on to the green, sheltering among the ruins of Donnellys' old mill.

'Why didn't you buy it?' Julie asked, breathless, as she leaned against the old stone wall.

'It reminds me of Sara's.'

'And what if it does?'

'I don't want to be dressed like *her*'. A sullen line had formed around the corners of Aine's mouth.

'Look!' Julie caught her arm. 'What's happening over there?' A crowd had gathered outside Donnellys on the Main Street. People were shouting; there were angry voices.

Aine shaded her eyes. Two men stood crouched, bareheaded, sleeves rolled up, facing each other. She moved up closer. One of them looked like Willie. Yes, it was Willie Sara. She recognised the thin stooped figure of Willie. A few paces away a tall swarthy giant stood glowering over him, fists raised. They had had been banned from Donnellys' and were continuing their fight on the street. Merciful God, Bull Kerrigan will kill Willie Sara! she thought, I'll have to find Colm.

'Aine!'

'Let go!' she cried, as Julie tried to hold her.

She fled down the street and across the square, thin spindly legs leaping between sacks of potatoes and creels of turf. Women with baskets of eggs and firkins of butter stood staring after her. She picked her way boldly through knots of men. Standing at street corners, they were rugged fishermen, elements of the seasons mapped on their faces. They spoke in low muffled voices, soft as the southern winds that blew around the hills of Connacht.

She kept on running.

A minute later she arrived at Gogartys' and wrenched the door open. A low buzz of conversation greeted her. Men in homespun pullovers stood at the counter gazing into their pints of stout as if they were measuring the depths of the universe. Others sat on stools talking of politics and war. Colm's back was to the window, sandwiched between old Daniel and Tim Hegarty. They discussed the currach races to be held in Cragann the following Sunday.

'You never can tell, Pat Hartigan can pull as good as the next.'

'If the wind changes round to the north—'

'Colm!' she hissed.

Colm turned, face dark with stubble, hair dishevelled. He looked as if he hadn't slept a wink in weeks.

She strode up and tugged his sleeve. 'Quick!' she gasped, 'Willie Sara's fighting Bull Kerrigan outside Donnellys' pub. The Bull will kill him!'

Colm put down his glass. A dark flush crept around his throat and into his face. He drew himself up to his full height letting his gaze rest on her. 'Willie can fight his own battles,' he snapped, and continued his conversation with the men.

Phil Gogarty arrived with a pint and placed it on the mat in front of him.

Colm reached out and took one long draught.

Aine, no longer, hesitated. She marched to the door and wrenched it open. 'You're useless!' she cried, glaring back at him, 'useless!'

'Can't you give us a kiss and forget Willie Sara!' a lazy voice shouted from the back.

'Shut your mouth, John Pete, or I'll shut it for you,' Colm threatened, glaring across at the speaker.

A loud burst of laughter broke from the counter. Aine's lips tightened. Memories of yesterday had faded. So this was the company he was keeping; these were his friends! She slammed the door shut and dashed back to Gogartys'. Willie Sara was leaning against the gable, blood oozing from his nose, right eye closing. The Bull pranced up and down like a wound-up jack-in-the box. Onlookers were shouting, goading them on. Some rooted for Willie, others for the Bull.

She pushed her way roughly to the front of the crowd, rose up on her toes and shouted, 'don't soil your hands with a *bodog* like that, Mr Kerrigan. A man like you has something better to do.'

The Bull stiffened, half-turned round.

Aine waited, scarcely daring to breathe.

'Maybe you're right now, girl,' he muttered, spitting on his hands, 'he's not worth the bother. I've beaten his sort before, men ten times the size of that old galoot.' He grabbed his stick, jammed his cap on his head and swaggered off down the street.

The people had already scattered.

'Give us a hand,' she said, beckoning to a man standing by the wall. Between them they hoisted Willie to his feet. Half dragging, half walking him, they arrived at Slatterys' where she asked for a basin of water and sponged the congealed blood from his face. 'Don't do that anymore,' she warned, catching his eye, 'or there's no knowing where you'll end up.'

Willie Sara grinned. 'Arragh, what! T'would take a lot more than that to leave me for dead.'

Frowning, Aine said nothing. The day had become suddenly overcast. The sun was going down in the west. A few minutes later she left the town, crossed the bridge and set out for Cragann.

On reaching the house she went straight to the kitchen. No sign of Delia. She had probably gone for her evening walk to Cartra. She threw herself into the armchair. A sickening thought gripped her. Willie could have been killed ... killed! She punched the cushions with clenched fists. He could have been beaten to death and Colm wouldn't have cared!

Chapter Twenty

Sometime around nine the following morning, Aine awoke to a knocking on the door. 'I'm up!' she cried, banging her knuckles off the linoleum-covered floor.

'They're all gone over to the hay,' Delia called out, 'this spell of weather mightn't last.'

She snuggled back into the pillows and closed her eyes. Down on the shore the fishermen shouted to each other across the water. Hartigans' sheep dog gave a loud bark. All familiar sounds! Suddenly, memories of Gogartys the previous evening came rushing back, Colm's face, laughter of the men at the counter. 'Wait till I get him!' she hissed, 'he'd no right, no right to speak like that and Willie his friend!'

In one leap she was out on the floor. She padded to the bathroom and turned on the taps filling the bath with sudsy water. After a quick wash and towelling, she struggled into her clothes and clattered downstairs to the kitchen.

Delia was busy pottering in the scullery. Hearing the movement in the kitchen she poked her head around the door. 'If you don't hurry they'll have finished the hay by the time you get there.'

Aine gulped down her breakfast; a bowl of porridge with milk; cup of tea. She snatched up her cardigan, threw it over her shoulders and hurried to Holohans' farm.

Half way across the hill there was a change of temperature. A biting wind blew from the sea causing her to shiver. Buttoning her cardigan she began to walk faster. To her right lay Holohans' field. Surrounded by stone walls and bushes, it sloped down to a rocky patch of land called the Puchan.

Nobody quite knew who owned the Puchan. Covered by thistles

and ragwort, the neglected strip of land made its own contribution. At the fall of each year a bumper crop of smooth pink mushrooms grew along its borders, enough to make an epicurean's teeth water. Further south, there was another stretch of land marked by ruins of settlements. Abandoned houses were scattered here and there, deserted by families who had exchanged their holdings for the price of their passage to America. There was a fairy wrath, its ring of stones pointing upwards.

The men were sharpening their scythes as Aine reached Holohans' farm. Anybody that could bind a stook, children, old men who had sat all summer in the chimney corner, were called in to help. Even old Daniel, with his sardonic eye, stood and watched the swinging scythes men. Anxious to have the hay saved before night Pa Holohan and his team pitched it quickly on to stacks, sweat running down their backs.

Dressed in a flowery pinafore and sunhat, Aine raked out the hay using a long wooden rake. With each thrust of the rake the fresh scent of newly mown hay drifted towards her. A few yards away Colm and the young Hartigans gathered it into stooks. Clean-shaven and cool, Colm's movements were swift and sure. From the corner of her eye she watched him. Not one bit concerned about yesterday, nor about how she was made a fool of. She didn't count at all! She plunged the rake into the stubble and dragged it furiously along the ground.

Towards midday, Maggie Holohan arrived with tea and sandwiches. A picture of industry, Maggie wore a navy-blue overall patterned with pink roses. Her hair was braided and coiled neatly around her head. Every year it was Maggie's responsibility to look after the needs of the helpers.

Perched on a haystack beside Julie, Aine ate her lunch; two slivers of cottage loaf with cheese and a hunk of currant cake washed down by three cups of strong sweetened tea. Satisfied, she lay back against the hay and looked up at the sky. It rose in a blue dome above them, whitening out towards the horizon. Birds chirped noisily in the hedges, rejoicing in an Indian summer.

'Strange, Colm didn't come over,' Julie remarked, wrapping her cup in newspaper and placing it back in the basket. She glanced across to where the men worked. Colm and Tim Hegarty were leaning against the haystack, mugs of tea in their hands. Pat Hartigan lay slumped between them, asleep.

'Why should he? Don't you know Colm is busy, drinking with his pals and stacking up money?'

'Aine!'

'Pity you didn't see him at the fair. Sloshed! Behaving like any old gurrier!' She sat up straight, eyes blazing.

'I didn't know he was in town' Julie said, astonished, 'I didn't lay eyes on him all day. But then I could easily have missed him as I went home early. Tim said he would call on the way.'

Aine shook the crumbs from her skirt and settled her hair under her hair-band where it had loosened during the morning's work. 'When I told Colm yesterday that the Bull was beating up Willie, do you know what he said?'

'What?'

'That Willie could look after himself. He kept on drinking as if he hadn't drunk a drop in weeks.'

'Well, that's how it is with them. The way to an Irishman's heart is through his pint.'

'You believe that?'

'Of course. Don't take any notice of Colm. It was a bit much to expect him to abandon his pint just to save Willie Sara.'

Aine's mouth tightened. 'Willie would die for Colm. He could have been killed yesterday twice over and Colm wouldn't have cared!' She leaned forward. 'Julie!'

'Mmm.'

'Why do you think Colm acted like that?'

Julie picked up a straw. She peeled it slowly, twisting it around her finger. 'You know about the fishing boat?'

'The one he's thinking of buying? Of course! It's been on the cards for sometime.'

'Well, Colm made a deal with Willie. Recently he arranged go into partnership with him. They had it all fixed up. They went down to Galway to settle the price. The very last moment Willie got a qualm and pulled out.'

So that was it! Willie Sara had inherited a bit of money from his aunt in the States, quite a substantial sum, somebody said. Rumour had it that he was going to invest. But, somehow, Aine could never imagine Willie Sara investing in anything, much less a sophisticated up-market fishing boat. He wasn't the type. On the other hand, that trawler, the one on which Colm had his eye, meant everything to Colm. She remembered how he described it, engine, funnel, the amount of cargo it would carry. In the end, she became as excited as he by the idea.

'So you can imagine how he felt,' Julie said, guessing her thoughts, 'they say he vowed he'd never again do a deal with Willie. But you know Colm.'

'When did it happen?'

'Only last week. I heard my Da telling my Ma ... he heard it from someone in the pub.'

'My God I ... I can't believe it!' Aine stood up, shook the hay from her dress and pulled the sunhat down over her eyes. The sun had reached its zenith. There was a dead heat over the land. A swarm of bees, evicted from their hives, were circling noisily around the haystack.

'By the way,' Julie said, eyeing her, 'you know that the guards were sent for yesterday?'

'Guards?'

'As soon as you left with Willie Sara two of the Belmullet gardai rounded the corner. They swooped on Gogartys meaning to break up the fight.'

'How did they know?'

'Somebody alerted them, someone who had been drinking in the pub.'

'Who?' Meeting Julie's eye she burst out laughing, 'Come on, Julie, 'she cried, 'I'll race you over.'

Aine reached the far side of the field a minute before Julie. She removed her cardigan, grabbed the long-handled rake and began raking the stubble feverishly. The Guards were sent for! Guards! Of all people! Calling in the Guards would have been anathema to Colm. But he might have told her, might have explained. After all she had known Willie as long, if not longer, than he.

Towards evening as Aine gatherd in the straw, packing it into sacks, she saw Johnnie the Post wheeling his bike through a gap in the hedge.

'It's a grand day!' Pa Holohan's voice greeted him from the top of the rick.

'A bit on the warm side,' Johnnie puffed, beating off the flies with his cap. Johnnie's feet were giving him trouble. He struggled lopsided across the field half-dragging the bicycle alongside him. Catching sight of Aine he took a long white envelope from his bag and waved it in the air.

'For me?'

He nodded. 'With an English stamp.'

Heavens! A letter from across the water! She couldn't remember when last she had received a letter. Quickly, she ran across the stubble to meet him. The envelope was addressed to herself in large black handwriting. Tearing it open she unfolded a sheet of thick white notepaper. On the top left-hand corner was the seal of Her Majesty, Queen Elizabeth.

'From her Royal Highness!' Johnnie exclaimed, peering at it over her shoulder.

Watching from the far side, Tim Hegarty shouted to Pat Hartigan. Having alerted Jamsie Dillon, the new farmhand, all three ran across the field and stood around her in a circle. Tim rested his elbow on Pat Hartigan's shoulder. Jamsie Dillon leaned against the handle of his hayfork.

'A job in the palace!' Pat Hartigan winked.

'Naw, it's a holiday in Windsor.'

'I always knew she could draw,' Colm's voice resonated in the quiet air as he slithered down the haystack and walked over towards them. 'She was at it the first time I saw her. Scribbling with crayons, drawing cats and dogs and one-eyed giants.'

'Hah! Her grandfather was the best drawer of hay around these parts,' Jamsie smirked.

'Hold your tongue, Jamsie Dillon,' Colm admonished, prodding him with his hay fork, 'you haven't the faintest idea of what you're talking about!'

'Jamsie Dillon's no fool!' Jamsie pranced up and down.

'It's from the Tudor Gallery,' Aine explained, looking up and catching Colm's eye. She was conscious then of nobody else in the field, nobody but Colm. He stood bareheaded, cap in hand, gazing quizzically down at her. 'It's a letter from an art dealer in London.'

'Read it to us,' he urged, 'read us the letter.'

Tudor Gallery,
London.

Dear Miss Fogarty,

I saw a painting of yours recently in London. In my estimation it's a most impressive piece of art. I hope to travel to Ireland next week and would like to visit you in Cragann to discuss the possibility of having your painting exhibited.

Yours faithfully,

Mark W Davis (Art Dealer)

'Well, I'll be damned! A who d' you know gobshite!' Colm exploded, a frown gathering between his brows.

'He'll be here anytime now,' Aine assured him, examining the postmark on the envelope, 'maybe today ... tomorrow ...'

'Heigh ho! Heigh ho! Her ladyship's off to London O,' Johnnie the Post's cracked baritone voice rang out across the fields. Like a shot, Johnnie fastened his mailbag, threw his leg over the crossbar of the bike and wobbled off out towards the road.

At six o clock that evening, Johnnie the Post stood watching from the window of his small thatched cottage on the hill. He saw a red sports car pull up outside Fogartys, a tall well-dressed gentleman jump out. In less than a minute he had mounted his bike and charged down the hill like a *si goath*. 'It's terribly grand,' he told Mrs Hegarty when he met her later at the Post Office, 'it has four doors and an opening on top of the roof.'

'You don't say! And the gentleman himself? Posh as a lord, if the truth be known!'

'You never saw the likes! His coat is as white as the chalk on Miss Cleary's blackboard. And he wears brown shoes, velvety-like.'

'Glory be to God! Not since the time of the Congress and Count John, himself ... Delia has struck gold at last. We won't be seeing much of *her* around here anymore!'

When Delia answered a knock on her hall door that evening, she saw a tall heavily built gentleman standing on the doorstep. He wore a white Panama hat and carried a brief case. Not a bit like the salesmen who normally called selling blouses and ladies headscarves. There was the traveller who came the previous winter with a case of ladies' underwear. She told him to go home out of that, he ought to be ashamed of himself! This gentleman was different. He looked as if he had gone up in the world. From the clothes he wore, you'd know he knew something about fashion.

'Miss Fogarty?'

Delia shook her head. 'If it's Aine, my niece, you're looking for, she's not here. She's over in Holohans bringing home the hay.'

'Oh, what a shame I've missed her!'

'But she'll be here any minute,' she added, quickly, 'you can step inside.

'So decent of you, Miss eh ...?'

'Fogarty, Delia Fogarty.'

The stranger followed her into the kitchen. In the soft evening light Delia's scrubbed kitchen held a welcoming glow. The midnight-blue dinner set standing on the dresser sparkled. There was a row of copper pots hanging on the wall. Wearing a starched white apron over her polka dotted dress, Delia stood, hands folded.

'Davis is the name,' he said, taking a gilt-edged card from the breast-pocket of his jacket and handing it to her, 'Mark Davis. I'm an art dealer in London employed by the Tudor Gallery. I saw a painting of Miss Fogarty's, recently, in the home of a friend of mine and came over to see if we could discuss the possibility of exhibiting it.'

'Well, well.'

'Your niece is ... a talented artist.'

'Won't you sit down, Mr Davis.' Delia drew the leather-backed chair from under the table and offered it to him. From the corner of her eye she watched him. Brown suede shoes, immaculate white socks. If only Aine would hurry up home! Bending, she began to stoke the fire and fill the kettle with water for tea.

Mr Davis sat back in his chair and crossed his legs. A small smile touched his lips. 'A client of mine in London,' he said, 'a patron of the arts, is interested in your niece's painting.'

'She has plenty of those things stacked in her studio.'

'She's a gifted young woman. Must have a wide clientele.' He coughed delicately as the aroma of turf-smoke entered his lungs.

'She's been painting since she was a child. I remember the first day she took a brush in her hands. There were smears and squiggles everywhere. Paint marks all over the place. I couldn't get any good of her since.'

'Regarding her latest work, you've no idea when she did it?'

'The one with the strange looking bird?'

'Bird?'

'Well, you know, something that looks like a robin, round shaped.'

'Not quite. This painting has a face at a window; it's very evocative.'

'She's painted so many. It's hard to keep track of them. It could be this one or that. Maybe it's the painting she finished off recently, the one she was so secretive about. She never said anything to anyone but one day upped and went with it. I never laid eyes on it since.' In desperation, Delia looked at the clock. Where was the child? Would she never come home? She eyed her visitor shrewdly. Prosperous looking gentleman with an equally fine bank account, no doubt! She heard the scraping of the latch on the back door. 'You'll stay for a while?' she asked, hurriedly.

'Well, I ... With regard to hotels ... can you suggest ...?' He let his brown eyes rest on her a moment.

'There isn't an hotel in Cragann. But we can put you up here. We've plenty of rooms. At the back of the house they're grand and warm.'

'That's decent of you, Miss Fogarty but—'

'Let there be no ifs or buts! Bye the bye,' she added, lowering her voice, 'Delia is my name. You can call me Delia.'

Chapter Twenty-One

All things considered, Aine was satisfied. A dozen or so golden-brown haystacks stood along Holohans' field. She donned her jacket and charged down the hill arriving breathless on Delia's doorstep.

'We've finished the hay,' she cried, wiping her shoes on the worn rubber mat outside. She stood, rooted. There was a stranger sitting in Delia's chair, a tall heavily built gentleman with glasses. He had dark brown hair going thin at the top. Delia sat opposite him, hands folded in her lap.

'This is Mr Davis,' her aunt said, rising and introducing him.

Aine eyed the visitor. He looked like a tourist or somebody who would be home on holidays. On the other hand, the Panama hat and those sparkling white trousers reminded her of a golfer.

'How do you do!' Mr Davis said, standing to shake hands.

'My niece has been working in the fields,' Delia explained apologetically, noting Aine's unkempt appearance, 'she's been giving them a hand with the hay.'

'Sounds a useful occupation to me! Working in the fields offers many opportunities. What do you think, Miss Fogarty, eh?'

Aine stared. She thrust her soiled hands into her pockets. Her fingers brushed against the crumpled letter lying there since morning. Could this be the art dealer? He wasn't like any of the dealers she knew. Chubb Nelligan, the horse man in town was a swarthy looking fellow with a bulbous nose.

'Delighted to meet you,' Mr Davis said, smoothing back his crisp dark hair. 'The moment I set eyes on your work I decided I'd have to come over and see you. Your painting, if I might say so, is of very high standard.'

For some unknown reason Aine didn't feel flattered by what he said. She hadn't considered the Cave painting in that particular light. Even if she had, there was something about the tone of his voice that irked her. Where in London had he seen it? Probably in Catherine's house. Her eyes followed the movements of his hands. Large and muscular, they were like those of a sculptor or a surgeon. A ring with a red stone glinted on his index finger.

'You must be hungry,' Delia said, snatching up the magazines and newspapers from the table and thrusting them into the wall-cupboard, 'I'm sure you'd like something to eat.'

'Well, if it isn't too much trouble.'

'Oh, none whatever. One extra mouth won't make much difference. We don't have many visitors in Cragann.'

Neat as a pin, Delia prepared the evening meal. Wearing her polka dotted dress under her white apron, she marched in and out to the dining-room carrying plates of food. She took a homemade loaf from the bin and placed it on the breadboard. Removing a vase of hydrangea which Aine had brought from Mulranny, she left them in the scullery. The raffia table-mats, a present from Rosemary, were taken from the press.

'This work which we hope to exhibit,' Mr Davis said, sitting back in his chair, 'when was it completed? I mean it must have taken ages to execute seeing its complexity.'

'Well ...' said Aine.

'All this nonsense about exhibitions!' Delia rushed in from the scullery. 'Things happen around here without anybody being told.'

'The exhibition will be on a small scale. We put on these shows occasionally to accommodate our clients.'

Delia checked the table. Milk, sugar, bread, everything in order. 'Tea is ready!' she called, 'sit here at the top. Oh, but you must!' She drew out a chair and patted the cushions.

Just as Mr Davis was about to sit down Pangur sprang up from her hiding place among the cushions, arched her back and spat. 'Oh, what a lovely tom!' he exclaimed, leaping back.

'Well, as a matter of fact, Tom had four beautiful kittens last week,' Aine remarked, sweetly.

'Take her out!' Delia ordered, glaring at her, 'take out that animal, d' you hear me? Don't worry,' she added, turning to Mr Davis, 'we'll have her put down. She's becoming quite a nuisance lately.'

'Who said Pangur is going to be put down?' Aine scooped up the cat and carried her out to the scullery.

Tea-time was a solemn occasion in Fogartys. Delia presided over the table and recited Grace. She poured out tea from a silver teapot with a long spout.

Mr Davis praised everything; the strong black tea; the juicy blackberries in the tart. He ate four slices of soda bread with salted butter. The spare ribs of bacon he eyed warily but when Aine took one in her hands he followed suit. 'The cross on the soda bread,' he asked, pointing to the home-made loaf, 'what does it mean?'

'There used to be a custom in our house never to bake bread without crossing it with a blessing. Whatever rises must be levelled out ...'

'Unless my memory deceives me it was Plato who said that.'

'I wouldn't be sure. It's a long time ago.'

'Never mind, I'll have another slice of bread. 'Hmm!' he remarked, looking around the kitchen. 'What a charming old house! It reminds me of the grand houses in London with all those beautiful antiques.'

'Where in London do you come from?'

'The inner city. I was born within ear-shot of the Bow bells.'

'Is your mother alive?'

'Oh, she passed away years ago.'

Delia pressed him to another cup of tea.

'Why, yes, thank you. There's nothing like a refreshing hot drink to chase away the blues. 'Now about this work of yours, Miss Fogarty' - he turned to Aine - 'you painted it all on your own?'

'Of course! Who could have helped me?' Aine was amazed that he should ask such a question. 'You don't think my art teacher had a hand in it, do you?'

'You see,' he said, with a faint smile, 'where masterpieces are concerned, we have to be careful.' He glanced out the window. Under a fast-changing sky Cragann Bay appeared dark and threatening. Enclosed by Nephin hill on the north and Cartra on the east, the tiny harbour bore a menacing look. The tide was going out leaving a trail of seaweed strewn along the strand. Across the road, a bunch of starlings were huddled together on the telegraph wires, cold and wet. Strange, he thought, that such an amount of talent should come from a backwater like this!

Delia sprang from her chair. 'My niece will show you around, Mr Davis. She'll introduce you to the beautiful places around Cragann.'

'If that's OK with you, Miss Fogarty?'

Aine shrugged.

'I'm sure London has its own beautiful scenery,' Delia pressed, making a final attempt to draw information from her guest before he set out for the walk.

'When my business expanded I moved to a more prosperous area. I now live on the outskirts of the city in a large suburban house called *Edenvale*. On a fine day you can see it, rising above the river. I've collected some valuable pieces of porcelain and Chippendale. Always had an eye for the good thing.' He sniffed an imaginary piece of snuff and adjusted his glasses.

Delia nodded. Just as she expected, a gentleman from the Big House. Her eyes shone.

Aine glanced at the clock. 'Let's go!' she cried. 'In an hour's time it will be dark.' Reaching for her jacket she threw it over her shoulders.

Mr Davis rose, flicked a speck of dust from his coat and stamped his shoes on the floor as if suspecting them of harbouring manure.

Outside, the air was chilly. He drew the collar of his mackintosh up around his throat. As they strolled through the village, his suede shoes and immaculate white socks became spattered with mud.

'Has he nothing else to wear besides those hush-puppies?' Aine wondered, staring contemptuously down at the brown suedes.

As they passed Brannigans, Sara Hartigan emerged from the side door carrying a loaf of bread. On seeing the stranger her eyes widened.

Aine pretended not to notice. She fixed her gaze on an imaginary ship appearing over the horizon.

'Going to Doora?' Sara called, hoping to gain a foothold with the visitor.

'Yeah.'

'You've picked up a new companion, I see.'

'Yeah.'

'Is he staying long?'

'I'll tell you when we're to be married. You'll be the first to be invited to the wedding.'

'Wedding! Mr Davis looked up. He had a difficulty in understanding the language of these people. Even the Fogarty girl, in spite of her English connections, lapsed into an incomprehensible gobbledygook whenever she met with her own.

'We were discussing a couple who plan to get married next month, perhaps. Depending on whether the matchmakers turn up.'

'Matchmakers!'

'That's what they do around here, make matches, matches upon matches.'

He rubbed his chin thoughtfully.

As they crossed the bog to Doora he stopped suddenly. 'I say what a colossal piece of land!' They stood still admiring the view. Out beyond the lighthouse huge breakers rolled, crashing against the cliffs. Showers of spray shot into the sky taller than the mast of a ship. Further over towards the horizon the islands languished in a blue haze, long narrow strips of land in the shadow of Nephin hill. Around them miles and miles of turf-cutters' bog stretched endlessly. Like ghosts in the middle of nowhere they stood gazing.

'Well, what do you think of it?'

'Such dreadful waste! Not a house to be seen anywhere. If this were England we'd have reclaimed it long ago. Every inch of land would be used for tillage or crops or developed into a model village. It's difficult to believe that all this exists and so many people homeless!'

To reclaim Doora! Of all the crazy ideas! Was the Englishman mad? Nobody in Cragann would dream of such a thing.

As they passed the dolmens the grizzly-faced monuments stared balefully out at them.

'Do you attend many celebrations and unveilings? ' he asked.

'Oh, yes,' she replied. She hoped he wouldn't pursue that subject. Parties in Cragann were invariably a flop. What with Colm drinking, Pat Hartigan fracturing his ankle, Julie getting sick ... 'It isn't easy to get transport,' she said, vaguely, 'there aren't many cars around here.'

'I appreciate your difficulty. You're very isolated, quite a distance from the mainland.'

'Cragann isn't exactly an island. Years ago it was separated from the town but now the bridge links the two together.'

'You've heard of the Frazers,' he said, changing the subject, 'Lord and Lady Frazer. They're patrons of the arts in London and very dear friends of mine—'

Noticing that he was gasping for breath, she stopped to tie her shoelace, giving him time to recover. After a minute or two they resumed their walk.

'I visited the West Bank in Paris last summer. It was an unforgettable experience. Came across some exquisite miniatures. Just before I left I found a copy of a Rembrandt letter hidden among the artefacts. A most extraordinary find!'

Aine yawned. She stared at the boundary wall separating the bogland from the adjoining field. Some of the stones had fallen leaving a gap in the hedge. She'd have to tell Pa Holohan this evening. His cattle might stray. With a start she realised that Mr Davis was speaking.

'I was just saying' - he sounded annoyed - 'that perhaps you'd like to pay a visit to London. I'd introduce you to the Tylers and Beresfords. They'll be up for the season and will, most likely, throw a few parties. You'd meet some of the celebrities, painters and sculptors from London's West End.'

That might be exiting. Some of those people might be a link with her past. Maybe somebody out there had known her mother ... She realised with a start that she was thinking of the twin, her mother's

143

sister, the woman who haunted her dreams.

As they approached the cliff, the roof of Pluais na gCaorach sprang into view. Sculpted from sandstone, it rose towards the sky like the dome of a Gothic cathedral.

Mr Davis fell silent.

'Can you see it?' she asked excitedly.

'I beg your pardon.' He was making obvious efforts to recover his dignity.

'There's where I did my painting. My only light came from a hurricane lantern.'

'Ah! So this is where you got your inspiration!'

She glanced down at his suede shoes. Impulsively, she offered to take his umbrella.

They began their slow descent to the caves.

Chapter Twenty-Two

When Aine recalled that journey down she was conscious of two things: one was the extraordinary beauty of the surrounding cliff. Alpine mosses, lichen and algae grew everywhere in an extravagant blaze of colour. The other was the stark terror in Mark Davis' eyes whenever she chanced to look back.

She followed a well-trodden glacier path and descended the steep incline. The sea, which had been lifeless for days, now burst into spume as it struck the rocks. Mr Davis followed down slowly. He was making good headway but it was his corpse-like pallor that drew her attention. His customary ruddy complexion had become ashen; his full lips were drawn tightly together. Strands of hair fell in disarray over his forehead. Whenever he stooped a bald patch appeared on the crown of his head.

'Keep a tight hold of the rock!' she cried.

There was no reply. All she heard was his breathing, in and out like the wheezing of a melodeon. Near the base of the cliff he missed his footing. 'Ouch!' he groaned. There was a slither of stones. A shower of gravel descended on her head.

'Are you all right?'

'Aagh!'

Would he succeed in finishing the journey? She visualised his body all broken up arriving home on a stretcher. Maybe she shouldn't have brought him. Delia had taken a fancy to him. Never before had a visitor received such treatment, placing him at the head of the table and giving him the best bone china. Wow, it could all end up in a match!

Mr Davis made heroic attempts to balance himself. In the end he grasped a ledge, took one leap and slithered awkwardly on to the shingle. Shaking the dust from his clothes he took a comb from his pocket and combed his hair. 'Phew! It reminds me of the Alps. My friend and I went on a climbing expedition last summer. The sheer fall of these cliffs would fill one with awe!' He whistled softly.

'It won't be so bad going back,' she said coldly, ignoring his remark, 'but you'd better hang on to a ledge. If you fall it will be a soft landing.'

He gave her a bleak smile.

'Have you ever piloted a ship?' she asked, minutes later, as she twirled his folded umbrella.

'My goodness ... no! I've very little knowledge of seafaring. I was raised in the city.'

'The city's OK but it's not as exciting as the sea. Listen to the breakers out there. They'd make your heart sing. But you've got to respect it. It has a heartbeat like everyone else. Sometimes it's slow. Other times it goes at a gallop. Listen! It's quickening again.' She pointed across to the surf lashing the islands.

'Who taught you all this?'

'Willie. Willie Sara is a fisherman in Cragann. He has travelled the world from Magellan Straits to the Cape of Good Hope and back. Some day, maybe, I'll sail myself.' In fact,' she said, thrusting out her chest, 'like Granuaile, I might own a few ships.'

'Granuaile, who is he?'

She laughed. 'Granuaile was a woman, a pirate queen, though in many respects she resembled a man. She cut her hair short like a boy and commanded a fleet of thirty galleys. Her armada was based out there.' With a sweep of her hand she gestured towards the coast.

'Irish?'

'Oh, yes. She plundered every sea-worthy ship that came within range of her telescope, especially foreigners that bore an enemy flag. In the end, she was captured by Lord Bingham and imprisoned in Howth Castle.'

'You seem to admire her.' He threw her a dubious glance.

'Of course. Who wouldn't admire a courageous woman? We could do with a few people like her around here. Maybe they'd keep old Maggie Reynolds in place.'

'By the way, I'd like you to stand for a photograph.' He opened a small leather case and took out a camera.

'Where?'

'Over there, close to the cave.'

She took up her position outside Pluais na gCaorach, locked her hands in front of her as Delia had taught her, put one foot before the other and stared straight at the camera.

He adjusted the lens and frowned into the viewer. 'If you could arrange your hair to the left, parting to the right; that's it!' Studying the effect he shook his head. Leaving the camera on a rock he walked over towards her. 'Allow me!' With a free hand he loosened her hair, fluffing it up till she felt like a younger version of Greta Garbo. 'Not quite the arrangement I had in mind,' he said, standing back. 'Your hair needs styling.' He focused the camera, clicked and then clicked again.

Aine fell silent. Stealthily she rubbed her scalp, the part he had touched with his fingers. It was as if a foreign body had invaded her and was crawling around inside.

Mr Davis shifted his attention to Pluais na gCaorach. He gazed at the dome roof sculpted from sandstone fanning out at the base. In its pristine innocence it looked like an early Christian oratory. Water dripped from its walls making a sound like tinkling bells. He stood back staring. Suddenly, he wheeled around. Aine saw another Mark Davis. He began to pace back and over, measuring the cave with his eye, admiring it, rubbing the walls with his hands. 'What a stunning piece of work!' His voice shook with excitement. 'It must be millions of years old, one of the oldest—'

'Sshh!' She put her finger to her lips.

'What does the name mean in English?'

'Sheeps' Cave. Some years ago sheep used to wander in here from the hills. There were so many of them drowned that the farmers had to put a stop to their wanderings. They don't come here anymore.'

Like a schoolboy he whipped out his camera. Kneeling on one knee, he photographed the cave from different angles. 'Ahh!' he exclaimed, pleased with himself.

Looking at him, Aine was reminded of the Sergeant, the nights he'd pocket his winnings having played a game of twenty-five.

As they entered the cave, a pencil of light escaped from the inside chamber. It stole across the floor dividing the darkness.

'There's somebody here!' she whispered, turning to him, 'there's a light inside!' She advanced slowly on tiptoe, steadying herself, keeping in close to the wall. Nobody had been seen in the cave before. Nobody ever came there. It was rumoured that corpses of drowned sailors were found a long time ago in Pluais na gCaorach. Old Daniel had it that a ghost appeared there at a certain time every year. It was the ghost of the captain of the Marie Celeste, he said, the brigantine that disappeared off the coast of America and was found later drifting in the North Atlantic, captain and crew having vanished. An uneasy feeling crept over her. Could this be the captain returning to report what had happened? She was about to turn back but Mr Davis had forged on ahead.

As they reached the end of the tunnel she got a strange smell. It was earthy and pungent unlike anything endemic of the sea. In the light cast by a lantern she saw a bulky figure stooped over, what appeared to be, a metal cauldron. Vapour passed from the cauldron through a coiled pipe into a wooden keg. In a flash she knew it was poiteen. 'Pat Neddy!' she cried, as the tattered old figure swung round. She found herself staring into the heavy jowelled face and red-rheumy eyes of Patrick Edward O Donohue.

'I told you to keep out of here.' He glared angrily down at her. 'Go away! Get out of my sight or I'll kill you!'

'You tried it before but you didn't succeed,' she retorted, not knowing exactly why she said it.

'I won't have you prying into other peoples' business. This is my private property.'

Aine said nothing. If Pat Neddy were drunk, most likely he'd be dangerous. Dim-witted as he was he'd be cunning and wouldn't be easily outstripped. She could hear his breathing, shallow like a run-down bellows. A seagull flew past the mouth of the cave. She glanced across at her companion.

The art dealer raised his hand in protest. 'Miss Fogarty is showing me around. I wanted to see the place that inspired her painting.'

'Miss Fogarty! Miss Fogarty! Since when did that one become Miss Fogarty? I remember her father when he didn't have a shoe on his foot. Fancy Johnnie Fogarty's daughter knowing how to paint! Painting how are ye! Hah! She doesn't even know who her mother was!'

'Oh, I say!'

'And none of your fine manners either, Mr gentleman. If you've come down from Dublin spying on me, I'll have you know something different.'

'To hell with yourself and your poiteen!' Aine burst out. However insane the old reprobate might be she didn't feel like standing back and accepting his insults. 'This cave is as much mine as it is yours. Neither you nor anyone else will keep me away from it.'

Pat Neddy raised his fists.

'Your liqueur smells fine, my good man,' the English man rushed in, 'how much do you charge for it?'

The old man paused. He retreated towards the poiteen still, staring at the stranger. 'You want some, eh?' His watery eyes glittered.

'Perhaps I could taste it first.'

Pat Neddy turned to the cauldron, filled a baby-power bottle with poiteen pouring some of it into an enamel mug and handed it to him.

Mr Davis eyed it dubiously. He swigged it around a few times before lifting it to his lips. 'By Jove!' he exclaimed, as the fiery vapours trickled down his throat, 'your moonshine is powerful stuff. Fill me a bottle. I'll take it to London.'

Pat Neddy grinned, delighted that he had found an accomplice. Measuring the poiteen with his eye, he poured some of it into a lemonade bottle and handed it to him.

Mr Davis counted out a few coins and dropped them into his hand. He shoved the lemonade bottle into his pocket and followed Aine back through the cave.

As they crept through the tunnel, they could hear the sound of coins jingling and the mad laughter of Pat Neddy, tittering at the good of it all.

Darkness was falling as they walked back through the village. A velvet sky hung above them displaying myriad clusters of stars. With her finger, Aine traced the Great Bear and the Little Bear, so many light years away.

Approaching the Barracks, the burly figure of the Sergeant could be seen standing at the Barrack wall. Hearing their footsteps he opened the gate and crossed the road. 'Are you out for a ramble?' he asked, glancing from one to the other.

'We are, Sergeant.' Her heart began to thump. From the corner of her eye she could see the shape of a bottle protruding through the lining of Mark Davis' pocket.

'You're a stranger around these parts?' the Sergeant remarked, peering at Mr Davis.

'He's a friend of Delia's. Came over from London on a visit.'

'Ahh! I hope you like our country, Sir?'

'He finds our accent a bit difficult,' she explained quickly.

Mr Davis sneezed. Taking a handkerchief from his pocket he blew his nose.

Aine felt sweat break out on her forehead.

'You're keeping a good eye on him, I see.'

'I'm doing my best, Sergeant.'

'Well good-night then, both of you!'

'Good night, Sergeant.'

Trembling, she took Mr Davis' arm and guided him to the centre of the road conscious of the Sergeant's sharp beady eyes staring after them.

Chapter Twenty-Three

Mark Davis became a frequent visitor to Fogartys. When in Dublin on business he would drive down to Cragann. He was most generous, bringing a bottle of Sandy Man's Port to Delia, a bunch of flowers or pound box of Black Magic to Aine.

Delia loved him. He flattered her, laughed with her. Her house reminded him of the great houses in London, he said, the old grandfather clock ticking in the hall, the leather armchair.

With Aine he was different. He watched her carefully under hooded eyes as she sat cross-legged in her chair, a well-fed cat on her knee. Her elfin face and ivory skin were as delicate as a piece of porcelain. There was a wildness about her, as she loped along the road exclaiming with delight at the sight of the first swallow. But those fierce blue eyes, that determined chin! Ahh!

One Saturday morning after Mark's departure to London, Aine arrived early to breakfast. Delia was already down standing by the mantelpiece staring into the fire. The table was set for two. A ray of sun splashed across the tablecloth gilding the rose-patterned teacups. The cat was curled up in the armchair asleep.

'Aine.'

'Mmm?'

'Mr Davis and I have been having a chat.'

'Well?'

'He said you had great potential, that you could earn your living from painting.'

'Really?'

'Listen to me, girl! You're old enough now to take up a job. A career in painting mightn't be a bad thing at all. Mark thinks that with a little bit of effort you could make your fortune.'

Mark! Since when did Mr Davis become Mark? Blinking the sleep from her eyes, Aine took an oatcake off the griddle and slapped it on to her plate. Drawing out a chair she slumped down into it.

'He has asked you to paint?'

'That's the first I heard of it.'

'Didn't he discuss it with you?'

'He admired my work; that's all.'

'What did you say?'

She shrugged. 'I didn't say anything.' Flicking the crumbs from her lap she sat back yawning. If only Delia would go away and forget all this nonsense about painting. Inspiration didn't come at the drop of a hat.

'The sooner you decide to earn your keep, Miss, the better. The cost of living is soaring.' Delia rose and raked the fire. She went to the scullery to collect the laundry checking the clothes to be left out for ironing.

'Why are you suddenly so interested?' Aine called after her. 'For ages you couldn't bear to see me paint. Now it's nothing but painting night and day!' With a piece of bread, she began to mop up the grease gathered around the edge of her plate.

'Hurry and clear the table!' Delia retorted, 'Nora Hartigan will be around in a minute to do the Wednesday cleaning.'

Preparations were being made for the Halloween festival. The gathering was to be held in Delia's. There were two or three rambling houses in Cragann, places where young and old met. First there was Holohans and Brannigans, though Pa Holohan had complained recently of an arthritic knee; he didn't feel able for the revelry.

On the eve of All Hallows the neighbours came around for a game of twenty-five or they'd sit by the fire telling stories. Afterwards there would be the usual hop. Willie Sara played the accordion and they would dance the night.

This year Halloween would be different. There was a stranger in their midst. Foremost in their minds was the dancing. Who would Mr Davis invite out to dance? Maybe he'd take a fancy to Sara

Hartigan. In anticipation Sara dolled herself up. She wore her new pointed shoes with buckles, red tartan skirt and frilly blouse.

Mr Davis had never attended a Halloween party. The idea of it intrigued him greatly.

'Did you ever dance a half-set?' Delia asked, one evening shortly after his arrival.

He shook his head. 'We do waltzes and foxtrots mostly in London and of course the Charleston.'

'Charleston?'

'Did you never see a Charleston being danced?' He began to wriggle his hips. 'You put your right foot in, your left foot out ...'

Aine began to giggle.

'My niece knows how to dance a half-set,' Delia explained, quickly. 'She won a prize last year at the Feis.'

'Wow!'

In the afternoon Mark said he would drive to Belmullet to take a look at the shops. 'Care for a spin?' he asked, glancing at Aine

She shook her head. 'Belmullet's such a stuffy little town. Who'd want to spend an afternoon in a place like that?'

The truth was, Aine was reluctant to travel with strangers. Few, if any, frequented Cragann and fewer still darkened the doorstep of Fogartys'. Whenever they did, she invariably went out of her way to avoid them. It was time, Delia thought, that the girl put an end to her nonsense. 'For heavens sake, child,' she said, 'put on your coat. An afternoon in town will do you all the good in the world!'

Minutes later, Aine was sitting in the passenger seat of Mr Davis' sports car. As they sped threw the village the wind lifted her hair spreading it out like a sail.

Dark and mysterious in a Panama hat and sun-glasses, Mark looked like Clark Gable or one of those famous film stars. Resting his arm against the rolled-down window, his other hand gripped the steering wheel.

As they drove past Holohans' field Tim Hegarty and Pat Hartigan lifted their caps in salute. Out thinning turnips, they were anxious to have their work finished before frost set in that evening. Leaning on their spades, they whistled after the sports car.

After some minutes' travelling Aine noticed a cameo of two young girls in sunhats hanging on the dashboard. 'Who are they?' she asked.

'What?' he shouted, tapping his ear. 'I'm afraid I'm a bit mutt an' Jeff.'

'You're what?'

'Oh, I beg your pardon. I mean, I'm a little on the deaf side.'

'Who are the girls in the picture?'

He removed the cameo and handed it to her. 'It's an antique I picked up at Christies. You seem to admire nice things.'

'Sometimes.'

'Sometimes?'

'Well I don't admire antiques just because they're antique.'

'I see.'

Finding it difficult to hear him over the wind she placed the cameo back on the dashboard. They lapsed into silence. The car travelled smoothly along. It was early in the afternoon so they met with very little traffic.

As they came within sight of the sand banks at Oiligh Aine brightened. She rolled down the window and gazed with admiration at the undulating dunes. Beyond them, white-capped waves broke in jagged lines along the beach. The bay stretched for miles to meet the Atlantic. She shifted her gaze to the road ahead. Suddenly she sat up straight. 'Watch out!' A streak of fluff shot across the road heading for the opposite bank. A young hare, tufts of white on its ears, ran for its life pursued by a boy with a sheepdog. Mr Davis jammed the breaks and swerved, missing the animal by a fraction of an inch.

Aine lunged forward, chin colliding with the dashboard. The car came to a sudden halt.

'That stupid animal!' he exclaimed, getting out to examine his car. 'Those peasants should all be locked up, crossing a highway like that to give chase to an animal!' Satisfied that there wasn't any damage done, he climbed back into the driver's seat. Whistling softly, he changed gear and accelerated.

Amazed, she studied him in the mirror. Did he always react like that? If there had been an accident or somebody killed what would his first reaction be? She recalled how Pa Holohan had searched all night when one of his animals had strayed.

'Have you ever visited the London boutiques?' he asked, as the shop fronts in Main Street came into view.

She shook her head. Rubbing her forehead, she found that a bump had formed where she had hit the dashboard.

'You'll have to see Bond Street. Oxford Street too is a great place for fashion. And of course there's Harrods. You could spend hours browsing around Harrods.'

She frowned. London for her meant something different. It was Kensington Gardens in springtime; or listening to Peter Pan playing his pipes; Hyde Park on a Sunday morning hearing the orators yell out their ideologies from the top of soap boxes; or ... St Paul's Cathedral, as it chimed out the hours high up in the Belfry with its six hundred and twenty-seven steps going right to the top.

As they approached the town, Mark slackened his speed. Traffic was beginning to thicken along Main Street. Cars crawled bumper to bumper ahead of them. Shops and petrol stations had swung into business. Passing Cattigans' Hardware her eyes lit up. 'That's just what we're looking for!' She pressed her nose against the pane of glass.

'What's that?'

She pointed to fishing tackle on display outside. 'I'll be going on a fishing trip, shortly.'

'Where to?'

'Out to the Great Bull lighthouse. We go there every year when the weather settles.'

'Who are we?'

'Colm, Tim Hegarty and myself. If you want to come along—'

'Now that's an idea! I always wanted to visit a lighthouse.' He pulled up outside Mackeys, the drapers. Said he'd like to buy her a gift. 'How old are you?' he asked.

'Going on nineteen.'

'Then how about that?' He pointed to a green silk dress hanging in the window. 'Suits your colouring, don't you think?'

'Her eyes widened. 'Oh! But it's so grand.'

'Try it on. I like nothing better than to see a beautiful woman dressed up. It makes me feel good walking beside her, seeing the glances of the men and stares of the ladies.' He gave a short throaty chuckle. 'What do you think, eh?'

She made no reply.

When the shop assistant arrived she nodded her approval on seeing the fitted-on dress. 'Suits you, madam. Catches the tone of your skin, lights in your hair.'

Mr Davis stood back admiring. 'I say! A face like that would launch the proverbial ships.'

'We haven't any ships in Cragann, only a few old fishing boats.'

'Parcel it up!' he ordered, 'I'll take it back to the car.'

Nobody planned Halloween. It just happened.

Willie Sara strolled into Delia's, accordion strapped over his chest.

Sara Hartigan arrived and began tapping her toes on the red-and white tiles. She stole a glance at Colm. With a visitor around perhaps he'd give her a few dances.

Soon everybody was out on the floor. Going up and down, up and down; the Hartigans, Tim Hegarty, Colm and Aine. Even old Daniel Cassidy danced a few steps. 'Yehoo! Over and under we go, around the house and mind the dresser! Yehoo!'

Colm swung Aine off her feet, his boots shooting sparks like the blacksmith's hammer striking the anvil.

When the half-set was over they sat down to cool. Willie played the hurdy-gurdy waltz.

'Where's Mr Davis?' Delia asked.

'He's up in the room.' Tim Hegarty nodded towards the brown panelled door leading to the sitting room.

'Come out and dance, Mr Davis, don't let good music like that go to waste!'

There was no reply.

Delia hurried to the sitting room returning minutes later with Mark at her heels.

Mark loosened his tie and removed his jacket revealing a gleaming white shirt underneath. Taking Aine's elbow, he piloted her on to the floor.

Delia sat with her knitting beneath the blue and white statue of Our Lady. She sat quietly and watched. One plain ... one purl ... one plain ...

Aine's green taffeta glistened and shimmered in the firelight. Hair swept up and wearing high heeled shoes, she looked some years older than her age. Mark followed her around in the dance, in and out, over and under, keeping respectable time to the music.

Suddenly Sara Hartigan appeared on the floor. She took Mark's arm and guided his steps. They whirled and dived, Sara's hair brushing the face of the dancers.

The music stopped. Mark walked back to his place, mopping his brow with a red silk handkerchief.

Night descended. A full moon cast its light in through the kitchen window. Delia lit the lamps and pulled the curtains. The tall white tilley lamp sent out a soft glow. Willie Sara buttoned his melodeon and placed it back in the case.

'Are you coming home?' Sara called, beckoning to Colm.

Colm shuffled his feet and drained his glass. He was beginning to show signs of having had too much to drink.

A few yards away Aine stood smiling beside Mark.

'Are you coming?' Sara repeated.

Colm snatched up his cap, jammed it on his head and charged out the door.

Aine looked at Julie. 'Come on,' she said, 'we'll walk you home.'

Having accompanied Julie as far as Brannigans, Aine and Mark quickened their steps. The night had turned chilly. A silver moon cast its light along the bay. A handful of stars studded the sky. Suddenly, the sound of voices shattered the night's stillness. Straining her eyes, Aine saw the familiar figures of Pat Hartigan and Tim Hegarty staggering home, arms entwined, singing:

And if there's going to be a life/ hereafter ...

Somehow, I'm nearly sure there's going to be ...

Drunk as lords, their slurred vowels resounded through the fields and down the valley.

On reaching Fogartys' Mark stood outside. 'Do you ever get tired of this sort of thing?' he asked.

'What sort of thing?'

'All these people, their crude merrymaking, drinking habits. They're not your cup of tea, are they?'

Aine stiffened.

'You were born for something greater!' He slipped his arm through hers. 'Come over to London with me. It's teeming with life.'

She stood motionless. Below them waves lapped softly on the shore. Further up among the hills a running stream gurgled and sang its way to the ocean.

'You don't have to answer me now,' he said, quickly. 'Think about it. Let me know when you've decided.'

'Yes, Mr Davis.' She was too amazed to say anything else.

'Please call me Mark,' he said.

Chapter Twenty-Four

Winter went out in a rage. On the last day of January rain fell in buckets over Cragann. The sea writhed in madness. People remained indoors waiting for the spell to pass.

With the approach of Spring the skies began to clear. The sun rose in a triumphant blaze over the land. Feverish activity began, replenishing stores, setting of seeds. Mark Davis' sports car could be seen more often at Fogartys'. He seemed to fit into the Fogarty household. What impressed Delia most was his refined accent and the way he could handle a drink. She watched as he drank his sherry, long fingers curled around the stem of the glass, as the coastguards did long ago when they attended the Castle Ball.

'There's a man who knows how to drink,' she remarked to Aine one night after Mark had gone out.

'So what?'

'Unlike some others around here who never know when to stop!'

'Such as?'

'Well, Colm Holohan for a start.'

'You always blame Colm for everything. What's wrong with someone lowering a few pints?'

'Nothing, provided he can keep his head!'

The following Sunday after lunch, Mark passed around photographs of his home in London. 'There it is!' he said, pointing to a three-storey red-brick building surrounded by poplar trees. 'You can see the gardens and land stretching to the river.'

Delia nodded. Just like the Big House at Oiligh where the Carters used to live. *Evendale* he called it. *Evendale!* Now a place like that would do justice to Aine. She pictured her standing in the long hall on a summer's evening receiving her guests, hair swept to the top of her head. Afterwards her photograph would appear in *Social and Personal*. She watched as she poured over the photographs with Mark, her well-shaped head up close to his. Aine was every inch Rosemary's daughter. Ah! Some day Aine Fogarty would beat her Wellington boots into slippers.

On the way home from Mass the following Sunday, Delia broached the subject of Mark Davis to her friend Mary Brannigan. 'What do you think of him?' she asked, hoping for some encouragement.

'He seems an honourable sort of gentleman to me. But then you never can tell—'

'Oh, he's so honest! You could safely tell him your sins. Would you believe it, last Saturday morning he took charge of the house while Aine and I were out shopping.'

'Now isn't that something!'

'But do you think they're a well-matched couple,' she persisted, giving her a sidelong glance.

'Definitely! Definitely! It seems to me that they're ... ah ... made for each other.'

But deep, deep down in the secrecy of her heart Mary Brannigan had reservations about the compatibility of the couple. Had their stars really crossed? Or was Delia, from her throne in Cragann, gently putting out her little toe and giving things a push? Which ever, Mary wished that her own daughter, Julie, would set her cap at somebody as eligible as Mark Davis. Julie hadn't an ounce of sense, skylarking with a commoner like Timmy Hegarty.

'You think he'll make her a good husband?'

'Of course! With all that attention he's paying her, over every month from London, buying her fine clothes and jewellery. What else could any girl want?'

Delia pursed her lips. Indeed! What else could any girl want? Secretly, she began to plan the wedding. She wrote to Switzers for catalogues of wedding dresses. Clucked her tongue at the prices of the material. With a similar pattern she'd make a better dress, herself. She fancied white slipper satin, but she'd leave that decision to Aine. After all, she'd be the one who'd be wearing it, though it was obvious to everyone that the girl hadn't a glimmer where fashion was concerned.

Meanwhile, with the arrival of Spring Aine's thoughts were elsewhere. Her eyes followed the rhythm of the tides as they ebbed and flowed rising in great mounds out beyond Carrageen; the fishing boats, as they glistened and shimmered in the sun. Those bright frosty mornings awakened in her a longing to be out on the sea again.

'What do you think of her?' Colm asked one day, plying a final coat of paint to a yacht he had recently acquired.

'Looks OK to me. But what about that fishing trip, the one to the Bull?' She picked up a stone and began knocking off the barnacles stuck to the gunners of the yacht.

'What did we decide?'

'In a few weeks time ...'

'Oh! righty oh! You make the sandwiches. I'll round up the crew.'

'About Mr Davis?'

'What about him?'

'He wants to——'

'Bring him along! There's no separating you two those days, is there?' Carelessly, he began to whistle the chorus of *The Blackbird*.

She watched as he gathered up his tools, muscles rippling in his arms. Suddenly she stiffened. Did he intend to invite Sara? What did Sara Hartigan know about hoisting a sail or handling a rudder? Why, she couldn't tell the difference between a paper boat and a yacht! A wind from the sea caught her dress. Reeling, she grasped the side of the boat to balance herself.

The following morning they set out from Cragann for the Old Bull Lighthouse. Armed with sandwiches and flasks, Aine had prepared for a long day's fishing off the Old Bull.

With help from Pat Hartigan and Tim Hegarty, Colm hoisted the sails rippling and flapping in the breeze. As they moved out into the deep he started up the engine. Sails filled up; the yacht shot off over the clear blue water.

161

After they passed Carrageen the yacht slackened. Aine helped with the fishing rods, unravelling the tackle. Pat Hartigan cast his line overboard. Colm kept his eye on the sail in case it should pucker and cause the boat to slacken.

Sitting in the stern staring into space, Mr Davis looked as if he were attending his own funeral. Shoulders hunched, the collar of his freeze coat was pulled up around his throat.

He could try to look more cheerful, Aine thought, crossly. After all, this was their annual fishing trip.

Out beyond Carrageen the breeze freshened. The yacht leaned over, slicing the water as it fell away in green cataracts. The receding shore looked like a picture postcard. She searched the landscape for Fogartys'. 'Look! Over there to the right!' she cried, pointing a finger.

Mr Davis levelled his binoculars in the opposite direction.

'No! Straight across from the cliffs.'

'You don't have to tell me the points of the compass!' he snapped, mouth puckering like a child's.

Aine fell silent. She trailed her hand in the ice cold water. The yacht ploughed steadily forward. He must have been brought up spoiled, she thought. Maybe his mother raised him single-handed. The boat swung on its side. She glanced at Colm. His gaze was fixed on the horizon, brows knitted tightly together.

Tim Hegarty hauled in a mackerel. It lay wriggling on the floor, blood on its gills. He extracted the hook from the mouth of another fish, cut a piece off its side for bait and cast the mutilated body, still alive, overboard.

It was then Mr Davis got sick.

Never before had Aine seen anyone so green. Bending over the side of the boat Mark's body writhed in agony. She stared, helplessly, at the heavily clad figure enveloped in yellow oilskins. Could this be the same man who swaggered into Renehans a few days previously? 'Are you all right, Mr Davis?' she called.

There was no reply.

'Hold on tight. We'll arrive at the lighthouse in another few minutes.'

He sat hunched, face like stone. 'This wreck of a yacht isn't seaworthy,' he said, pulling the collar of his coat up closer.

'It managed to take us out safely,' Tim pointed out, in an effort to cheer him.

'I hope it will carry us back,' he snapped, gathering himself together for another bout of sickness. 'Augh! I'm dying ... Take me home, I'm dying!'

Seagulls screamed and scooped low for fish. Colm sat with his hand on the tiller staring straight ahead. The Old Bull loomed up in front of them, its whitewashed tower glistening in the sun.

'I want to go back,' Mark Davis moaned, 'please turn the boat around.'

A herring gull surfaced too near the yacht but took off again in panic.

Aine felt hope slipping away. She caught Colm's eye and signalled him to return.

On the journey back the yacht began letting in water. She grabbed an aluminium saucepan used exclusively for bailing, removed her sandals and rolled up her dress. On her two knees she scooped out the water slopping around her ankles.

'My shoes are drenched!' Mark complained peevishly, stamping his feet.

She glanced down at his brown suedes. Limp and shapeless, his long feet looked like two sick animals.

Colm continued steering.

Eventually, the listing yacht sailed drunkenly into Cragann Bay. Colm and Aine pulled the ropes, lowered the sail and dragged it on to the beach. Water splashed over the floorboards, where Tim's four mackerel beat their tails up and down in a pool that was no longer shallow.

Chapter Twenty-Five

Spring gave way to summer. On the slopes of the hills the fields became heavy with the weight of crops. White blossoms grew on the potato stalks; poppies flickered in the breeze. Down on the shore waves lapped, making furrows in the clean smooth sand. Not a speck of seaweed could be seen. Seagulls scurried around rocks spangled with barnacles teaching their young how to fish.

One sunny afternoon, at the beginning of June, Mark drove down to Cragann. As he approached the village he saw Aine outside the house feeding a brood of Rhode Island Reds. She wore a white cotton blouse and a pair of rolled-up denims. A broad-brimmed hat shielded her face from the sun. 'Get down you greedy rascals!' she admonished, as three fat roosters pecked one another, going all over the place. Throwing them a handful of grain from a dish she whooshed them off, laughing, as they flew in on top of her.

'What a sight for sore eyes!' Mark bore down on her from the top of the road.

Startled, she looked up. In the glaring sunlight Mark's tailored suit, white collar and tie looked peculiarly out of place.

'May I help?' he asked, extending his hand for the basin of chicken food.

She shook her head. 'You'd ruin your suit. Better destroy one set of clothes than two.'

Together they strolled up the path, his arm around her shoulders.

'When did you arrive?'

'Got into Dublin this morning. Picked up a car at a garage in Naas and drove straight to Cragann. Phew! It was hot on the journey down.'

'You didn't waste any time.'

'Not when it meant seeing you!' He pressed her hand gently.

As he smiled she noticed the gold fillings in his teeth.

'Did you get much painting done?' he asked, moving to open the garden gate.

'Whenever I had time.'

'What do you mean, when you had time?'

'Oh! You know, there's so much to be done, weeding, digging, all that kind of thing.' She pointed to drills of potatoes and vegetables set near the wall.

Bending, he pulled a blade of grass and ran it between his fingers. 'What about the fishing?' he asked, closing the gate and putting it on the hasp, 'Who accompanies you on those trips?'

'Mostly Colm and Willie.' She felt herself blushing remembering the day they went fishing to the Old Bull, the day Mr Davis got sick. Involuntarily, her eyes travelled to his feet. He wore a fashionable pair of hush puppies. The brown suedes must have got a hasty ending. 'Sometimes Willie lets me row when the weather is fine', she added, avoiding his glance.

'Does painting not take priority over everything else? Surely you know that artists spend hours polishing their craft. Genius, they say, is ninety-nine percent perspiration and one percent talent.'

'You mean art is the result of hard labour?'

'Precisely. There's a well-known theory that culture, environment, practice, really determine what we are. Not inheritance or birth.'

'You believe that?'

'Of course! I come from a working class background, myself. My father was a ... well, a wheeler and dealer. Over the years - my mother who was of French origin - stinted and saved to send me to college. Hard work and determination got me where I am today, with I suppose, a little bit of luck and er ... a pinch of diplomacy. If I had depended on genes ...' he gave a harsh laugh, 'I wouldn't be where I am. But to return to the subject of painting, if you haven't been practising then I suggest you begin. Your unique style is popular at the moment. There's a market out there which, I suggest, you home in on.'

They had arrived in Delia's front garden. Aine stared at the bushes. Something stirred among the evergreens. A long sleek body crept through the undergrowth. Grabbing the handle of the sweeping brush she shook the branches. 'Get out, puss! shwshsh! out! It's Pangur,' she explained, looking at him, 'she's at her latest occupation, stalking the robins. Lately, she's been bringing them home, carrying them in through the open window.'

'Do you hear me, Aine?' He caught her arm in a vice-like grip.

She drew back quickly. 'Let go,' she protested, 'you're hurting me!'

'Your paintings could make a fortune!'

'A fortune for whom?' Breathing hard, she disengaged her arm and stood glowering up at him.

'I've told you already your work is admired. We hope to exhibit it in the Tudor one of those days. There's a possibility of sale.'

She stiffened. Who said anything about selling? She had discussed the possibility of an exhibition only. She bit her lip in frustration. Who'd ever dream of buying her work? She'd only be a laughing stock, a figure of fun around London. Artists would think she was crazy. A young ignoramus from the West of Ireland! How could Catherine have thought of such a thing? She gave a furious shake to the evergreens, dug her heels into the mounds of earth spilling over from the flower beds.

'Listen, my dear! Your painting has great potential. It's different from the ordinary kind of stuff. People get tired of the same run o' the mill.'

'Oh, forget it!' she cried, 'let's go inside. I'm hungry!'

Back in the kitchen she stoked the fire and put on the kettle. Having rummaged in the pantry she found a fresh batch of scones Delia had baked that morning. She whisked a few eggs and tipped them into the pan trusting that with a bit of luck the mixture would turn out to be an omelette.

Returning to the dining room with plates of food, she found Mark at the table leafing through a Country Woman's magazine. Outlined against the window, his thick red neck and powerful shoulders reminded her of a bull-fighter. Whatever his genealogy he must have been fed plenty of hot gruel! As she approached, he placed the magazine back on the shelf and walked over towards her. 'Mmm!' he sniffed, peering over her shoulder.

'Savoury omelettes,' she said, stacking the plates on the plate rack.

'Ahh!'

'They'll just about whet your appetite.' She set places for two. Served the omelettes with salad and cottage cheese, together with some thick slices of Delia's brown soda bread covered with salted butter.

'I was just thinking,' he said, as he sampled her cooking, 'that you'd make a great housewife.'

She laughed. 'Delia wouldn't agree.'

'Well, whatever about housekeeping, what about your art?'

'Art?'

'Did you ever think of painting a shocker?'

'A what?'

'Something outrageous that would shock the critics, jolt them out of their complacency.' He rubbed his hands. 'What's popular to-day you could sweep away over night with a new genre.'

'Mr Davis!' She put down her cup, drew herself up straight. 'When I paint it's not to create a fashion. I paint because I want to paint, because I've got something to say, a truth that won't change with the seasons.'

A very admirable sentiment, my dear! But you don't seem to realize what's happening. Over in London your painting has caught the imagination of the public. Out on the streets they're whistling your theme song.'

'What do you mean?'

'The music ... the aria in your painting, it's been heard on the airways.'

She stared blankly at him.

'Listen!' He hummed a few notes, paused and then whistled them.

Her hands flew to her face. 'Oh, God!' she cried.

'My dear, as if you didn't know. A BBC team who visited the Gallery, discovered it. The notes were well camouflaged at first but one of the camera men had an idea. He used a mirror, one of those pocket mirrors you find in a lady's handbag. Eureka! As if by magic a whole series of minims and crotchets became visible. Catherine and I ...'

Aine wasn't listening. She sat motionless. Somewhere from the past a voice ... a song ... It echoed through her brain, pulsated through her blood as if it were being played on an amplifying machine.

After lunch, the following day, Mark set out for town. He had to book a room for a colleague of his in Slatterys' hotel. The shooting season had begun in the West. If bookings weren't made early a visitor would have no accommodation and would, consequently, be deprived of one of the season's greatest entertainments.

Delia donned her coat, changed into her outdoor shoes and set off for a ramble up Cartra.

Aine sat alone in the kitchen. She still brooded over what Mark had said ... a melody in her painting ... heard over the airways ... After some minutes, she rose from her chair, went to the bookcase and took out a volume of Encyclopaedia Britannica. As she leafed through the pages she drummed her fingers off the mahogany book shelf. To her horror she found she was tapping out the tune which Mark had whistled in the kitchen that morning. She closed the Encyclopaedia and fled to the sitting room.

In the harsh mid-summer light the old Victorian sitting room looked shabby and grey. Its jade green fireside suite, bought after the house was built, showed signs of wear. The multicoloured rug covering the hearth looked threadbare. In a corner near the window stood a piano, its walnut wood reflecting the flickering light of the fire.

Heart racing, Aine lifted the lid of the old Steiner. Not since her childhood days had she played it. Years back, she had taken lessons from Miss O Reilly in town where she had been taught the scales and banged out the notes of the *Spinning Wheel* and *the Barcarole*. As her fingers touched the keys she began to play. Timidly, at first, then with confidence, she played the complete melody. Plaintive and sweet, the music filled the room, then died away, a whisper across life's half-door. Spellbound, she rested her hands on the keyboard. The clock in the hall struck eight. Somewhere outside a child cried. The door opened. A finger of light crept across the floor. Delia stood in the doorway gazing across at her, clutching a folded umbrella. 'Where did you get that music?' she asked.

Chapter Twenty-Six

Aine shuddered as if she had been awakened rudely from a dream. She stared at her aunt not understanding what she meant.

'That music, where did you get it?' Delia asked, harshly, advancing into the sitting-room.

'Mr Davis—'

'What has Mr Davis got to do with your father's composition? He used to sing and play that piece to you on his violin.' She stood still, face like a stone, etched against the light.

Aine said nothing.

Delia walked to the window and looked out. Stars studded the sky. The moon was full casting its light along the bay. 'I can still see him sitting there in that chair, violin under his chin, playing *Song of the Dawn*. Sometimes I forget that he's dead. I expect him to walk in the back door whistling. Your father was a great musician. People passing along the road used to stop and listen to him play.' She turned, walked back and sat on the edge of the chesterfield. Flames leaped and hissed in the grate casting their shadows along the walls.

Aine rose from the piano stool. Her limbs felt heavy almost refusing to carry her. A paralyzing fear gripped her. If it really was her father's composition, where had she heard it before? Suddenly the answer exploded in her brain like a ball of fire. A crazy excitement seized her. 'You're absolutely sure it's his?'

'Of course, I am. He composed it the summer before he died. There's a copy of it in the trunk along with the rest of his work. We'll have a look to-night in the attic; that's where he stored it. But first, I'll prepare the supper. Mark will be here any minute.'

After supper Delia lit the hurricane lantern. Mark Davis had not returned. Together, she and Aine climbed the narrow stairs leading to the attic.

In the soft rays emitted by the hurricane lamp Aine saw her father's trunk standing in the corner. It had been there for years, virtually untouched. A pile of suit cases stacked to the ceiling were on the side of the room where the roof sloped to the floor. An aroma of sawdust from the worm-eaten furniture made her eyes water. There were two broken chairs and a battered washstand lying on its side.

Delia unlocked the trunk and slowly lifted the lid. On the inside was a label bearing her father's name and address: *John Fogarty, Hampton Gate, London, passenger to Ireland*. Had he planned to travel on a return ticket?

She removed a pear-shaped case from the bottom of the trunk. Inside was a violin, still in perfect condition. A chamois duster and two pieces of rosin were hidden in a pocket underneath. Extracting a briefcase, shabby and worn, she laid it on the floor beside the violin. 'He was very careful of his music,' she said, 'never let anyone touch it. All these are his.' She pointed to a pile of dog-eared manuscripts which had fallen out on the floor. 'Some of them were written in Ireland, others abroad. He wrote this piece here one summer while in Brazil. Rosemary said he composed it while they awaited their passports.'

Peering over her shoulder, Aine saw a jumble of crotchets and minims penned untidily on a yellowing manuscript sheet. There were notes scribbled on the margin, crossed out and rewritten. Some of the pieces looked unfinished.

'Ah, here we are, *Dawn Song!* This was his favourite.' Reverently, Delia picked up a manuscript bound with black leatherette. 'He composed it one morning between four and five o' clock, after the Dawn Chorus. It was one of his best.'

'Let me see!' Aine's voice trembled. With clammy hands she leaned forward and moved the lantern up closer. The manuscript sheet showed a series of squiggled notes, some blotted with ink difficult to decipher. She read them aloud, hummed them softly. It was the tune she had played on the piano!

'That says all that he stood for,' Delia said, unaware of her niece's agitation, 'his love of the sea and the mountains; the mornings he rose early to climb Cartra. It's all there. That's the voice of John Fogarty.' Placing the manuscript back in the trunk she stooped to pick up the lantern.

'Wait!'

'What is it?'

'I'd like to take a look at it again.' Aine pointed to the discoloured sheet of music.

'Be sure and leave it back where you got it,' her aunt said, handing it to her.

A minute later, clutching her father's manuscript, Aine trundled downstairs after Delia.

Later, that evening, Mark pulled up outside Fogartys'. He opened the gate, walked up the path and tapped on the kitchen window. 'Anyone at home?'

'Come in, come in!' Delia replied, opening the hall door, relief registering in her voice. 'Thought you were lost or that you had deserted us.'

'Sorry about that.' He followed her into the brightly-lit hallway. 'I met a colleague of mine in town and we had a few drinks. You know how it is, one thing follows another.'

'Ah!' she said, 'you must be hungry. I'll put a slice of bacon on the pan and a few newly laid eggs.'

'Oh, no thank you. We dined at the *Emerald*. Thompson, an old friend of mine, said he'd call out here before he goes back. Says he would like to see your work,' he turned to Aine. 'But I say, you're looking rather peeked. Anything wrong? Nothing dreadful has happened, I hope.'

She shook her head. 'Just a bit tired. I spent a long time in the garden weeding.' As she spoke an aroma of perfume – something like the scent one got from Delia's roses - wafted towards her. Mmm! Sara would know what it was. Sara was familiar with all the perfumes from those fat American parcels her mother received in the post. Funny how Englishmen had such curious habits! It was everyone's right to be different, of course. But all the same, you wouldn't expect a gentleman from London to be girlish. It would take a lot of cajoling before any of the Cragann boys would wear perfume like that!

'Don't forget the flowers for your parents' grave,' Delia reminded her.

'I'll cut them in the morning. They'll have a better chance of staying fresh.' She disappeared upstairs to get her cardigan.

'Tomorrow will be the anniversary of her parents' death,' Delia explained, turning to Mark, 'they'll be sixteen years dead tomorrow.'

'What a shame her parents can't see her now! They'd be proud of their talented daughter.'

'Her mother was English, you know, a twin, the poor girl.' Her other-half was a good-for-nothing damsel. She turned her out when she married my brother. They say she's somewhere in London. Never comes near us. Not that I'd ever want to see her again.'

'Dear, dear! What a tragic story! Dreadful for Aine and for your noble-hearted self! But I say! I've got some letters to write. I must catch the post in the morning. So if you'll excuse me ... By the by,' he said, as Aine returned, 'what about that painting you're working on?'

She shook her head. 'I didn't have much time. There were jobs to be done.'

'Hmm. There's an exhibition opening shortly. It would be an ideal forum for your kind of work. But since you're not ready—'

'Oh, there's tomorrow,' she said, 'after I return from the cemetery tomorrow.'

Chapter Twenty-Seven

Towards noon next day Aine stood at the cemetery gates. For the first time since they met she felt reluctant to meet Catherine. Some inner voice told her to go back, to stay away from the cemetery.

She sat at the side of the road and gazed across at the pearl-grey strand in Portree; beyond that, the islands, smoky-blue, like giant pieces of ice. The sea, in one of its moods, looked dark and threatening. Overhead, seagulls wheeled, screaming.

She rose and mounted the steps as the figure of a woman approached. Tall and slender, Catherine threaded her way daintily through the rugged terrain until she reached the ruins of Saint Sorcha's church. She wore a black ermine coat and furry hat and her small feet were ensconced in ankle-strapped shoes. Frowning, she stared at the wall opposite her. Aine followed the direction of her gaze. A bunch of starlings tussled for a worm. One of them, craftier than the other, had succeeded in monopolizing it. Catherine coughed and clapped her hands.

'They're worse than us humans!' Aine called, loud enough for her to hear.

She turned and walked slowly back, zigzagging between the graves. 'Hello!' she greeted.

'When did you arrive?'

'I got into Dublin yesterday. Drove to Belmullet and stayed in the *Emerald* last night. The *Emerald*'s a comfortable hotel, I must say.'

Aine frowned. Who else had mentioned the *Emerald* recently? Shrugging, she fixed her attention on the woman in front of her. What would she have to say about the painting? She suspected now that the inspiration she received that night in the cave came from a source bigger and more powerful than herself. To trade it would be worse than sacrilege. Looking up, she met her gaze.

'Sit down,' Catherine invited, making space for her on the wall. 'What's worrying you, my dear?'

'Have you ever been harassed by anyone?'

'Harassed?'

'You know, bulldozed into doing something you don't want to do?'

'Really, I can't say I have.' Her lips curled into a small smile.

'That stupid art dealer!'

'Who?'

'Mr Davis. He's trying to persuade me to paint for the market. He's offered to take me to London. My style of painting is fashionable, he says.'

She gave a husky laugh. 'That's a splendid idea! Why don't you accept his invitation? London is teeming with opportunities. You'd build a spanking good reputation in no time. That's if you're serious about art.'

Aine said nothing. She dangled her feet off the wall hitting her heels against the cold stone.

Catherine watched her. Could the girl be persuaded to leave Cragann? She was old enough now to decide for herself. That painting of hers might be useful, far more lucrative than she realised. But she'd have to tread carefully—

'There's Colm. 'He needs me to give a hand with the fishing.'

'For heaven's sake, child, what has Colm got to do with it? I'm sure he'll find plenty of ... eh ... other fish in the sea. Mark Davis, I can assure you, is a wonderful guy. Well positioned.'

Aine looked at her. Something in the tone of her voice puzzled her. What would *she* know about fishing or about life in Cragann? Easy for her to talk, coming as she did from a well-to-do background.

'If Mark has offered to help, you'd be a fool not to accept. I've known him for years. He's a brilliant assessor, can smell out the genuine article anywhere. Come to think of it, he did say something favourable about your painting, dear.'

She sat up quickly. Was this it? Was this the offer she had been waiting for? Excitedly, she pushed a loose strand of hair back from her face. Whatever she might say she'd have to stand firm, insist on her rights. The painting wasn't to be sold. A wind blowing from the sea caught Catherine's coat flinging it open. Aine saw a long oval brooch glinting on her dress. 'That ... that brooch?' she stammered.

'Well?'

'It looks like a mizpah.'

'You've seen a mizpah before?'

'Yes, my mother used to own one. It was found on her dress the day she was drowned. Her sister, I'm told, has an identical one. My mother was a twin, you know—'. She stopped short. Something about the expression on the older woman's face struck her as odd. Her vivid blue eyes had become clouded, dark as night. Her finely chiselled mouth had hardened into a thin line. Suddenly, she drew back in horror. 'Oh, God' she cried, 'you're my aunt, my mother's twin!'

An amused smile crossed Catherine's face. 'So you've stumbled on the truth at last, my dear. I'm Catherine Taylor, your mother's sister. This brooch was given to me by my parents on my eighteenth birthday. Rosemary, your mother, received an identical one.'

'You're ... you're my mother's twin!' The words seemed to stick in Aine's throat. She rose, took a step backwards, dug her fingers into the ledge behind her pulling at the withered grass.

'Precisely.' Catherine's eyes were mere slits. Her beautiful face had sagged. Taut lines appeared at the corners of her mouth. 'Now that you know who I am perhaps we can talk. Maybe we can arrange for you to visit us in London. Your relatives—'

'Why didn't you tell me?'

'But, my dear!'

'Never mind your endearing words, your sugar-coated lies. You've been coming here, year after year, under false pretences. I used to think, once, you were my mother, my dead mother. As I grew older I knew, knew it was impossible. But you could have told me, told me the truth. You kept on pretending.' Aine felt as if the ground around her was beginning to open up. She was falling ... falling ... into a bottomless pit.

'Aine, let me explain.'

'There's nothing left to explain. You didn't stand by my mother when she needed you. Neither did you stand by Delia and me. We were in Cragann all those years. You never came to visit us.'

'Please listen!'

'What else have I done only listen. You took advantage of me, made me look a fool.'

'The reason—'

'Don't talk to me about reason! Reason doesn't enter into this. You're my mother's twin, the only sister she had.'

'I was afraid you'd despise me.'

'I do despise you. I despise all that you stand for. After all those years you continue to deceive me!' She turned, strode towards the tomb, laid the flowers she had picked from Delia's garden at the base of the headstone. Without a backward glance she raced down the steps and on to the road.

'Aine!'

She kept on running giving no indication she had heard. She sped down the road towards Cragann. The wind was against her all the way. Cold and sharp, it lashed her cheeks and stung her eyes making them overflow with tears. On the brow of the hill, close to the dolmen, she saw the outlined figure of an old woman. Leaning on her stick she was staring down into the valley. On the cold evening air the echo of her laughter, loud and shrill, was like the high-pitched cackle of a witch.

Chapter Twenty-Eight

When Aine got back to the house Delia was busy in the garden watering the flowers. She flung open the gate, rushed past her and charged upstairs.

'Aine!'

There was no reply.

Delia dropped her watering can and hurried indoors.

Aine had disappeared upstairs and had locked herself into her room.

'Aine!' Delia shouted, banging her fist on the bedroom door, 'open that door!'

'No!'

'Aine, what's wrong with you? Unlock the door at once!'

There was a moment's silence. A key turned slowly in the lock. The door flew open. Aine stood there bleak-eyed, small face blanched.

'What's the matter with you?'

'Catherine Taylor is here.'

Delia's hand flew to her throat. She stared blankly at her, trying to interpret what she said.

'She's over in the cemetery. She's been coming here, year after year, for the past ten years or more. But I didn't know till to-day who she was.'

Delia turned to go downstairs then changed her mind. She walked past Aine into the room and sat on the side of the bed. 'Sit down, child,' she said, motioning her to a chair, 'where did you meet her?'

'Over in the cemetery.'

Delia closed her eyes. Her face took on a flint-like expression as if she were bracing herself for some impending disaster. 'I'd have discussed all this with you before, only I didn't believe she'd come back. It's a long, long time, so long that people have almost forgotten.' Rising, she walked to the window and looked out. The sky was dark; all of nature was silent. 'Your grandparents, the Taylors, were an unfortunate family. Everything they planned went against them. But their greatest tragedy was the loss of their daughter. Rosemary was a beautiful child. Her father, in particular, adored her. As she grew older her twin became jealous of her. She couldn't bear to see her receive so much attention. There were arguments, fights. Catherine went so far once, I'm told, as to have threatened to kill her. When Rosemary married John Fogarty she saw her opportunity. She schemed, lied, did everything she could to blacken her reputation. The upshot of it all was that your mother was disinherited.'

Aine sat, hands locked tightly in her lap. Outside on the lawn birds chirped noisily in their nests. The boatmen on the shore could be heard talking to each other as they prepared for another night at sea. 'What did she do?' she asked, through set lips.

'What *could* she do? She just walked away.'

Who'd ever think that this woman and her former friend were one and the same person? Why did there have to be rivalry, one person out to get another, Cain out to get Abel? Had her mother discovered the truth of it long ago? Had she learned the hard way and shrugged them all off, deciding that heaven can only be won when those closest are wrenched from one's grasp?

As Delia got up to go Aine heard the throb of an engine on the road outside. She ran downstairs. A black motorcar had pulled up at the gate. There was a banging of doors. 'She's here,' she cried, 'Catherine Taylor is here!'

Peering out the window, Delia saw a tall, fashionably-dressed woman walk up the pathway, a haughty expression on her face, spring in her step.

'Delia, my dear, how are you?' Seconds later, Catherine stood on the doorstep. 'Working hard, as usual, I'm sure. You never did take life easy, did you?' Face flushed, a hint of triumph in her dark eyes, she embraced her sister-in-law. 'Do you remember the old days—?'

'What brought you here?'

'I meant to get in touch with you before but—'

'Why did you deceive her, let her believe you were somebody else?'

'But my dear Delia!'

'You have great cheek! You've been coming here, year after year, without lifting a finger to help that child. You've made a fool of her, filling her with all kinds of lies.'

'I meant to—'

'You meant to do many things. Hell is paved with intentions like yours. What about your mother's inheritance? The child was second beneficiary to the will. You never offered her a penny. Where's all the money gone?'

'*Netherby* was in need of repair after my parents' death. I intended to recompense her afterwards.'

'Hah! Another of your precious intentions! Why do you come here, anyway? Why do you visit her tomb seeing you didn't even show up at the funeral?'

Catherine flinched. Her eyes became clouded, pools of fathomless grey. Her mouth trembled. She fumbled in her pocket for a handkerchief but no tears came.

Delia refused to relent. Her eyes blazed. Years of anger suddenly erupted pouring out like hot lava. A lifetime of buried grief was unearthed. Outside, carts trundled heavily home from the bog; a dark barked After what seemed an age she turned and opened the kitchen door. 'Put on the kettle,' she called to Aine, 'we need some tea. You might as well come inside,' she said, turning to her visitor, 'what's done cannot be undone.'

Struggling to regain her composure Catherine followed her sister-in-law into the kitchen. She sat down, took out a mirror and began to repair the ravages done to her face.

Delia opened a press and took out her rose-patterned china. She arranged the cups and saucers and began to pour out tea from a silver teapot. 'Are your parents still alive?' she asked, offering her visitor a scone.

'My mother died the year after Rosemary was drowned. And

three years later my father joined her.'

'And yourself, where do you live now?'

'My husband and I live at *Netherby,* the ancestral home, some nine or ten miles outside London. Here's my address.' She took a gilt-edged card from her handbag and handed it to her.

Delia pursed her lips. She was about to say something when Catherine rose to go. 'As I've already said to Aine, some day, perhaps, you'll visit us.'

Aine rattled her teacup.

'Definitely!' Delia replied, her mouth grim, signalling her niece to be quiet, 'definitely Aine will visit you. Nothing surer than that!'

A minute later, Catherine Taylor waved goodbye and climbed into her shining black motorcar.

Aine stood motionless at the gate, long after the sound of the engine had died away.

Chapter Twenty-Nine

Years later, Aine would remember with a sigh the gilt-edged card left by Catherine on the kitchen table. Innocuous and innocent though it looked, it was to be the instrument later which would open up vistas, vistas of which she had never even dreamed. *Netherby Hall, Seven Oaks*, she read, holding it up to the light. A wistful smile crossed her face. What would she not give for a glimpse of *Netherby Hall*?

Sitting on Delia's high chair, she propped her head in her hands and rested her elbows on the table. The name *Netherby* conjured up all that she could imagine of her mother's home, purple twilights; shadowy pathways; footsteps echoing down stone steps. And dungeons, deep, deep, buried in the bowels of the earth.

'Tell me about your home,' she asked Catherine, one evening, as they sat on the cemetery wall overlooking Portree. It was a fine summer's evening. Blackbirds and thrushes filled the air with their music.

'You'd have to see it, my dear, to realise how beautiful it is. The gardens are a maze of labyrinthine walks, sculptured hedges, tiny picturesque bridges.'

'And the house?'

'The house is Georgian. A fine mahogany balustrade balcony overlooks the hall. Motifs of birds and flowers decorate the ceiling. We entertain lavishly, exotic wines, various kinds of game.'

'Are there any paintings?'

'Oh, yes! Massive portraits. Gentlemen with corkscrew moustaches and ladies wearing low-cut gowns and chignons.'

'All very grand?'

'Majestic, my dear.'

'Ah!'

Sitting opposite Delia at the table Aine clenched her fist.

She recalled her expression, those guileless blue eyes and dulcet tones as she sketched for her, scene after scene, of her idyllic childhood. Not by as much as a flicker of an eyelid did she reveal who she was. The memory of that betrayal stayed with her. Sleeping or waking she would dread seeing again that terrible betrayal in another person's eyes. The gilded card, clean-edged and decorative, symbolised all that she stood for. What a fool she had been! How could she have been so blind not to have guessed? She jumped up, walked over to the range and opened the top of it.

'Stop!' Delia cried. 'Give it to me.'

'I'm not going to *Netherby Hall*. I don't want to see that woman again.'

'You've as much right to *Netherby* as anyone else. Your mother was one of the Taylors. She'd own half the estate if she were alive to-day.'

'My mother is gone. Why keep on lamenting someone who's dead?'

Delia sat back in her chair and closed her eyes. Still smarting from the shock of Mark's sudden disappearance, she was determined now that nothing would come between Aine and this last opportunity. 'Listen!' she said, 'Catherine Taylor is a wealthy woman, a woman of influence. If you want to be successful, a recognised artist, this is your chance.'

'If only she had told me!'

'Did Mark ever let it slip that he knew her?'

'Mark! Mark's a bigger scoundrel than Catherine ever was. He drove down here like a lord. Thought we'd be impressed by his finery and posh accent. Hah!'

'Mmm. Well, two wrongs won't make a right. But all the same, if you want to be an artist I think you should go.' Delia waited. The child would have to go over. There was no other way. She'd have to get in with that woman. Get well in with her. What was there here in Cragann for somebody like her? Besides, if her painting was good enough for Catherine Taylor, then it was good enough.

Aine frowned. She paced back and over, hands clasped tightly in front of her.

Delia watched, angle of her chin, swirl of her skirt, backwards and forwards ...

'Very well,' she said suddenly, 'I'll go!'

Delia rose from her chair. 'I'll bring the suitcase down from the attic. You can be putting a few things together.'

Aine began her preparations for London.

She worked non-stop filling her studio with water-coloured landscapes. Some of them she completed in the house, others were painted outside in the fields or down by the shore. She was determined to have a sizeable portfolio to take with her to London. From long hours of practice her tones became richer. Looser patches of colour were often set beside patches of white. Though eager to impress, she refused to imitate the real world. She pencilled her drawings imaginatively, reorganising the essential elements around which she composed a picture. Instead of using light and shade she modulated her painting with tonal colour.

Some days later she was over in Brannigans visiting Julie. It was early in the morning. Brannigans shop hadn't opened. Unwashed beer glasses cluttered the counter, left there since the previous night. The air was heavy with the smell of stale Guinness.

Sitting cross legged on the counter the girls nibbled sweets from a jar of liquorice all-sorts.

'I've news for you, Julie!' Aine said, digging her hand into the sweet jar and drawing out a bead-coated liquorice.

'News?' Julie's eyes narrowed. She flicked an expert eye over Aine's slender figure. 'Don't tell me—'

'Nope!' Aine laughed, taking a swipe at her with a folded-up newspaper.

'What then?'

'I'm going to London.'

'What! What on earth put that idea into your head? Don't tell me you're going on your own.'

'Why not?'

'For heaven's sake, Aine, you haven't an ounce of sense. People like you went over there before. They were never heard of again. You're not forgetting Mags Donnelly, are you?'

'What about her?'

'Preggies, d'you remember? She came home without a penny in her pocket and dying of hunger.'

'I'm not Mags Donnelly. And besides, I've an aunt living over there. I'll be moving in the highest circles, mixing with the right kind of people.' Aine pushed the sweet jar over towards her cousin and popped a liquorice-all-sort into her mouth. 'Where a person like me is concerned, there's no need to worry. My relations are rich. They've lashings of money. Come to think of it, those parties they have will be fun, meeting all those aristocratic weirdoes.' She stopped chewing, wrapped her arms around her knees and began rocking to and fro.

I'll wave my hat to all I meet ...
And they'll wave back to me ...

Julie stared, aghast. 'For heaven's sake, Aine! We might never see you again! This might be our last time together.'

'Don't be an idiot! You know full well I'll come back. Keep an eye on the cat. If Pat Neddy catches her at large he'll throttle her.'

'Aren't you afraid of the sleazy night-clubs? And all the prostitutes they tell us about? And what about work? What will you do when you get over?'

Aine began to hum the *Emigrant's Farewell*, whistling bits of it between her teeth. 'Sleazy night-clubs! You don't have to go further than Dublin for that kind of thing. As for work, Catherine will look after that. There are plenty of fine jobs to be had in London.'

'Hmm! Catherine Taylor is it?' Julie drew herself up to her full height. 'I wouldn't be too sure about her if I were you. According to rumours the lady is no great shakes. Don't expect too much from her ladyship.'

'I'll meet Mr Davis. Mr Davis said London is teeming with opportunities.' Aine made an effort to appease her cousin. Knowing Julie she had decided not to tell her the whole truth, not for the present, at least.

'Well, don't say I didn't warn you.'

She jumped off the counter and shook out her skirt. She was about to leave when the shop door opened.

'Ah! This is where you are!' Delia stood in the doorway waving a long white envelope. She cast a quick look around her ... the unwashed glasses, litter of sweet papers ... The sooner Pa Brannigan shows a leg, the better, she thought. 'I was looking for you everywhere,' she said, turning to Aine. 'Here, this was in the post. Must be from *her*.'

Frowning, Aine took the letter. Catherine hadn't wasted much time. Strange how anxious she was to see her over in London! Using Pa Brannigan's carving knife she slit open the envelope and unfolded a sheet of thick white notepaper.

> *Netherby Hall,*
> *Seven Oaks,*
> *London.*

Dear Aine,

Enclosed is a postal order for thirty pounds, price of your passage to London. Your painting will be exhibited next week in the Tudor Gallery. I look forward to meeting you before then.

Yours affectionately,

Catherine.

'You can change it in the Bank.' Delia said, eyeing the folded slip of paper. 'You'll get better value there than in the post office.'

Eyes shining, Aine slipped the postal order into her inside pocket. Seeing Julie's lip beginning to quiver, she rose quickly. 'Tooraloo!' she cried, embracing her, 'I'll write when I get over!' Raising the latch on the shop door she stepped out on to the pavement.

Chapter Thirty

Strange things were happening in Cragann. At the end of the summer two foreign trawlers sailed into the bay from Howth; another came over from England. Fishing for sharks, Daniel Cassidy said they were. The trawlers were fitted with harpoon guns and engineers on board pumped oil from the livers of the fish into big steel barrels. The captain of the *Recruit*, one of the visiting trawlers, sought help from local boatmen and Colm Holohan was made overseer down on the slipway.

'You never saw the likes!' Daniel exclaimed, eyes rolling, 'Pat Hartigan up to his ocsters in piping hot blood and livers slithering all over the place. The sight would do you no good.'

'Huh!' Delia grunted, 'Old Daniel would be far better employed if, instead of his joking, he hobbled to the slipway and gave a hand with the unloading!'

On the eve of her departure Aine sauntered down to the shore. She stood in the shadow of the old boathouse and watched the boatmen tread water as they loaded provisions on to waiting currachs. Seagulls screamed, flying in every direction. Her gaze followed the movements of the men. She sensed their excitement, tensing of muscles, as they loaded and unloaded cargoes. She would miss their good-humoured banter, their wry comments. Close by, five or six up-turned currachs lay on the grass like sleeping watchdogs. Would all this be the same when she returned or would old customs have given way to new? Then she brightened. Tomorrow morning she'd be saying goodbye to her old life ... bound for glory and the city lights! 'Colm!' she called, as Colm's tall figure appeared on the slipway.

'I'm busy; it'll have to do later.' He beckoned to one of the men and together they heaved a huge crate on to a waiting punt.

'I only came to tell you—'

'Put it over there, John.' Colm walked knee-deep out into the sea. He gave the punt a shove, sending the fisherman and cargo skimming out over the water.

'I'm leaving.'

'You're what?'

'I'm leaving Cragann.' Breathless, she arrived down beside him on the shingle, hair blowing in the wind. 'I'm going over to London tomorrow. I'll stay with my relatives, the Taylors.'

Colm dropped the fish box he was carrying. He stood facing her, mouth drawn into a thin line. 'I suppose it's that Davis galoot. I hope he'll look after you.'

'It's nothing to do with Mr Davis. I've been thinking about it for some time. Opportunities are good over there. I'll … exhibit a few paintings … sell some, maybe.'

'And when will I see you again?'

'After I've made a bit of money. There's going to be an exhibition in the Tudor next week. Catherine is a member of the Jury. I think she's interested in the Cave painting.'

Colm's face clouded. 'I see. Well if that's how it is I suppose you'll have to go.' He gazed out to sea, forehead puckered like a child trying to assemble a jigsaw and finding some of the pieces missing. 'I'm hoping for a break myself.' He glanced at her quickly. 'I've bought a new fishing boat, started some deep-sea fishing. I'll hire a few lads from around.'

'You've bought a new boat!'

'Yeah. Fifty foot long. Steel hulled, eighty horse power engine, hydraulic steering. Everything you could think of.'

'Wow!'

'She's even got trawl doors, net, wheel house and mast light on top.'

'What kind of catch?'

'Oh, deep sea only. No lobsters. She'll go after white fish and prawns.'

Aine's eyes shone. 'And her range?'

'She can go as far as the Porcupine Bank.'

Amazed, she stared at him. Face flushed, his eyes had taken on an amber brilliance. 'Where did you get the money?'

'Savings.'

'Savings!' In her wildest dreams she couldn't imagine Colm saving anything. He had never saved a penny in his life. Besides, when did he ever have money? There was nothing to be got from fishing around Cragann.

'Well, as a matter of fact,' he shuffled his feet, 'I made a bit on the side, smuggled a few barrels.'

She burst out laughing.

'But if that's how you want it ...' He turned away. A gentleman with a foreign accent had approached him asking for directions. Colm accompanied him up towards the road.

'Colm!' she called, but Colm had already gone out of ear-shot.

That night, the day's work done, Cragann boatmen assembled in Brannigans. Captain O Neill, skipper of the *Recruit* ordered drinks for all the helpers. Brannigans looked bright and shining. Great fat bottles of whiskey lined the shelves winking in the light of the tilley lamp. Glasses sparkled, reflected in the long oval mirror. A buzz of conversation came from the men at the counter punctuated by loud bursts of laughter. Stories were exchanged between the fishermen of Howth and those of Cragann.

Willie Sara drew out a stool and sat in beside Colm. He settled his pint, arranging it strategically on the table mat in front of him. 'Herself is leaving us tomorrow,' he said, gazing at nothing in particular.

'Yeah.'

'What do you think of it at all?'

Colm shook his head. 'That good for nothing art dealer!'

'Hah'

'You should have seen him the day of the fishing trip, a cowering idiot, afraid to look at the guts. Himself and his suede shoes! Suede shoes how are ye!'

'What with her having those rich relations, maybe she'll do well after all.'

'She hasn't any training. Not enough clout for their kind of world.'

Willie scratched his head and took a mouthful from his pint. Colm drained his glass and ordered another round.

Mary Brannigan arrived with the drinks. She placed a pint of Guinness topped with creamy froth in front of each of them, dropped the money into the till and handed Colm his change. 'Plenty of activity these days,' she smiled.

'Aye. Cragann never had it so good.'

Picking up a duster Mary began mopping up spills. A tall handsome woman with russet-brown eyes, she was one of those people who refuse to be daunted by the messiness of life.

Willie Sara raised his glass. 'Slainte!' he said. He took one long draught and pursed his lips, savouring the bitterness of the Guinness.

Colm hunched his shoulders, cleared his throat and leaned towards Willie. 'You know,' he said, after a second or two, 'I had plans.'

'Plans?'

'Plans for the two of us.'

'Eh'

'Yeah. I made a bit of money on the fishing. The new trawler, don't you know?'

'She's a fine cut of a boat.'

'As good as you'd get around here. I had hoped to expand the trawling, employ a few men and build up the business so there'd be plenty for the two of us. And there she is off ...' He swivelled his glass around, staring vacantly at the rows of whiskey bottles.

'She'll come back.'

'Yeah, after she's discovered the kind of rotter he is.'

'You think she'll do well?'

'Naw! Not a chance. There's no future for her kind over there. She's no money. Her pictures won't sell.'

Willie Sara nodded, gloomily.

Colm glanced at the clock on the ledge above the door. Having drained his glass he wiped his mouth with the back of his hand. 'I'd better be off,' he said, 'I'm meeting a chap on the pier. He's leaving for London tomorrow morning.'

Chapter Thirty-One

Aine awoke to the sound of footsteps crossing the landing and descending the stairs. At first she didn't understand what was happening. Then it dawned on her. She was leaving Cragann. The thought stunned her. It was as if somebody had stabbed her, stabbed her a long time ago and she was beginning to feel the pain. But wasn't this the opportunity she had waited for, the chance to see London, rub shoulders with the rich, the influential?

Lulled into her old feeling of immunity, she jumped out and pulled back the curtains. The sun had risen over Achill casting its light along the bay. Clouds banked in the west were beginning to scatter. The village was awake.

In the kitchen Delia rekindled the fire adding a few sods to it. Dressed in navy overalls and slippers, she wore that grim look which Aine had got to know so well. Porridge reheated, cooked since the night before, was left to simmer at the side. 'Eat a good breakfast,' she said. 'Have you got everything, change of clothes, shoes, portfolio?' Her voice took on a business-like tone as if she were totting up bills. 'Bring your kilt and your velvet bolero. There will be parties ... fancy dress balls.'

Suitcase locked and everything in order, Aine sat down to breakfast; a bowl of porridge with milk, cup of tea. As she ate, she fidgeted with her spoon staring at the rose-patterned breakfast cups as if she were seeing them for the first time. On the road outside someone revved up an engine - Pa Holohan getting ready for town. Down on the shore fishermen could be heard shouting to each other as they shouldered their currachs. Colm would be donning his oilskins, preparing for another day's work.

'Be careful with your money,' Delia warned, 'keep your purse around your neck; they might rummage in your things. And when you get over, write. Write and tell me how you are.'

Aine said nothing. There was plenty she would like to have said. Words burned within; but not this morning, no, not this morning when the thought of travel buffeted her stomach. Having checked her ticket she picked up her coat, said goodbye to her aunt and boarded the bus for Dublin.

As she was leaving Cragann she gave a quick look back. In the morning light the old stone building looked shabby and gaunt. She would miss that hulk of granite, the sleepy windows and the wind-blown oleria leaning against the gable. Delia stood in the doorway peering from behind dark-rimmed glasses, her thin figure receding as the bus pulled slowly away. Aine blew a space in the glass and waved. She would miss all those old and familiar things. She put her case on the rack and straightened her beret, stealthily brushing away a tear. She was on the first leg of her journey to London.

Late that night the Western train pulled into Dun Laoghaire. It came to a sudden halt alongside the mail boat, appearing out of the darkness, a huge black hulk.

Aine thrust her head out the window. Portholes were lighted up and winked like lighthouses in the dark. Lifeboats hung on davits lashed to the deck. High up were the funnel and masts. She had never seen a vessel so big. Along the pier came the sound of music. A lone musician was playing the *Croppy Boy* on his violin.

She collected her suitcase, left the carriage door swinging behind her and staggered after the crowd, handle of the case cutting her fingers. A ship's officer checked her ticket waving her on towards the deck of the *Cambria*. The passengers disappeared into alleyways, up ladders and on to other decks. The ship trembled beneath the force of generators and ventilating fans. She dropped her case beside the rest of the luggage and watched while a jersied seaman covered it with a tarpaulin, lashing it down with ropes. Red-necked country men gathered around the bar drinking pints. They spoke of Crew, Finchley, Camden town, places of which she never heard. The air was blue with tobacco smoke. She thought she heard a familiar accent. 'Are you from the West?' she asked, turning to a youth as he ordered himself a drink.

The young man stared.

She darted away before he could make a reply.

Her view from the deck told her the gangway was gone. Mooring ropes lifted from their bits were splashed into the sea and winched on board. The telegraph bell sounded from the bridge; the engines throbbed. They were leaving Ireland.

As the ship sailed from Dun Laoghaire she stood on deck hoping to catch a last glimpse of the Irish coast. But a storm of hail obscured the lights. The wind running along the sides lifted her hair playing a ghostly tune on the aerial wires. The *Cambria* rose and dipped, speeding along towards Wales.

Snug in her warm coat and Delia's woollen scarf, Aine paced back and forth. Further out, beams from the Bailey flashed through the darkness slipping across black seas and breaking like sharks' teeth. As the deck became unsteady she clung to the railings. Across from her two young nuns sat huddled on a life-raft. Wearing long black veils and voluminous skirts they reminded her of magpies, angelic faces framed in corrugated white. She had heard of nuns. Old Daniel Cassidy's sister, Nelly, became a member of the Holy Servants but the gardener set his eye on her ... The younger of the nuns became seasick. Her companion took a bottle of liquid from her handbag and offered it to her. Aine guessed it to be either holy water or poiteen.

'Keep your eyes tightly closed, Sister,' the older nun advised, 'in that way, you won't see the horizon.'

'I'm dying! Oh, my God, I'm dying!' The corpse-like nun was too far gone. Leaving all dignity behind, she lurched to the side of the ship retching violently.

Dejectedly, Aine descended to the lower deck. The steps were wet and slippery. An ashen-faced man lolled in a chair, raw porter pouring from his mouth. Children clung to their mothers, anxious and queasy. She entered a toilet. It was awash with urine. Her head spun.

Ascending the upper deck again she found a wind-swept seat and sat beneath the lifeboats. Close by, two jersied seamen hosed filth into scuppers. She rose, shook back her hair and paced the deck once more.

The *Cambria* sailed into Holyhead in the small hours of Saturday morning. Aine walked down the gangway, clothes crumpled, sticking to her legs. Following the other passengers, she received her first glimpse of the *Irish Mail* train as it pulled in at the platform.

Years later, she would recount with a smile her first impression of the great *Irish Mail*. Red plush seats and linen chair backs greeted her as she entered the carriage. She sank into a seat near a window nestling her head against the soft upholstery. A grey-haired elderly lady wearing an ermine coat and carrying a poodle sat down opposite her.

'Dear! dear!' the old lady panted, wiping her brow. 'Its been a dreadful rush. Quiet Cassie!' The poodle wriggled in her arms struggling to be free. 'Travelling far, my dear?' She looked at Aine.

'Seven Oaks.'

'You're Irish! Such charming people, you Irish. My great grandfather emigrated from Ireland. From a place called Monagahan.'

'I've heard of it.' Aine looked around to see where the other passengers had gone. There was a gentleman two seats away hidden behind a newspaper.

'The advantage of a first class carriage,' the lady said, caressing the poodle's head, 'is that there's plenty of space. And Cassie loves her little trot, don't you, Cass?'

'First class carriage!' She jumped up and examined her ticket, blood mounting to her face. 'I'm in the wrong compartment!' She snatched up her suitcase, rushed to the door and hurried along the corridor. The carriage doors were about to be closed. She collided with a porter going in the opposite direction. 'I'm looking for a seat,' she panted, tugging his sleeve, 'I've a third class ticket.'

The porter replied in a foreign language.

'I'm Irish!' she cried, trying to make herself understood, 'Irish.'

He replied in a sing-song tone pointing to carriages further down. Afterwards, she learned he was a Welshman speaking in his native tongue.

The second carriage she entered had hard seats and no chair

backs. The air was heavy from lack of ventilation. She sat beside a red-faced man with a peaked cap whom she had seen prostrate from sickness earlier on in the night.

The man with the cap unravelled a parcel of sandwiches from a tightly strapped case. 'There's nothing like a bout of sickness to give you an appetite,' he said. 'Would you like a chunk of bread, Miss, or sup of the crathur?'

She shook her head, pointing to the wrack where her lunch lay intact.

'Tell me, where did you come from this morning?' he asked.

'From Mayo,' she replied, despondently, seeing the shores of Cragann recede further and further.

'And you're travelling on you're own all day?' A small, foxy-haired man with rolled-up sleeves sitting in the corner, asked.

'I'm going to my aunt's. My aunt is living outside London in a place called Seven Oaks.'

'That's a long way off, a long, long way from here to London. How d'you intend getting there, Miss?'

'Oh, I'll be taking a taxi. There'll be plenty of taxis at the station.'

'I wouldn't be taking any taxi if I were you,' the man with the cap said. 'Go by the underground. The underground is cheaper.'

'The underground?' She wrinkled her brow. 'How do you get to the underground?'

'Listen!' He leaned towards her. 'All you have to do is take the Northern line, it's black. Change at Tottenham Court and take the Central line, that's red, to Liverpool Street. Then the Main Line to Seven Oaks and you're there.'

Aine thanked him. By this everyone in the carriage was listening intently.

A burly looking navvy in the corner put down his beer bottle on the floor and looked at her. 'Are you colour-blind?' he asked.

'Colour-blind?'

The navvy lowered his voice and leaned forward. 'There was a Mayo man once who went down the underground. He was colour-blind and you know what?'

'What?' Her eyes widened.

'He was never seen again.'

Smiles creased the faces of the passengers.

The navvy sat back humming Mac Alpine's Fusiliers.

A minute later the whistle blew. The great steam engine hissed, belching up smoke. The train chugged slowly out of the station gathering speed as it left Holyhead.

Early next morning Aine arrived at Euston. She rose and stretched; every bone in her body felt stiff and sore. Suitcase in hand, she stepped on to the platform. The morning had grown cool, but the air in the station reeked of coal and soot. To her right, people were descending an escalator. She walked over slowly and placed her suitcase on the first step. To her horror it began to go down, down, until it had gone out of sight. Throwing caution to the winds she followed after it, lost her balance but regained it again.

Down in the underground there was an entirely new culture. It looked like a place that never saw the sun, a twilight-world in between the real and the illusory. The cold air made her cough. A train rushed into the station. A crowd surged towards it as its doors opened. Aine followed with her suitcase.

Having descended the train at Tottenham Court Road station, she stood a moment on the platform, unsure of her bearings.

'What can I do for you Miss?' A man in a gabardine coat, low brimmed hat shadowing his face, approached her.

'Can you tell me, please, how to get to Liverpool Street station? I came over from Ireland this morning to visit my aunt in Seven Oaks. Somebody told me to go by the underground.'

'Have you any money on you, Miss?'

'Yes, but it's in my suitcase.'

'Well, just you follow me. I know where to take you.'

She turned to pick up her case. 'Oh God, my suitcase! I left it on the train.' Looking around, she saw the doors of the train still open and jumped on board.

Later that evening, Aine arrived in Seven Oaks. It was raining heavily; she hailed a taxi.

'Where to, Miss?' the taxi man asked, opening the window of the cab.

Netherby Hall, she replied.

Chapter Thirty-Two

The road narrowed after Aine left Seven Oaks. The taxi tore with slick sounds along the open countryside. There were no houses till they came to a high stone wall running parallel with the dusty road.

'Another half-mile,' the taxi man called. 'You see that clump of trees, Miss, on the brow of the hill sloping towards the valley, that's *Netherby*.'

Aine was silent. She felt a sudden stab of fear. Gone was the excitement of the previous evening. She was like a child now about to begin her first day at school. Would she know the answers, know when to sit and stand? Delia had taught her to speak when she was spoken to, to use the right cutlery. As they drove through the wrought-iron gates, she mustered the last bit of self-confidence she possessed.

The avenue to the house was long and winding. Above them a colonnade of trees cast their shadows. Everything around them was silent. Even the engine of the car sounded more subdued. The driveway broadened to a wide sweep. They turned a corner and there was *Netherby*. It was lovelier and more graceful than she had ever dreamed. On either side grasslands and closely-cut lawns spread out before them. The terraces sloped to the gardens and the gardens to a river.

The taxi drove to the front steps and pulled up before a panelled hall door. Aine descended feeling sick and chilled after the long journey. She climbed the steps and rang the doorbell. A girl in uniform appeared. She wore a black silk dress, white collar and cuffs and seemed to be around her own age.

'I wish to see Lady Catherine Taylor,' she said, a nervous

contraction in her voice.

'You can step inside. Madam is expecting you.'

Years later, she would remember with a smile that slim childish figure in a corduroy coat ascending the steps of *Netherby* clutching Delia's suitcase. She would recall, too, her first glimpse of the great central hall, the cedar wood floors, ancestral paintings, and the mahogany staircase with the dark stone passages beyond.

She followed the maid to a well-lit room of splendid proportions. Its sumptuous beauty stunned her. There were three large windows reaching down low, almost to the level of her knees. Sculpted marble decorated the chimneypiece. A thick rosebud-patterned carpet covered the floor and on either side of the fireplace were high-backed armchairs in gold brocade. A walnut cabinet stood in the opposite corner on which there were two tall Chinese vases filled with roses, tulips and orange lilies. An oil painting of a lady in crinoline, reflected in one of the gilt mirrors on the wall, drew her attention. She tiptoed over to examine it. The initials V.T. were inscribed on the lower left hand corner. Proportions a little inaccurate, she thought. Suddenly, the door opened. 'My dear!' Catherine exclaimed, crossing the room, arms extended to embrace her.

Aine found herself enveloped in a soporific cloud of sweet-smelling perfume that tickled her nostrils, causing her to hold her breath to prevent herself from sneezing.

Catherine moved to the window and pulled down the blind but not before Aine had seen her heavily made-up face. There was no sign of tiredness or wrinkles. She wore a charcoal-grey dress of woollen material. A pink scarf, knotted at her throat matched the tone of her lipstick. 'I see you've been admiring our paintings,' she said, nodding towards the portraits, 'they're mostly my grandfather's. The poor old dear was an artistic genius. His works are legendary. Unfortunately such talent often skips generations.' Her face hardened. 'But how are you, my dear? Tired, after such a long journey?' She turned and rang the bell. 'Flora will make you some tea.'

The maid entered a minute later carrying a tray of tea and muffins. Having placed it on the table she withdrew quietly. For somebody so young, Aine thought, she didn't as much as blink an eyelid betraying the fact that they had already met.

After tea Catherine smoothed down her dress and stood up. 'Well, my dear, you've had a very long day. You'll be glad of an early night. We're having some guests over tomorrow. I've invited Mark Davis and a few friends to join us.'

'Oh!'

'Mark is my agent. He's been with me for years and is most efficient. You'll find all the guests very interesting; each one is well versed in art. But I thought a few new items of clothing might help.' She flicked an eye over her blue gingham pinafore and white blouse. 'There are a few dresses hanging in your wardrobe—'

'Oh, but there's no need! I've brought my new skirt and blouse and bolero to match.'

'Tut! Tut! An attractive *Dior* creation will make all the difference. Flora will help with your hair.'

'My hair?'

'You know, a little touching up here and there. Well, let me see. A different style, perhaps, would be interesting.'

'But really—'

'If there's anything else, my dear, just let me know.' The steel glint which Aine had got to know so well appeared once more in her eyes, a glint as sharp as the point of needle. She rose abruptly and rang the bell.

Flora appeared in the doorway. 'Ma'am?'

'Show Aine to her room, if you please. Good night, my dear. Sleep well!'

Aine followed the maid through a well-lit hall, up a wide sweeping staircase. The ceiling was decorated with an elaborate rococo plasterwork similar to that of the drawing room. There was a gold-faced clock on the landing.

A cold current of air greeted her as she entered the bedroom. There was no heating, only an empty fireplace. The walls were Chinese blue matching the floral eiderdown. A Queen Anne dressing table of inlaid rosewood, delicately finished, stood in the corner.

Beside the table was a pale Chippendale chair.

'Lady Catherine has very good taste,' she observed, looking around.

Flora crossed the floor, smoothed down the wrinkles in the eiderdown and checked the cabinet for toilet requisites. 'The house was always like this,' she said, primly, 'it's a Georgian house. I heard Mrs Moffatt say that the idea originated with Lady Catherine's grandparents. It was redecorated later when she and her sister were children.'

'Mrs Moffatt?'

'Oh, that's the housekeeper. She looks after the running of the house. She's been here since her ladyship was a child.'

'Does Mrs Moffatt ever mention Lady Catherine's sister?'

'Well, not really. But I did overhear a few things. Seems some kind of feud broke out between her and her family. They say she married beneath her. Her parents were furious so they disinherited their daughter. But the girl had a child. She's the one who will inherit *Netherby*. But come here, Miss, until you see the view.'

Stumbling, Aine moved to the window. Her thoughts were in turmoil. The girl was mistaken of course. She'd overheard a piece of gossip in the kitchen and jumped to conclusions. Strange, she hadn't connected her with the disinherited twin. Following the direction of her hand, she saw a plantation of trees rising in the distance, tall and straight against the horizon. Closer to the house was a field where a few horses grazed. There was a glint of running water. Further west she saw an orchard, flower gardens and the roofs of greenhouses. 'Who looks after it all?'

'The head gardener, Luke. He's been here many years now. Sir Richard, himself, with the help of two apprentices, devotes a lot of time to *Netherby*. Of course Mrs Moffatt and the maids take care of the inside.'

'You work very hard?'

Standing with her back towards her, Flora's rotund figure stiffened. The starched cap covering her hair quivered ever so slightly. 'Her ladyship's good to us. As long as we obey orders we get plenty of time off. Wages aren't bad.' She closed the window, fastening the shutters with a snap, refusing to be drawn into further discussion of the Taylors.

Aine wondered how Flora succeeded in remaining a member of Catherine's retinue. Did she not sometimes wish that her ladyship would go and take a jump for herself? What wild twist of fate had bound that woman and her mother together, giving them a common identity, common heritage, only to recast them again, several years later, in different moulds? 'We'll meet at breakfast,' she said, turning to her.

'I won't be looking after the dining room tomorrow, Miss. It's Gillian's turn.'

'But won't you have breakfast, I mean with the family?'

'Oh, Lord's sake, no. I'll be breakfasting downstairs with Mrs Moffatt and Luke, the butler. Only the gentry eat in the dining room.'

When Aine turned to ask another question the housemaid had gone. She looked around, awe-stricken, at the splendour of the room. Not in her wildest dreams had she imagined anything so beautiful, so many exquisite objects, glassware, linen, silver engravings. She opened the wardrobe and took out one of the dresses. Made of velvet with a scalloped neck, it was enhanced by a lace stole. She rubbed it against her cheek and using the mirror on the dressing table, looked into it. The small pale face of the girl in the mirror caught her attention. For a brief second, the china-blue eyes of Lady Catherine Taylor seemed to stare back at her.

Next morning, the first thing she heard was the sound of folding shutters. A blaze of sun struck her pillow. 'Oh?' She blinked into the sunlight.

'You'll be late for breakfast, Miss,' Frowning, Flora stood in the doorway staring across at her.

Aine yawned. 'I'll be down in a minute.'

Half an hour later, she stood fully dressed on the dining room floor. It was a long spacious room facing south. In the centre was a mahogany table laid for breakfast. A white linen tablecloth, stiff as cardboard, matched a set of serviettes shaped like cardinals' hats.

Over the fireplace hung the family crest bearing a coat of arms engraved in gold. Underneath it was an angry lion standing on his hind legs, leering. She walked over and read the motto: *Aquila non capit muscas.*

'Well, what do you think of it?'

She spun around, quickly.

A tall grey-haired man stood looking at her. His face was thin and bronzed. Dressed to go out, he wore a grey tweed jacket with riding breeches. Having crossed the room in quick strides, he stood beside her examining the crest: *Aquila non capit muscas.* Eagles don't catch flies. Heavy stuff, what?'

'Yes, it's a bit,' she frowned. 'Eagles think flies are too far beneath them.'

'That's what they'd like to believe.' There was a hint of irony in his deep voice. About to turn on his heel he changed his mind. 'Have you seen our gardens?'

She shook her head.

'Tomorrow at noon if you're down, Luke will give you a guided tour. He's an expert gardener.'

'I'd like that very much.'

'You'll enjoy a walk around the lakes. This time of year there aren't many swans but it's still very beautiful. Lady Catherine and your mother used to swim there as children.'

'You remember my mother?'

'Of course!'

The swiftness of his reply caused her to look up.

'But you must see the lake,' he said, hurriedly, as if conscious of having committed an indiscretion, 'it's an artist's paradise.'

'I haven't had time to see anything yet,' she confessed, 'there's a river, isn't there, flowing through the fields?'

'Yes, that's the Avon. It's excellent fishing ground. Do you know anything about inland fishing?'

'We've only got the sea in Cragann.'

'Then I'll get you a fishing rod and we'll see what we can do. It's quite simple, really.'

Aine thanked him. She was about to ask a question when the door opened and Catherine breezed in. Wearing a jade green, v-necked dress, she carried a distinctive air of authority. Her coral cream skin, soft as satin, seemed to glow. But her eyes! Aine couldn't help noticing her eyes. In the harsh morning light they held an unnatural brightness. Lines were embedded at the corners of her mouth.

'I see you two know each other already.' Her glance darted from one to the other.

For some inexplicable reason Aine felt herself blushing, as if she had been caught in some kind of clandestine behaviour.

'Richard dear, would you mind telling Luke to send up some fresh vegetables this evening. We're having guests to dinner. And oh! yes! Aine and I are meeting Mark and some friends this afternoon. Aine would like to make a few contacts, wouldn't you, my dear?'

Aine fidgeted with her hands. The prospect of a leisurely afternoon on the river began to recede further and further. It was being made clear to her now who was in charge at *Netherby*.

Chapter Thirty-Three

The ordeal of meeting Catherine's visitors was Aine's first hurdle. Early next day, she returned to the drawing room to await their arrival. She was surprised to find Catherine already there arranging flowers. Tulips and daffodils spun this way and that in open-mouthed vases. Sitting on a low chair near the window she helped her gather the falling petals. Could this be the cool-headed woman who greeted her the previous evening? Arranging a few daffodils wouldn't account for all this starting and stopping and display of nervousness.

The sound of a car could be heard on the gravel sweep. There was a banging of doors; the doorbell rang. Mark swept through the hall into the drawing room. Dressed in a white cotton suit and Panama hat, he looked more self-confident and relaxed than when last she had seen him. A gentleman in a bowler hat accompanied him.

'Good journey over, my dear?' he asked, kissing her lightly.

'Yes,' she replied, coolly. Inwardly, she recoiled remembering that day in Cragann, the day he fluffed out her hair before taking the photograph.

When the guests arrived Catherine glided around the room, pausing at the cabinet to dispense drinks. Eyes lowered, a petulant expression had settled on her delicate features.

Sitting opposite Aine on the sofa was a tall dark-haired lady. She wore a knitted silk dress over which was draped an ermine scarf. Mark introduced her as Sarina. She held a cigarette holder in one hand and nervously tapped a golden cigarette lighter with the other. Beside her sat a sandy-haired gentleman in grey, pince-nez balanced on his aristocratic nose. Mark addressed the couple as Sir Nicholas and Lady Frazer. The gentleman who accompanied Mark remained standing until Catherine persuaded him to be seated. Of medium height and stout build, his clean-shaven face lay in repose but his grey eyes flickered.

'This is Aine,' Catherine said. 'She has just arrived from Ireland.'

'Anna!' Lady Frazer echoed.

'No, Sarina. Aine, as pronounced Awnyeh in Gaelic.'

'Oh, dear! You'll have to excuse my Gaelic. What have you been doing with yourself, Aine, since you came to London?'

'Nothing very much. I arrived only yesterday. But Sir Richard is arranging for a fishing trip on the river.'

'Fishing? Ha! Ha! Kitty, m'dear, we must rescue the child from that boorish husband of yours. Did I hear someone say she's Rosemary's daughter? How terribly interesting! History repeating itself, eh?'

Catherine paled. Her beautiful face became pinched. 'Aine may be Rosemary's daughter but she's also my niece. She doesn't need any help from my husband.'

'My!' Sarina drawled, breathing rings of smoke into the air. 'We do get rattled rather easily, don't we?'

A different parlour maid entered carrying a plate of layered chocolate cake on a silver tray. Catherine took the plate and passed it among her guests refilling their Chinese teacups.

'You said you were interested in fishing,' the stocky gentleman called Mr Turner addressed Aine.

'Oh, yes. At home they trawl the Atlantic and gut the fish themselves.' A flush of excitement suffused her face. 'Mostly mackerel and herring,' she added.

There was an awkward silence.

Sir Nicholas adjusted his pince-nez. The gentleman with the flickering eyes coughed. Aine learned later that he was Mr Henry Waters, a well-known art critic for the *London Times*.

'How very resourceful we are!' Sarina sneered. 'Kitty, my dear, you produce such unusual protégés.'

'Actually, Aine devotes most of her time to artistic pursuits,' Mark hastened to point out. 'You've seen her painting in the Tudor. An example of tremendous talent, don't you think.'

'Quite so, quite so.' Sir Nicholas helped himself to another slice of cake.

'I'm sure you've all received an invitation to the whist party at Willoughbys,' Catherine said, changing the subject. She uncrossed a long sheer stockinged leg and looked around the room with a nervous scrutiny. 'Lord and Lady Ashdown will be there, also the Beresfords. It promises to be a very exciting evening. Unfortunately, Richard cannot come. You know how he detests such evenings.'

'Tut! Tut! What a bore! But what about you, Aine?' Sarina's bangles jingled as she put up a gold lorgnette. 'The Irish are sharks at cards. Nicholas attended some bizarre whist drives over there, didn't you, Nick?' She cast a knowing glance at her husband.

Sir Nicholas nodded, his mouth full of chocolate cake.

'In Cragann they play mostly Twenty-five,' Aine explained. 'Delia often wins a pig's head or maybe a turkey. She invites the neighbours, Willie and old Daniel. Sometimes they play a-hundred-and-ten.

'Ahem!' Mr Waters cleared his throat.

'Have you read on the *Sunday Gazette* the new prices for silverware,' Sir Henry asked, turning to Mr Waters.

'The market is frightening. They're pricing us out of our homes.'

'More tea, Henry?' Catherine pressed.

'S'il vous plait.'

'Milk?'

'Un petit poudre.'

'Yes, the news from abroad is bleak,' she agreed. 'Our men overseas don't seem very hopeful either. Still Britannia will always rule.'

'What's the scene like in Ireland?' Sir Nicholas asked, pointing his pince-nez at Aine. Having worked for sometime in the diplomatic corps, Sir Nicholas prided himself on being an authority on the affairs of that country, though he often thought that he merited more accolades than he actually received.

'The scene?'

'Oh, you know, post war trauma and all that. Have you people regained confidence?'

'What do you mean? We've always been confident. Our fishing

trade is mostly with France. It's one of the up-and-coming fishing trades in Western Europe. French trawlers come regularly to Cragann. We get a good price for our lobsters—'

Sarina Frazer's eyebrows shot up. 'Good gracious, child, you sound so bourgeois! I thought Rosemary said—'

'Forgive me, Mark frowned, 'Aine has a busy schedule ahead. Perhaps we could defer this interesting conversation till later.'

Sarina yawned. 'Nick, darling, you're not forgetting our Bridge party, are you?'

Her husband shook his head.

'I'll collect you tomorrow evening at seven,' Mark said, addressing Aine.

After the guests had gone Aine decided to take a stroll out of doors. She ran upstairs to change her shoes. Catherine had left strict injunctions about changing one's shoes before taking a stroll in the garden. When she reached the landing window she stood and looked out. The sun seemed sharper, more dazzling than that to which she was accustomed in Cragann; the sky more defined.

She paused on the corridor to examine the portraits. There were paintings of the Taylors, grandparents, uncles, aunts, cousins; one of Catherine on horseback; another of Richard and herself on their wedding day. No trace of Rosemary anywhere, as if she had never existed.

Crestfallen, she returned to her room and closed the door. On leaving, minutes later, she heard the sound of voices coming from somewhere along the corridor. A man's voice was raised, angry. *'She's a visitor for God's sake. Can't you abide by the rules?'*

She stood still, holding the handle of the door.

'... a spoiled brat just like her mother before her ...'

'The only honourable thing to do ...'

'Honour! Who wants to talk about honour? My mother wasn't in her right mind, I tell you. Why, she didn't even know what a codicil was!'

'You must recognise the child's rights.'

'That girl's no child. She's more like a—'

She closed the door quickly. Descending the stairs leading to a cobblestone yard outside, she arrived at the kitchen garden. Along by the wall, growing in rectangular boxes, were several rows of mixed herbs, thyme, garlic, sage, interspersed with root vegetables. A wrought-iron gate opened on to a flower garden. She found herself standing at a picket fence against which grew a mass of climbing roses and sweet pea. Opposite was a red brick wall sheltering an herbaceous border of sunflowers, lupines, sweet William and lavender. She stood, uncertain, gazing at the roses.

'A great summer for the English rose,' a voice called cheerfully in a Scottish accent. Startled, she spun around. An elderly gentleman with streaming white hair and corn flour blue eyes smiled across at her. This must be Luke, the gardener, she thought, relieved. He was dressed in navy plus fours and a white shirt. 'It's wonderful!' she replied. 'Such richness of colour! You do this, yourself?'

'Och, aye. It becomes second nature when you're trained for it. I spent a few years in the Botanic Society's Garden in Regent Park.'

'Mmm! And this is verbena?'

'The verbena looks after itself, least troublesome of the lot. What do you think of my rejuvenated irises? They've received a bit of a shaking up, recently. Just like the delphiniums, they need special treatment. Have to be cut at the base and given a good feed, water and mulch. If the slugs don't get at them they should produce another lot of spikes in September.'

'Everything seems to be moving around here,' she laughed. She pointed to the concentric circles swirling around the water-lilies. Seed heads and masses of bluebells swayed in the breeze.

'Candleberry bells,' Luke said. 'Sir Richard, himself, planted those.'

'Sir Richard is interested in gardening?'

'Och, aye. He's a fellow of the Linnaean and devotes much of his time to the study of English gardens. He reads a lot of books on horticulture. Angel's fishing rods,' he remarked, as they passed a cluster of tall rod-like flowers bending to and fro.

'What's that over there?' She pointed to an unfinished structure resembling an ancient Greek temple. Beams of pinewood were laid across pillars of stone and trellised with wild roses.

'Oh, that's the pagola. Made after a model they saw in Venice. It was just being built when her Ladyship was drowned. They never bothered with it since.'

Frowning, she stared across at the unfinished pagola like a child confronting a mystery. 'And the nymph sitting on the edge of the washbowl,' she asked, after a minute, 'she has something in her hand?'

'It's a conch shell. She's listening to the sea. A great favourite with her ladyship, Rosemary. Lady Catherine wanted to have it removed but Sir Richard objected.'

Luke accompanied her along the walks. He pointed out the line of alcoves, an alcove for every letter of the alphabet. Then he left her to explore the remainder of the garden on her own.

It was approaching noon. The sun was at its zenith. Noticing a Japanese tea house among the trees she walked over towards it. Painted white, it was built of trellised wood with a curtain of honeysuckle hanging around the door and covering part of the wall. She pushed aside the honeysuckle and entered. Feeling hot and tired from the sun she sat down and leaned her head against the latticed framework. Suddenly a breeze lifted a branch of honeysuckle. On the wall opposite was a small oval photograph. Moving closer she found it to be that of two young girls, nine or ten years of age, in sundresses and floppy hats, sitting on wicker chairs. Between them sat a middle-aged lady wearing a hat with flowers. A table laid for afternoon tea stood in front of them. The smaller of the two girls was smiling revealing a gap in her teeth. One of her socks had dropped to her ankle. The other girl sat up stiffly, a pouting expression on her face. Aine took the photograph off the wall and held it between her hands. It must have been hanging there for years, a piece of forgotten history. Something like a stab of pain went through her. She stood still, listening to the wind rustling the leaves outside then returned the photograph to its hiding place.

'Which of the two girls is Rosemary?' she asked, meeting Luke on the gravel, a few minutes later.

'The lady with the gap in her teeth.'

'Your garden has interesting things.'

'Yes, hasn't it,' he laughed, as if something exciting were about to happen. 'I detest those pattern gardens, myself, where flowers are degraded to crude colour to make a design. We'll have to hire you to give a hand with the landscaping!'

She wheeled around. Somebody was calling from the house.

'Luke!' Flora shouted, running down towards them. 'Her ladyship wishes to have a word with you.'

Looking up, Aine saw a face withdraw quickly from an upstairs window.

Chapter Thirty-Four

'Would you care for a drink?' Mark asked, rubbing his hands officiously, as he called to collect Aine at *Netherby* the following evening.

Aine shook her head.

Without further ado Mark took the decanter from the drawing room cabinet and mixed himself a whiskey and soda. 'We'll drive to the Tudor first,' he said, swirling the contents around in his glass, 'the exhibition is opening at seven. We can have dinner at the *Royal* afterwards.' He glanced at his watch, finished off the remainder of his drink and rushed out the door.

Aine shivered. Whatever warmth the sun in the French windows might offer, it did little to alleviate the gloom of the panelled walls or soften the smiles of her ancestors. What mad impulse was driving Mark? Wasn't it she, after all, who was exhibiting the painting? Frowning, she picked up her coat - the turquoise woollen Catherine had given her - and followed him out.

Mark left his car at the Pavilion. They walked the remaining distance to the Gallery. Throngs of people streamed past Buckingham Gate up Victoria Street giving her her first real taste of London. Red buses, black taxis, whizzed by, hooting. Neon lights glowed and glimmered over shop windows and cinemas. High up on the steps of St Paul's an old man in rags played his accordion. A tinker woman with her freckled faced son stood in an alley way, begging. She rummaged in her pockets and threw them a few coins.

As they approached the Gallery her spirits soared. This was her moment, the moment for which she had waited. How often had she dreamed of it, tripping along the heather-coated bogs in Cragann or walking at evening on Portree strand. She pictured the critics, imagining how they'd question her. Where had she trained? What would her next painting be? Tingling with excitement she followed Mark up a flight of steps leading to an octagonal cut-stone building supported by Doric pillars. Passing through a glass swing-door they entered a foyer.

Everywhere people were hurrying, Chinese, West Indians, tourists of all nationalities and creeds. There were Americans, maps in their hands, eager to absorb the European culture. Having climbed the last flight of steps, they came to the Turner Room where the Art Exhibition was being held.

A low buzz of conversation greeted them inside. There was a nauseous smell of paint mixed with the odour of perfume. Most of the guests were invited. Gentlemen with beards and silver pince-nez and ladies in off-the-shoulder evening dresses sipped glasses of chardonnay. They discussed Picasso and Cezanne, comparing them with pioneers of other European schools. Press photographers hovered in the background. Catherine was engaged in conversation with the Frazers and a gentleman in a tuxedo suit who had flown in from Paris that morning to open the exhibition.

'Delighted to see you in London, Monsieur Renard,' Mark greeted him.

The gentleman bowed. Said something in French.

'This is Miss Fogarty, a modern watercolorist.'

'Charmed, Mademoiselle! You're one of our pioneering artists, I see. There's a new era beginning for watercolorists. I look forward to seeing more of your work.' A pair of deep-set, smiling blue eyes looked kindly into Aine's.

'Except for Turner and a few other notables,' Catherine noted sweetly, 'watercolorists are still only second class artists. But Aine's going to break the mould, aren't you, darling?' She laughed, her tinkling laugh.

Aine fidgeted with her gloves. Her heart beat faster. Monsieur Renard liked her painting, liked it well enough to have paid her a compliment.

They moved on further down the room. Paintings were everywhere, arranged several rows deep. They filled every inch of wall space. She peered at the titles: *Beach on the island of Poros; View of Cardigan Bay.* She admired the diagonal brush strokes on the Welsh cliffs, the untouched paper giving the effect of foam. Advancing to the next painting she read: *Durham from the River.* The artist had changed the lighting direction to dramatise the bridge. There was an exotic looking view of Venice, another of a market day in the Provence village of Gourdes and a painting of a Greek island villa. Eagerly, she looked around for her own. At last she saw it hanging in a space above the door, virtually invisible. It looked different ... brush work strong ... colours almost garish. She felt a sudden stab of fear. A voice in her head whispered, *you're not going to make it!* She looked wildly about. She couldn't see anyone she knew. A lady behind her nudged the gentleman next to her. 'Look darling, what do you make of this?'

'Which one, dear?'

'The painting up high hidden above the door.'

'Mmm. Quite ordinary, really. A face at a window. So bourgeois!'

'Darling, you're looking at the wrong one. It's a bird. A bird trapped in a storm.'

The gentleman shrugged. 'Does it really matter? It's too far away for anyone to see.' They moved further on down the room.

Aine's face burned.

'I see you're admiring your painting,' Mark said, stepping up behind her. He took out his spectacles and hitched them on the bridge of his nose. 'Looks rather good, eh?'

'Most of the others are sold,' she replied resentfully, pointing to the stickers on the frames.

'Mmm. And for quite a good price, I'm sure.' He opened his catalogue and checked the price list. 'Well, we had better make a beeline for dinner. If we don't go now the places will be filled.'

Half an hour later they were walking down High Street. It was twenty to seven, too early for dinner. They sat in the lounge of the *Royal* and waited. People surged in but they succeeded in finding a table in a corner. Around them conversation buzzed in an excited babble of languages.

A waiter carrying a tray laden with drinks threaded his way between the tables, shedding the drinks as he went. 'Benedictine, Monsieur?'

Mark nodded.

'I hope Monsieur's pictures are going well.'

'How did he know?' Aine asked, after he had gone.

'That I deal in paintings? That's not too hard to guess, my dear. Those fellows read the papers.'

'I see.'

The head waiter at the door beckoned. They followed him into the dining room. It was brightly-lit with lilac-gray walls and windows opening on one side to Elton Square and on the other to Victoria Station. They were lead to a table near a window. Bowing, the head waiter recognised Mark from other occasions.

Cool and debonair in a lounge suit, Mark exuded an air of self-confidence. 'What will you have,' he asked, scanning the menu.

'Oh, anything will do. I don't really mind. Bacon and cabbage, as long as there aren't any slugs. I don't like slugs. They sweat out their houses as they go.'

'Come now, be a little more daring. Try something Italian or French. What about Pasta All' Arrabiate with mushrooms and bacon, eh? And a bottle of red wine,' he added, beckoning to the waiter. He sat back, a satisfied expression on his face.

'Mark'.

'Well.'

'I wonder what the critics will think.' She leaned across the table towards him.

'Of what, my dear?'

'Of the Cave painting.'

'I wouldn't worry about that. Critics have the strangest ideas. They never seem to agree on anything. You've met Jacques Renard, haven't you? Now there's a fellow who knows his peanuts.'

The waiter returned with platters of grilled bacon, mushrooms, spaghetti and a julienne of vegetables. Mark poured ruby-red wine into her glass. He then filled up his own. 'To us, my dear,' he said

216

smiling, raising his glass.

She gazed stonily at the glass of wine and the platter of spicy food left in front of her. 'My painting doesn't have a sticker like the others,' she burst out, 'nobody wants to buy it. That's what makes artists famous, isn't it? I mean when viewers are willing to pay that kind of money for their work.'

'Mmm, more vegetables, dear?'

She shook her head.

Mark coiled worms of spaghetti around his fork. He lifted his glass and tasted the wine.

Blushing, she struggled with the spaghetti, casting a furtive glance across at him. He was staring impassively out the window. In the end, she pushed away her plate and sat toying with her fork.

Having finished his meal Mark gave a burp of satisfaction. He wiped his fingers on his table napkin, lit a cigar and sat back, smoking. 'My dear,' he said, after a while, 'concerning your painting, we've come to the conclusion, Catherine and I, that it hasn't got what takes.'

Aine flinched. 'But Monsieur Renard—'

'Monsieur Renard is a good-hearted fellow. I know old Jacques. He's got a heart of gold. But the truth is, your painting doesn't attract the interest of the viewers.'

'You didn't give it much space, did you? Nobody had a chance to see it. It was hidden at the top.' She eyed him fiercely. Around her people were laughing, talking, finishing their meal. Cups rattled.

Mark shrugged. 'Wall space wouldn't make much difference. But don't get me wrong,' he held up a placating hand, 'your work is of very high quality, that is, as far as water-colours go. Unfortunately, nobody here seems interested. 'However, he pulled at his cigar and watched her closely through a ring of smoke, 'there's a chance yet that something can be done.'

'What do you mean?'

'Listen!' He stubbed out his cigar on the ashtray. Leaning forward, voice lowered, he said. 'Perhaps we could do a deal, you and I?'

'What kind of deal?'

'A business arrangement. There are some top notch galleries in London. I happen to know some of the managers. It's not going to be easy but with a little bit of influence ...' He flicked an imaginary crumb from his jacket.

Aine glanced at her wine. Still untouched, it winked and laughed mockingly. Was this to be a cause for celebration? Oughtn't she to sit back and drink to Mark, to herself, to her own future as an artist? But the word celebration, suddenly, had a hollow ring. The proposed deal - if it could be called that - sounded spurious. She rolled up her table napkin into a ball and pushed away her glass deciding that if she tasted the wine it would turn sour on her lips. 'Very well,' she said, lowering her eyes.

'There's one condition, my dear. To defray costs I have to ask for commission.'

'How much?' She wondered where she was going to get the money. Colm? No. Willie Sara might have a little put by. Maybe he'd give her a loan until she had sold a few pictures.

'The standard payment for an agent in London is fifty percent of the profit. And that, of course, will include your portfolio rights, you understand?'

'Yes.'

'I believe in having all my contracts transacted legally. So I shall ask my solicitor to draft a document which you will be requested to sign. I'm sure Catherine won't mind being witness. In the meantime, mum's the word. I'll meet you in *Netherby* tomorrow at eleven. Ok?'

She nodded.

Going home that evening she sat in Mark's passenger seat, hands clenched in her pockets. Cold and hungry, she would have given anything for a plate of Delia's hot stew. Her leather handbag containing her gloves, together with the catalogue of prices from the Gallery, lay on her lap. The Cave painting had been listed and priced at a heavy sum. But it didn't really matter. Nobody had seen it. And even if they had they would have turned away.

'Enjoying London?' he asked, as he manoeuvred his car out of the snarl of traffic.

'Very interesting,' she replied. She stared vacantly at the rows of red brick houses. Fronted by wrought-iron railings, they had no gardens. White Venetian blinds were drawn tightly, shutting out every glimmer of daylight.

'Have you visited the Opera House yet?'

'No,' she said, shortly. She hoped he wouldn't ask her any more questions.

As they approached *Netherby* she asked to be dropped at the gates. Not daring to look back she ran up the avenue. It was raining heavily. Sheets of rain were driven against the front of the old stone building lashing the gravel. She arrived at the hall door, red-nosed, her clothes sodden, hair matted on her head.

'Oh. Miss, you're so foolish, you could catch your death!' Flora cried, admitting her.

As she sat by a roaring fire in the servant's hall, minutes later, drinking hot cocoa, the implications of the proposed deal with Mark became clear to her.

That night she wrote to Delia.

> *Netherby Hall,*
> *Seven Oaks,*
> *London.*

Dear Delia,

I've settled in at Netherby. It's a house full of mystery. You'd love all the finery, the white linen tablecloths, sparkling tea-sets ... and the beautiful exotic rugs. But more than anything else you'd adore the gardens. Peony roses and tulips grow everywhere. The rooms upstairs are very grand. There are tapestries on the walls and cedar wood floors ...

My painting is on display in the Tudor Gallery. It's not sold, yet ... but it will be.

Love,

Aine

P.S There's a photograph of my mother hanging in the tea house.

She sealed the letter and stamped it. An ironic smile touched her lips. Her painting was about to be sold! One by one, she began to summon up the events of that evening; the Cave painting hanging above the door where nobody could see it; comments of the viewers, one more foolish than the other ... Try as she might she couldn't recapture the melody. Her father's spirit had fled, banished by the grossness of a spurious deal. Exhausted, she fell into a troubled sleep. She dreamed she was running down a narrow lane. Her body became entangled in ribbons of spaghetti. The more she tried to extricate herself, the more entangled she became. The ribbons grew tighter, tighter, until she felt she couldn't breathe. She woke up screaming.

Looking at her watch she found it to be after four. She jumped out and lifted a corner of the curtain. A pale moon shone through the trees casting a silver path along the grass. In the distance she could hear the hard, dry, bark of a fox. Along the walk, by the gable of the house, there was a small red glimmer. It was the glow of a lighted cigarette. She dropped the curtain, climbed into bed and slept till dawn.

Chapter Thirty-Five

'Ahh! This is where you are!'

Startled, Aine turned her head. Catherine stood in the doorway of the drawing room. In the harsh morning light her luxuriant blonde hair showed signs of greying. It was the day after Aine's decision to sign over her paintings. Having considered the consequences, Catherine, Mark, whatever their motives might be, she had come to the conclusion about one thing: she couldn't face back to Delia without some measure of success.

'My goodness!' Catherine exclaimed, pealing off her gloves and throwing aside her mink coat, 'you're sitting all alone in the dark.' She glanced involuntarily at the silver tray set exclusively for three people.

'I'm waiting for Mark.'

'Well, take it from me, Mark won't be late. He's one of those few people who keep their appointments.' Having selected an armchair, she arranged herself comfortably against the cushions, crossed her legs and lit a cigarette. In the dark closed-in drawing room with its drawn eau-de-nil curtains, scrolled sofa and brocade chairs, the shaded lamp cast a soft light into the mirrors and on to the Persian rugs.

Sitting on a low chair, near the fire, Aine's pale blue dress almost blotted her out against the muted background. She clasped and unclasped her knees. Once or twice she caught Catherine looking at her, eyes narrowed against the smoke of her cigarette. It never occurred to her to doubt her authenticity or that of Mark. The latter might have behaved idiotically in Cragann, disappearing on the night of the ceilidh; getting sea sick on the fishing trip, but here in London, in the closeness of the drawing room, his authority went unquestioned. Catherine, for her part, was a woman of undefined consequence, a force to be reckoned with.

Sharp at eleven they heard the sound of the Daimler on the gravel sweep; there was a banging of doors. Mark raced up the steps and swept through the hallway. Wearing a dark grey overcoat, white collar and tie he carried a brief case. 'Everything in order?' he asked, removing his coat and hanging it on the back of a chair.

Catherine nodded.

Sitting up straight Aine gripped the sides of her chair. Her eyes darted from Catherine to Mark and from there to the orange-blue flames spluttering in the grate. Would Mark fulfil his promise? Would he carry out his side of the bargain? Suddenly, she felt afraid, afraid of the consequences ... of the menacing shadows ... ghosts that hovered.

Mark sat at the table, his back to the window. He opened his brief case, took out a long white document and placed it on the table, Conway Steward pen beside it. 'Now let me see! Ah, here we are!' He ran his forefinger along the bottom of the page, pausing on the dotted line.

'I'd like to have a look at it first,' she said, pointing to the document.

He handed her a copy.

She scanned the small black print. *Deed of Exchange* was written at the top. *This agreement is made- space- between Aine Fogarty (hereafter known as vendor) and Mark Davis (hereafter known as purchaser.)*

'Was this drawn up by a solicitor?' she asked, conscious of Catherine's razor-blue eyes staring coldly across at her.

'Of course! Of course! I went over all that with you yesterday.'

'Will we each receive a copy of it afterwards?'

'For heaven's sake, yes! Here!' he barked, jabbing his finger authoritatively along the line marked x.

She picked up the pen, half-closed her eyes. In one second she was transported back to the caves at Doora. She heard the thunder of the waves. Saw the lightning zig zag along the Cave walls; smelled the rusty oil lantern with its orange-blue flames ... She felt again the fire within, driving her relentlessly on, forcing her to make sense of the convoluted life which spread like a tapestry in front of her. As her fingers clutched the pen conflicting thoughts gripped her. What if Mark were deceiving her, using her for a purpose? What if—? But nobody said her painting was valuable, nobody, only old Monsieur Renard. And he praised it out of pity, pity for the poor ignorant girl from the West of Ireland. She leaned forward and flattened the document down with her hand. Somewhere in the house the telephone rang.

'Will somebody answer it?' she asked, glaring from one to the other.

Nobody moved.

The phone kept on ringing, shattering the silence of the half-empty house.

'I'll answer it, myself!' She jumped to her feet, rushed out the door and along the corridor, half walking, half running, pausing before the telephone table.

'Hello!'

'Is that Miss Fogarty?'

'Yes.'

'This is Brian Inglewood from the Tudor Gallery. We've got some exciting news for you, Miss Fogarty.'

'What's that?'

'The painting which you exhibited in our Gallery this week is sold.'

'Sold?'

'An anonymous buyer. He paid seven thousand pounds for it. Says he wishes to withhold his name for the present, at least. Naturally the sale is attracting attention. We've had phone calls from the *Times* and *Gazette*. They're asking for statements. Perhaps you'd let us know, madam, when you intend calling.'

'Oh!' Aine said, not knowing what to say.

'We've been advised to forward the money to your bank in Ireland. We've got all the data.'

'Thank you.' she said. She put down the receiver. Her painting was sold! Turning on her heel she collided with Flora, the parlour maid. 'They've sold my painting!' she cried, catching her by the arm and whirling her around on the corridor, 'my painting is sold!' She visualised the sticker, red as blood, on the top right-hand corner.of the picture. Visitors would see it, admire her style and compare her with other artists. Somebody liked it, liked it well enough to have paid seven thousand pounds for it! Overcome with excitement, she ran up the corridor going in the direction of the drawing room. As she approached, the sound of voices reached her.

'She mustn't know ...' Mark's voice was low, insistent.

'How much did you bid?'

'Not a whole lot. Later it should reach a good price—'

'It's sold!' she cried, bursting into the room, 'my painting is sold!'

'What do you mean?'

'I've just had a phone call. A man from the Gallery ... He said they've sold my painting.'

Sitting opposite Mark at the table Catherine's eyes began a sliding act. Her lips tightened.

As if catapulted from his chair Mark sprang up. 'Who the devil did this? I was the last to leave the Gallery last night. There wasn't a sign of a bidder. Nobody had ... The painting was still unsold.' He began to pace back and over. Suddenly he spun round. 'It's you!' he shouted, jabbing a finger at Aine, 'you! Who did you phone?'

'Mark!' Catherine placed a restraining hand on his arm.

Mark glanced from one to the other. He swept the documents into his case, snatched up his coat and charged out the door. A minute later, the roar of the Daimler could be heard on the driveway.

Aine sat back in her chair and closed her eyes. She locked and unlocked her hands. A feeling of intense joy gripped her. Her painting was sold; she was a recognized artist! But somewhere deep down in the depths of her heart she felt a pulsating pain, as if somebody close to her, somebody whom she loved, had died.

Sitting opposite her at the table Catherine began to manicure her already perfect nails. Only a slight tremor of the hand betrayed her emotion. Through the open window came the sound of music. Somebody was playing the piano, playing out his heart, the frustration of years. She recognised the tune. Old Daniel used to sing it in Brannigans' whenever he had an extra drop taken.

'My dear!' Catherine said, placing the nail file back in her handbag and addressing her, 'this latest piece of news is wonderful. I mean for a novice like you ... But who is the buyer? None of our clients showed a particular interest. A painting like that wouldn't attract the connoisseur. They're mostly R.H.A trained artists. It's a shock for poor Mark. We ... he had intended to market it properly. It would have been necessary to pull a few strings, of course. The poor dear went to such trouble having your painting assessed and mounted. You'll have to get in touch with—'

Aine scraped back her chair and stood up. With an effort she controlled her voice. 'Whoever the buyer is he liked my painting, liked it enough to pay that much money for it.'

'You'll have to discuss it with Mark, my dear. Mark is an authority on marketing. As I said before it's important to listen to your agent.'

Aine stared. Catherine's carefully made-up face showed signs of discomposure. Beads of sweat glistened on her forehead. 'My painting is gone. I won't be talking to Mr Davis. Get me my things. I'm going home.'

Catherine rose, crossed the room and opened the window wide. A scent of lavender and rosemary mixed with the resinous smell of the nearby pines drifted in from outside. On the front lawn the boy tending flowers whistled as he flattened the soil around a mound of pansies. She closed the window, returned and sat down. 'You realise what you're doing?'

'Of course. I'll have enough money to go on. I'll open a studio. Take in a few pupils—'

'But you can't do this. I mean it's too soon. Now that you're successful we'll have to celebrate, throw a few parties.'

'I don't want any parties.'

'But, my dear! I'm your mother's sister.' She stubbed out her cigarette and began to dab her eyes. 'Life is passing. I need people around me, young people like you who'd brighten things up. I feel sure you'll settle down, get used to the running of the house ...' Her voice took on a pleading note.

Aine stiffened. 'I'll pack my things. Please get me my suitcase. I'm going home.' In her mind's eye she saw Cragann, complacent and remote, sheltering in the shadow of the Mayo hills; Delia in her armchair knitting. Down on the shore the fishermen's voices, low and intense, as they bartered their night's catch out beyond the pier, the sound of surf rumbling ... She glanced at the woman in front of her. Face flushed, eyes glistening, she showed little sign of yielding. In the space between the blinds and the window frame Flora could be seen talking to the young gardener. Gesturing wildly, her round fat hands filled the gaps left in her speech. A minute later, she tiptoed into the drawing room carrying a tray of tea and muffins, a look of fierce pride in her dark eyes.

Days and weeks passed. One late afternoon, towards the end of August, Mr Waters, reporter for the *London Times*, called to see Aine at *Netherby*. Eager to interview her about the sale of her painting, he placed himself squarely in a chair opposite her. It was a sultry afternoon. A warning of thunder on the radio earlier hadn't materialised. The curtains in the drawing room were half-drawn.

Aine sat on her favourite low chair, knees drawn primly, together.

'How do you see the future of art in England, Miss Fogarty?' He leaned forward, pencil poised, awaiting her reply.

'I don't see it at all.'

'But you must see some possibilities—'

'None whatever.' She stood up and backed towards the door.

'Miss Fogarty! I say, Miss Fogarty—'

She fled down the corridor and across the landing descending the steps leading to the courtyard outside. Passing through the wicker gate she came to the rose garden. Daylight was beginning to fade. Deep among the trees an owl hooted. The solitary call of the bird emphasized the monastic stillness. Close to the lily pond water trickled from the fountain making a sound like tinkling bells. She could see it glinting. She sat on a seat of bamboo cane and gazed up at *Netherby*, the house she had dreamed of, stored up in her heart. She stretched out her hands as if to take some of it with her. But she knew, already knew that the vision had fled. There was nothing here only a broken dream. Along the walk somebody was singing. It was the song she had heard that day, many weeks earlier. As she listened she mouthed the words.

La ... st night she came to me ... she ... came softly in ...

So ... softly she came that ...

Richard said music was his passion, the elixir of life. Bits of the conversation they had had returned. *Be careful that you don't get entangled ... Freedom once lost ...'*

She felt she was trespassing. Turning on her heel, she retraced her steps and returned through the kitchen garden.

A week later Aine left *Netherby*. As she was saying good bye, Catherine stood on the front steps dabbing her eyes with a flimsy handkerchief. 'Something to remember us by, my dear,' she said, handing her a small square box.

Aine thanked her and put the box into her inside pocket. Richard gave her some petunias, which she carefully wrapped in a brown paper bag and packed in her case.

'Set them in thin soil,' he advised, 'they may need to be transplanted.'

'I'll do my best,' she promised.

He smiled as he waved good bye, a hint of scepticism in his dark eyes.

As she climbed into the taxi for Euston she bade farewell to *Netherby Hall*. Its tall grey windows stared coldly back at her. Whatever dark secrets it held would remain intact. Passing through the wrought-iron gates she leaned back against the red upholstery emitting a sigh of relief. Minutes later, the London taxi gathered speed. She was out on the highway.

Chapter Thirty-Six

A thick fog was rising from the river as Aine reached Euston Station. She stood, letting it sweep over her, swallowing it through all the pores of her skin, filling her eyes with it, nose, ears and mouth. She felt like shouting ... singing. She had gone beyond the reach of Catherine and Mark.

On the Mail Train home the passengers looked different. They had an air of expectancy about them, chatting to each other, laughing uproariously as if they knew each other well. Carrying heavy suitcases and overcoats, they were better dressed than those who had travelled out. Work seemed to have been plentiful on the buildings and in the factories.

She had scarcely settled in her seat when a man from Longford sat in opposite her. She read his address as he put his case on the rack. He removed his duffel overcoat and unfolded a copy of the *London Times*. Immediately, a photograph of herself in Social and Personal appeared in front of her. *Success of Irish Artist* was the caption. It was a close-up shot. Her face was elongated, out of proportion.

'Excuse me,' the man from Longford said, thrusting his head over the newspaper, 'I think I recognise your face.'

'Could happen,' she shrugged, 'haven't we all got a double of us somewhere.'

'Ah, sure you Irish girls when you leave the old sod lose the run of yourselves.'

'Would you think that now?' Squinting, she eyed the Longford man's beer belly. 'Some of you fellows, when you go over there wouldn't be too far behind us.' She poked her face up close to the newspaper. *Irish Artist Wins Fame Over Night*. Wouldn't Mark be delighted with that? Funny how excited he became about her painting! And Catherine, what interest had she in the matter? Stifling a yawn, her eyes wandered around the carriage. Someone had thrown orange peel on the floor. The air was heavy, reeking of soot and grit from the engine. She rose and opened the carriage door.

Outside on the corridor the window was tightly shut. She wrenched at the strap until her hands ached. Struggling with it, she jerked it a few times until it finally crashed open. She thrust her head out inhaling the cold night air. At the front of the train a fireman was stoking the engine. Smoke billowed from the funnel as it hissed and belched out steam. At the rear, a smaller engine prepared to push the great Mail Train up the slope and out of the station.

The whistle blew. The train rumbled slowly out leaving the suburbs of London behind. The passengers settled down; some were already asleep. The great *Irish Mail* gathered speed as it blasted through the night carrying her home.

On the boat over Aine sat in a corner near the lifeboats and slept most of the way. She dreamed she was back again in the rose garden at *Netherby*. She heard the water trickling in the lily pond. Smelled the verbena as it grew along the wall. In the shadow of the pagola stood the unknown singer. But superimposed on it all was the face of a woman, a woman standing at a window, watching. She awoke suddenly.

'I was afraid of disturbing you lest you get a fright.' A wrinkled Scottish sailor stood gazing, quizzically, down at her.

'What time is it?' she asked.

'Not far off the sixteenth hour.'

'Are we nearly there?'

'Any minute now. They'll soon be loosening the anchor.'

She stood up, gathered her belongings and ascended the upper deck. People were becoming restless, looking at their watches. She leaned over the side of the ship. Pieces of wrack, empty milk cartons and cigarette boxes, whirled past. A screaming seagull flew up into the air. She took out the box which Catherine had given her. Inside was a locket containing a photograph, a close-up shot of *Netherby*. High and resplendent in the sun, the old stone house stared proudly back at her. Surrounded by clipped hedges and lawns, its tall tulips stood to attention. The rose garden at the back was hidden, its crazy-patterned flower beds, Japanese tea house ... and the photograph of a child with wrinkled stockings, gap in her teeth. A surge of unforgivingness welled up inside her. She looked out to sea. Far, far out blue-black waves softened to a forgiving whiteness. Patches of colour intermingled, neither black nor white. That's what it was all about, neither black nor white. Suddenly, she saw the great Hall of *Netherby* as it really was, a sad house, a house hurrying to its doom. She held the photograph up to the light, tore it in two and tossed it into the foaming waters.

When the ship docked at Dun Laoghaire Aine stood waiting. The gates opened; she walked down the gangway, suitcase in one hand and portfolio in the other. A gust of wind lifted her dress whirling it around her head.

'Hey, Beautiful, what are you doing to-night?' a voice shouted from the bridge.

She glanced up.

Two cheeky young sailors leaned over the side of the boat, grinning.

'Bandy legged bootleggers!' she retorted, her face going crimson.

They roared laughing.

Haughtily, she held her dress and continued her way downwards. The smell of cooking fat mixed with brewed coffee wafted towards her from the galley making her head swim.

A minute later, she staggered up the pier following the other passengers.

Having boarded the suburban train she found a seat near a window. People were hurrying in all directions. She sank back against the soft upholstery and closed her eyes.

'Are you on your way home, girl?' an old man smoking a pipe, sitting opposite her, asked.

'I am.' She opened one eye, defiantly.

'They're terribly busy over there altogether.'

She nodded. She wasn't too sure who he meant. Flora or Luke?

Maybe it was old Moffatt who looked after them in the kitchen. Certainly it wouldn't be any of the partying bodies upstairs. That Sarina lady couldn't as much as stitch on a button.

A bald-headed man with a corkscrew moustache, melodeon under his arm, thrust his head into the carriage.

'A fine hurdy-gurdy you have there,' the man with the pipe said, winking.

'Aye, we'll knock many a good night out of it yet,' the melodeon player replied, baring pink-and-white gums. 'The Customs would wreck your head. Wouldn't you think now they'd leave an old fellow like me alone? What with all those loafers out there, cigarette lighters and God-knows-what sown up their sleeves and down their breeches. Arragh what, man!' He glanced around the carriage and squeezed himself in beside Aine.

The train pulled out from Dun Laoghaire and ran for miles along by the sea. Leaving the windswept seascape behind, it skirted the city. Backs of red-brick houses rushed past on their left. Smoke spewed from chimneys. Clothes swollen by the breeze blew in dingy backyards. In the distance tall office blocks and a cathedral spire reared their heads. This was Dublin, city of poets and dreamers; home of O Casey and James Joyce.

At Westland Row Station she boarded the train for the West. Chugging into the open countryside, it halted at every stop. A youth with a pony tail got in at Mullingar.

'God help us,' a red-faced man wearing a cap said, looking at Pony Tail, 'aren't we a bit confused in ourselves?'

'Too much buttermilk, they say, isn't good,' nodded the melodeon player, who had turned up beside them again after they had changed trains.

'Hurrah for Ireland!' Ponytail shouted, opening a noggin bottle of whiskey. 'Good stuff, hah!' He smacked his lips, wiping his mouth with the back of his sleeve.

They passed the outskirts of towns and villages. Telegraph wires rose and dipped. Outside Castlereagh potato fields were everywhere in flower. Stray sheep followed sparse bits of grass on rocky hillsides. In Roscommon the stone walls of Connacht became visible, monuments to another age.

Exhausted, Aine descended the train at Ballina. Her eyes were red, smarting from coal-grit and lack of sleep. Her clothes, smelling of grime, were sticking to her legs. Women, some of them pregnant, dragged their luggage along the platform to the bus office, drained of every bit of life.

That evening she mounted the bus for Cragann. The first star was out over the Atlantic.

'There could be rain before midnight,' the bus driver said, checking his passengers.

'There's nothing as plentiful between this and high heaven,' replied a man at the front.

'Travelling all day?' the driver asked Aine, opening the luggage-hold for her case.

Aine nodded.

'Your aunt will be glad to see you home. All kinds of goings-on in England now, I believe. Give me that parcel, Ma'am, and I'll put it on the rack.' A large woman had got in and was struggling with her luggage. 'They say Brannigans' was raided last night,' he added, addressing nobody in particular.

'Ora,' said the woman beside her, sitting up with a jerk.

'There was a good number caught. But somebody gave them the nod. When the Sergeant went in there wasn't a soul in the pub. The place was empty. Only ashtrays and half-empty pints on the counter.'

'Well, well!'

'And what do you think? Wasn't the barman standing by the counter, yawning, sleeves rolled up and counting his money? But I'll tell you this. They weren't going to get the better of the Sergeant.'

'Ahh!'

'He searched the whole house. Everywhere he looked he found somebody hiding. Daniel Cassidy had locked himself in the wardrobe at the top o' the stairs. Young Hegarty and Colm Holohan were hiding under Pa Brannigan's bed.'

'No!' said Aine. 'Did he give them a summons?'

'He wrote down their names in a notebook. Let them off with a caution.'

'By Jove!'

'Next stop,' a woman laden with parcels called from the aisle.

'Mind yourself getting out there, Ma'am,' the driver warned, opening the door.

Aine was faint from hunger. A cup of tea and a sandwich was all she had on the mail boat. The longest delay was at Coonihans. The driver, with some of the men got out for refreshments. After twenty minutes or so, they all climbed back into the bus wiping their mouths, smiling. She was on the last leg of her journey home.

As the bus rounded the schoolhouse bend Cragann lights sprang into view. She hadn't told Delia she was coming. Distracted as she was by the photographers, she didn't have time to send her word.

Chapter Thirty-Seven

'Well, look what the cat brought in!' Delia exclaimed, as Aine strolled into the kitchen at six o clock that evening. 'Where on earth did you come from?'

'London.'

'London!'

'I travelled over on the boat last night. Came down by train this morning.'

'You didn't stay long, did you? Here! Give me your case. There's a cake on the griddle. With a few spare ribs and a glass of hot punch you won't be long about warming.'

Aine glanced slowly around.

Everything in the kitchen was still the same. Delia's old armchair was standing in the corner; the Virgin in her blue mantle reigned from her bracket above the door; her aunt's knitting basket, chunks of wool spilling out over the sides; and Delia herself, presiding over the hearth, hands roughened from dicing onions and carrots on the chopping board.

'Richard sent over these.' She took the paper bag of petunias from her suitcase and left it on the table.

'What's that?'

'Petunias. They're a silvery mauve colour and flower for months—'

'You can put them in water. They grow uncommonly well around here.'

'He's wonderful with flowers, rockery and trellis, anything you could think of. You should see his assortment of sweet peas, magenta, orangey blues and deep pinks growing everywhere, even among the runner beans and climbing up the wall at the back door. Their perfume is heavenly. You'd get it from the kitchen window.'

'Mmm!'

'Last Sunday I went boating on the Thames. It was a scorching hot day. There were two swans paddling back and over. Come Summer, Richard said, there will be dozens of them.' Exhausted, she sank into a chair at the table and began to nibble a piece of apple cake.

'Tell me,' Delia said, pouring out tea for both of them, 'how is herself?'

'Who?'

'Catherine.'

'Busy attending openings and that kind of thing. I didn't see much of her, really. She organizes parties, sets things up, if you know what I mean.'

'Humph! A fine organizer she was always, a great schemer. But Mark, how is he?' There was an anxiety in Delia's voice which she could scarcely manage to conceal.

'Oh, he's alright.' Aine toyed with her spoon, eyes glued to her plate.

Immediately Delia sensed something. Aine hadn't played her cards! She hadn't pulled it off with Catherine and Mark. Her painting wouldn't sell; she'd never be mistress of *Evendale*. Rising, she opened the turf box and threw a sod on the fire. 'Did you meet all the grandees,' she asked, by way of changing the subject, 'ladies with double-barrelled names and posh accents?'

'If it's the Frasers and Mr Henry Waters you mean, I had tea with them.'

'What about your painting? Did they—?'

'My painting is sold, sold for seven thousand pounds!'

'Glory be to God!' Delia threw up her hands in amazement. 'Good gracious, child, you'll be rich. You're coming in for a fortune. Who's this you said has bought it?'

'They didn't say in the Gallery'.

'Seven thousand pounds!'

Aine frowned. 'I'm not returning to London. I've earned enough money to go on.'

Delia stared. What on earth would she do with the child? With a dowry like that she wouldn't find a husband between Cragann and New York. No ordinary Yahoo would be good enough for Johnnie Fogarty's daughter.

'I'll earn my living painting,' Aine said, divining her aunt's thoughts,' a sale like that will attract plenty of work.'

'Aah! I knew you'd succeed. You've taken after your mother. But we can talk about it tomorrow. Your room is ready. I was kind of expecting you.'

The following morning Aine woke early. Having finished breakfast she cleared away the dishes and headed straight for the shore. Walking along the water's edge she filled her lungs with kelp-laden air. A soft breeze caressed her face, ruffling her hair.

'You're home!' Julie called, waving excitedly from the foreshore, 'I thought you were gone for good!'

'Didn't I tell you, didn't I say I'd be back?'

'Well, you didn't stay long; did you not like it?' she asked, arriving down beside her on the shingle.

Aine frowned. 'The galleries and theatres and all that kind of thing were wonderful but—'

'How is Mark?' Julie's eyes narrowed.

'Mark won't be coming here anymore.'

'Oh!' Together, they walked up the beach, on to the green and sat on the wall outside Brannigans, swinging their legs as they were wont to do in the past.

'Aine.'

'Mmm.'

'Colm has been acting kind of strange.'

'How's that?'

'He's gone all silent. Went off to London and nobody knew where he was.'

Aine gave her a sidelong glance. Beneath them a stream gurgled in an unbroken rhythm running to meet the sea. She collected a few pebbles, counted them out, one by one, and dropped them into the water. 'How long was he away?'

'Three whole days. And you know—'

'What?'

'Colm is one in a million. He'd have done anything in the world for you. You let him go.'

Aine said nothing. The water beneath them continued to sing, meandering in and out between stones and falling in tiny cascades over a built-up dam. 'Come on!' she said suddenly, leaping off the wall, 'I'll race you home.'

Having parted from Julie, Aine retraced her steps. The evening sky had grown overcast. Ominous clouds were banked in the west. She pulled at a *buachalan* growing on the hedge and swung it to and fro. Strange, Colm hadn't put in an appearance. He'd probably gone off on his fishing boat, the fifty foot trawler with the hydraulic steering. She swung the yellow *buachalan* around and around at a frantic speed.

As she passed the boathouse Willie Sara was tinkering with his lobster pots. She ran across the grass to meet him.

'I heard you were home,' he said, without looking up.

'Yeah.' She shifted her weight from one foot to the other.

'Didn't you like it?'

'Well, sort of, but I wanted to come back'

'And what d' you think of the latest?'

'What's that?'

'Didn't you know? Colm has sold his fishing boat.'

She took a step backwards as if she had been hit.

'There was a man down from Howth one morning, lately. Before you could say Jack Robinson the boat was gone.'

The fifty foot, steel hulled trawler, the boat for which he had sacrificed so much! 'Are you ... sure?'

'Of course I'm sure. Ask Old Daniel; he'll tell you. '

'How much did he get for it?' she asked, dully.

'Thousands, they say.'

'Thousands?'

'Well, about seven or eight thousand, Daniel said the other night in Brannigans.'

Aine was silent. What on earth had possessed him? Now he had neither boat, nor job, nor anything ... 'Fool!' she cried, stamping her foot. 'Fool! Why in heaven's name did he do it?'

'What did you leave him for anyway? You knew full well you wouldn't find the likes of him again.'

'I didn't leave him.'

Willie put down the lobster pot he was mending and looked at her. 'What's wrong with you, Miss, is you're spoiled. Delia has spoiled you. Ever since you could walk you got what you wanted. Colm would have given you his last farthing. You with your high and mighty notions, expecting the devil an' all from your relations in London! As for that precious art dealer of yours! Hah!' He spat on his hand. 'He's not worth the bit of ground he walks on!' Having finished his task, Willie collected the lobster pots piling them up, one on top of the other.

Aine turned slowly away. A fresh wind blew from the sea tossing her hair. She drew her jacket around her hugging herself into it and walked aimlessly up the road, shoulders hunched. Suddenly she stopped, turned and dashed back to the house. She took the petunias uprooted from *Netherby* and climbed the road to Portree.

Chapter Thirty-Eight

Somebody had cut the grass. It was the first thing Aine noticed on entering Portree cemetery. Where the wind had blown, petals of wild flowers - crocuses, strange tiny bells and clumps of purple foxglove - lay in drifts along the turf.

She climbed the railings of her parents' grave, opened the brown paper bag and took out the petunias. With deft fingers she dug the soil and planted them, one by one, flattening the clay around them. Task completed, she sat down and gazed across at Portree. Colm's decision had stunned her. What untoward circumstances caused him to act like that? He had nothing now ... nothing! And Willie with all his *blather!* For some inexplicable reason she felt things were beginning to change in Cragann. A twig snapped behind her.

'You didn't waste time, I see!' Delia scrambled up the embankment clutching a spade and watering can.

Speechless, Aine stared at her. Never before in her whole life had she seen her aunt in the cemetery, neither for funerals nor for any other occasion. Her dishevelled appearance shocked her. Wisps of hair fell in disarray over her forehead. Patches of crimson dyed her cheeks. She left the spade and watering can at the side of the grave and walked over towards her. 'The petunias will need to be watered,' she said, 'you could fill the can at the stream.'

'Somebody was here!' Aine pointed out, ignoring her remark, 'the grass has been cut.'

Delia removed her hat, wrapped a scarf around her head and began digging. After a minute or two she straightened. 'The ground is quite dry; surprising how hard it can get!'

'I didn't think ... I never saw you in the cemetery before,' Aine stammered.

Her aunt donned a pair of leather gloves, collected the *scraws* and withered leaves and began stuffing them into a sack. She stopped suddenly. 'I haven't been here for years, not since the day your parents were buried. I got the notion last Sunday ...' Breathing heavily, she leaned back against the railings and drew her jacket around her. 'For a long, long time, I couldn't get it out of my head that it was your mother who caused John's death. If Rosemary hadn't gone out that day ...' Her voice trailed off.

Aine glanced at the petunias. For a brief second the tiny green leaves seemed to quiver ever so slightly. 'Here!' she said, impulsively, 'give me the can. I'll go for the water.'

As she walked across the sandy dunes a vast open space spread out before her. As far as the eye could see, daisies and buttercups studded the grass. Scutch and dandelions grew in stubborn mounds along the banks. A skylark carolled overhead. In the distance the sound of surf could be heard crashing on Ardbracken Strand. Her spirits lifted. Tripping along, watering can rattling at her side, she began to sing:

I'm a lone ... ly little petunia in an on ... ion patch ...

An on ... ion patch ...

An on ... ion patch ...

She found the stream hidden under a clump of rushes. As she approached she could hear it murmur, tumbling over rocks and losing itself further down as it reached the sea. She knelt on a grassy patch, placed the can at a strategic angle and filled it up to the brim.

On returning, some minutes later, she found Delia with an improvised hoe whacking the life out of a straggling blackthorn.

It was late when Aine left the cemetery. Her aunt had already gone. The moon was full casting its light along the bay. She took the short cut home along the strand.

When she reached the shore she removed her sandals. Marks of cartwheels showed where Pat Neddy with his donkey had been down earlier taking seaweed to Holohans' farm. Bird tracks criss-crossed the sand near the water's edge. Hoisting up her skirt, she paddled in the shallows. Immediately the water drew her. Pealing off her dress she placed it under a stone and waded in. The waves lifted her up rocking her gently. This foaming white world welcomed her. Its roars were a language she understood. A voice in her head shouted, never! never! never! That night in September … those other nights … Delia had invoked all the saints in heaven … She laughed aloud. Overhead the pole star watched, constellated in a blue-black sky. A solitary owl coasted, outstretched wings tilting from side to side, cruel eyes scouring the seashore. She lifted her head and stared him in the eye. 'Be off,' she cried, splashing noisily, 'be off, bird!'

The owl screeched, hovered, dangling its feet, almost brushing the sea. Tawny-feathered, its yellow rimmed eyes stared coldly down at her. Then he settled, folding his wings primly.

She turned on her back. Beyond the weed-covered rocks along the shore, she distinguished a tiny black dot. It moved slowly, resolving into a human figure as it went. Somebody going to Portree? Not Willie Sara. Colm and Tim Hegarty had gone to a boat show in Galway. She came to the conclusion that the person was a stranger.

She swam in closer to the shore. The man's shadow fell in relief on the moonlit beach. He lumbered along kicking the stones in a haphazard fashion. In a broad-brimmed hat and three quarter length coat, his gait seemed vaguely familiar. But her clothes! She'd have to locate her clothes.

She skirted the rocks and ran along the edge of the water turning in the direction whence she had come. She gave a quick look back. The stranger was catching up fast. She headed for the sand dunes and hid in the rushes waiting for him to pass. But to her surprise, instead of walking on, he paused, removed his hat and pointed to something in the sand. It was Colm! He stood, bareheaded, outlined against the sky.

She crept out from the rushes, head lowered, picking her way clumsily through the hard shingle, petticoat flapping.

'Get changed,' he said, handing her her clothes.

Teeth chattering, Aine drew her dress down over her head and removed the sodden petticoat. In an effort to restore life to her limbs, she thumped herself, chaffed her hands.

'Take this,' he said, offering her his overcoat, 'it might warm you.' He placed the heavy worsted trench coat over her shoulders.

She wrapped it around herself feeling its warmth seep in through her skin.

'How's that?'

'Better.'

'I'll race you over.'

They ran along the shore leaping over stones and clumps of seaweed and arrived at the place where the rocks meet the foreshore. Breathless, they threw themselves on the grass.

'Phew!'

'Colm'

'Mmm.'

She reached out and plucked a blade of grass. 'Why did you do it?'

'Do what?'

'Sell your fishing boat?'

He made no reply. She studied his profile, long rugged face, firm jaw line. So often had she longed to sketch him. So often. But how did he know she'd be here? Willie? Willie Sara ...? Then in a flash, she knew. It was Colm who had bought her painting. He sold his boat to raise the money. She sat still, eyes unseeing, staring straight ahead. Behind her the wind whispered, rustling the reeds in the foreshore. Waves broke on Ard Bracken. There wasn't a buyer! Nobody wanted it. 'Why did you do it?' she cried, turning to him fiercely, 'why? why?'

Colm shrugged. 'To get you out of his clutches. Anyone could see he was a fraud.'

'Oh, God!' She pounded the sand with her bare fists. 'I ought to have known ... ought to have realised—'

'You're a talented artist.'

'What do you know about art?'

'Not very much. But I know a gombeen man when I see one. I made inquiries in the Gallery. They had trouble with the art dealer. He didn't want to give you space. That Davis galoot was out to rob you. A man like that wouldn't waste time unless he saw something worthwhile at the end of it. He wanted your talent.'

Aine dug her fingers into the grass growing around a rock,

shredding its thick blades. Along the shore the west wind whispered. It whipped the sand into little eddies that scurried along the ground.

'Nobody wanted it,' she said, after a long pause, 'nobody wanted my painting. It was hanging up there a long time, up near the top. People used to stand and stare and ask silly questions. Is it a bird? Looks to me like a flower. They could never figure out what it was. One thing I know, I'll never be professional, never be a professional artist.' She scooped up a handful of sand letting it pour out through her fingers. 'It was all a dream ... just a foolish dream ... Everything else took second place.'

'You have a right to your dreams. I'd hate to think you hadn't another to replace this.'

She laughed. 'How will I explain it to Delia?'

'The money is yours'.

'And it's your painting.'

Frowning, he shook his head.

'What about the fishing boat?' she asked, eyeing him dubiously. 'How will you——?'

He reached out and covered her hands with his. 'Together we'll work it,' he said.

'Together.'

Glossary

Bainin:	Sweater made from home-spun wool.
Buachallan:	Weed with a yellow flower.
Blather:	Senseless talk.
Cnapan:	Pile or heap of seaweed.
Dilisk:	Seaweed growing on rocks under water, purple-brown in colour.
Duidin:	Clay pipe once used for smoking tobacco.
Gombeen man:	Cute rustic.
Poiteen:	Whiskey distilled from barley.
Puchan:	A piece of land said to be inhabited by fairies.
Si goath:	Fairy wind.
Slean:	A turf-cutter's spade.
Spalach:	Wet turf used for banking a fire.
Sugan chair:	Chair made from straw using a special weaving hook.

Una Trant, a retired Secondary teacher, was born and brought up in Co. Mayo and now lives in Dublin. She facilitates Creative Writing classes at Harold's Cross Adult Learning Centre.

Acknowledgements

I Could Have Danced All Night
Words by Allen J. Learner and Music by P. Loewe
Copyright 1956 Chappell and Co. Inc.

She Moved Thro' The Fair (Padraic Colum)
(C) COPYRIGHT 1909 BY BOOSEY & CO. LTD.
Reproduced by permission of Boosey & Hawkes Music Publishers
Ltd.

Galway Bay (Wise Publications)

Off To Dublin In The Green (Dominic Behan)

Every effort has been made to trace copyright holders of the excerpts of songs published in this book. The author apologises for any material included without permission or without the appropriate aclnowledgement and would be grateful to be notified of any omissions or corrections that should be incorporated in the next edition or reprint.